EAST OF INNOCENCE

EAST OF INNOCENCE

DAVID THORNE

CORVUS

First published in trade paperback in Great Britain in 2014 by
Corvus, an imprint of Atlantic Books Ltd.

10 9 8 7 6 5 4 3 2 1

A CIP catalogue record for this book is available from
the British Library.

Trade paperback ISBN: 978 1 78239 220 0
E-book ISBN: 978 1 78239 221 7

Printed in Italy by 🦁 Grafica Veneta

Corvus
An imprint of Atlantic Books Ltd
Ormond House
26–27 Boswell Street
London
WC1N 3JZ

www.corvus-books.co.uk

For Emmanuelle

Acknowledgements

My thanks go to my agent, Tina, and editor, Sara, for all their support, guidance and belief. Thanks also to my family, for being there. I am grateful to Nick and Ligeia for their help along the way, and to Sue Fry and John Hibbs for their early inspiration.

1

IT'S AN OLD joke, well-worn. What's the difference between God and a lawyer? The man sitting across the desk from me, eyes fixed on my face, doesn't look like he'd appreciate the punch line. God doesn't think he's a lawyer? No, that's not the problem right now. The problem, at this moment, is that this man seems to think I'm his salvation, some kind of avenging, all-powerful deity backed up by, and hence rendered invincible by, the full weight of the law. When the reality is I have no idea what the fuck he expects me to do.

His name is Terry Campion, someone I have known casually from school upwards. His father was TJ Campion, a volatile, troubled man who ran a used-car business on the north side of the Southend Arterial Road before bad luck or, more plausibly, a well-placed match burned it to the ground. The aftermath of the fire was fed by rumours that he'd sold a portion of his business off to some local hard cases who weren't impressed by the returns, which were on the very low side of TJ's promises. These stories were no more than playground gossip when I was a child, given extra colour by the sight of Terry, a lonely, solitary but defiant boy who quickly dealt with other children's jibes with his fists. I recall him once defending his family's reputation with his teeth, leaving a much bigger boy in tears, bite marks on the boy's stomach weeping blood. The son of his father, everybody said. He at least proved them wrong on that score.

'You always looked out for me,' Terry says. He sounds desperate. I looked out for him? The Terry I remember was two years below me and at the very periphery of my consciousness. More likely it's wishful thinking, some subliminal emotional persuasion to try to up my enthusiasm for his case. Because right now, I'm looking anything but enthusiastic.

'I don't know where else to go,' Terry says. 'There's nowhere.'

He's got a point. After all, he can't go to the police. He *is* the police, a career choice that always surprised me but, I suppose, was as good a way as any of escaping the shadow of his father's misdeeds. I, as much as anybody, can appreciate that.

'I'd like to help,' I say. And it's true, I would. I really would. 'But this…' I gesture at the discs he's placed on the desk. 'It's not anything I do.'

What Terry has brought with him, and what I've just watched, is footage from the CCTV of Gaynes Park police station, dated five nights previously. He'd called in a favour, got a duty sergeant from that nick to get hold of them for him, someone who owed him one, Terry didn't say what for. Copied, not stolen, he was quick to assure me, perhaps worried that I'd refuse to view them on some

2

petty legal point. He really doesn't know me as well as he claims.

Considering the upbringing he's had, the story he's just told me seems all the more unfair. Are some people simply born with bad luck hiding behind every coming hour, always minutes away from some unjust catastrophe?

Terry described to me his time as a policeman with the disillusioned, disbelieving air of a man who has recently escaped the clutches of a cult and cannot understand how he could have been so deceived in the first place. But after such an uncertain and confused early life, perhaps it's not surprising that he threw himself into the police force with such unquestioning vigour and abandonment; in its unambiguous righteousness and arrogant, self-assured camaraderie, he found a moral certainty he had never previously imagined existed. His guileless enthusiasm and uncomplaining conformism didn't go unnoticed; over the years, he was continually handed the assignments nobody else would touch. Policing sink estates where feral children spat and urinated on you from third-floor walkways, raiding crack houses filled with the odour of human faeces left in rooms where people with ruined lives slept; the jobs that only the truly fervent would take on without complaint. Back then, he accepted this work without question, seeing it as an opportunity to prove his commitment. Now, he told me, he saw it for what it was: the exploitation of a naive fool.

Whatever the truth of the matter, this willingness to go where nobody else would explains how Terry found himself one warm night on a 'prime' assignment, but one for which he was completely, crazily out of his depth: working under-cover, sourcing and then buying a quantity of marijuana from a Turkish man with terrible burn marks on the backs of both hands who ran a network of cannabis factories across Essex, mostly in the attics of rented properties.

The man was busted by the local drugs squad at the precise moment Terry was loading five kilos of the man's product into the back of his unmarked police car, a case of wrong place, wrong time that would make anyone question just what terrible crimes they'd committed in a previous incarnation. Unwilling to compromise his cover, Terry held up his hands, allowed himself to be arrested, cuffed, bundled through the frantic blue lights into the back of the waiting van.

'The problem began,' Terry told me, 'when we got back to the station. One of the officers, Baldwin, turns out he's some kind of zealot. Like, a real fucking headcase. We park up and I'm pulled out of the van, I've been sat next to this Turkish nightmare who keeps fucking spitting, he's been looking at me like I'm the reason he's here, right? Like I set him up or something. So I think, I need to prove my creden-tials, show I've got nothing to do with the police, so I give Baldwin a bit of lip. Nothing major, just tell him I want my brief, call him a cunt, like, what copper doesn't get that kind of shit all the time, right? Next thing I know, he's put his elbow in my throat.'

Baldwin struck Terry with the practised casualness of a man pushing a dog's snout away from the dinner table. Choking, hands cuffed in front of him, Terry staggered back against the van in the police station's car park. He

4

tried to say something, tried to say Baldwin wasn't allowed to do that, ready to come out of character if this was the way things were going to go down. Baldwin gave one of his colleagues an aggrieved look and that man, clearly well used to unquestioningly following the whims of his superior, took out his baton, took a step back and hit Terry in the kidneys, twice, then across his knees, beating Terry to the tarmac.

Terry may be twenty years from those defiant days defending himself in the playground, but his instincts for self-preservation, so long honed and if anything enhanced by the dangers of police work, remain sharp. He waited for his head to clear then raised himself up on one arm, kicked out at the policemen surrounding him, made contact. There was a collective intake of breath from them, amused rather than shocked, tickled that this little man on the floor felt he could go toe-to-toe with their undisputed might, thought he could compete. Somebody sang the *Rocky* theme, chuckling. They were as relaxed, as at ease, as if they were watching the game in their own home.

Then Terry, coughing out the blow to his throat, rocked back on his heels and punched Baldwin in the balls with both hands.

What followed Terry described to me as 'a fucking good old-school working over'. Having watched the footage, I can't help but think he's being deliberately glib. He was kicked back to the ground, helped up and punched, dropped and stamped on, battered with batons, the Turkish dealer all the while watching on, quietly thankful it wasn't him at the receiving end. The footage I watched was dark and hard to make out properly, the assault a flurry of action with only the occasional blow caught in detail as one of the car park's lights caught a raised hand or the gleam from a polished baton. But it gave a good idea of what happened. Terry's face across the desk from me, purple and cut and stitched and swollen, gave an even better one.

'So what?' I said. 'Report them, get them thrown out of the force. You've got the evidence, right? Good riddance.'

Lying on a cell floor bleeding, Terry told me, that had been exactly his plan. But then later, could have been ten minutes, could have been hours, he can't really remember, Sergeant Baldwin came back in with two colleagues; the same two, he believes, who'd inflicted the damage in the first place. Baldwin explained that they'd confirmed who Terry had eventually told them he was, a brother officer, and hey, listen, no hard feelings, right?

'No hard feelings?' said Terry. 'You've broken my fucking nose.'

'See, thing is,' said Baldwin, standing over Terry, 'thing is, I thought you were trying it on. Why I put you down.' He spoke with the slow assurance of a man who believes his place in the world is safe, inviolate. 'A mistake. We've all made them.'

Terry watched Baldwin through one eye, the other already closed, noted his lack of remorse, his unshakable self-belief, and knew that here was a very dangerous man. But years of looking out for himself had left him intrinsically disinclined to forgive and forget.

'We'll see what a tribunal thinks about that, shall we, dickhead?' said Terry.

Baldwin took a deep breath, fixed Terry with a stare that didn't know how to flinch.

'Let's not,' he said.

He'd done his homework, Baldwin, while Terry was on the cell floor, done some digging into Terry's private life, turned up a sister, a mother, the only family Terry had alive and all the leverage Baldwin needed.

'Say anything, word one, and I'll burn their fucking houses down, I'll have your sister raped. Understand?'

Terry, defiant and punchy as he was, knew when the game was up, knew when to wind his neck in. He lay back in his own blood, closed his good eye, sighed, said, 'Just fuck off, all right?'

'What is it you want me to do?' I ask Terry now. His family have been threatened with violence, he has had violence visited upon him by a team of policemen who think nothing of beating suspects into submission, who place their own moral authority above the law. This is not my territory; as I told him, this is not anything I do.

Terry swallows, shakes his head. He doesn't know. He doesn't know what he's doing here. He's desperate, at the end of his tether and thinks, because I'm a lawyer, I'll have the answers. When, as far as I can see, there's only one.

'Let it go, that'd be my advice. Drop it. You took a beating. Big deal.' I look up at Terry, raise my eyebrows, best I can do. 'You'll live.' But looking at him, at the set of his body, rigid in his seat and fists clenched, I just know that's advice he can't take.

'Either that or lodge a complaint, get the internal people on to it.'

7

'Baldwin and his mates'll be suspended. It'll go to a tribunal. Everyone'll know I grassed, end of career, and Baldwin, know what he'll do to me, to my family, before it even goes anywhere near a trial?'

'So, what...?'

I let it hang; Terry sighs, his shoulders drop. Whatever magical solution he was hoping for in the dilapidated office of Daniel Connell & Nobody, Solicitor, he now knows it isn't going to materialise. No protection, no huge media exposé, no glory. No gung-ho lawyer willing to assume the risk, go gunning for the bad guys. You're on your own, son, just like you've always been. There's a brief silence, then a passing bus makes my window shudder.

'Just keep hold of them. Look after them.' He nods at the discs. 'Anything happens to me, you'll do the right thing.'

Do the right thing? The truth is, I don't even want to be in the same time zone as these discs. I don't want anything to do with them, with this case, with Sergeant Baldwin and his out-of-control colleagues, with fucking Terry Hard-Luck Campion and his poor, blighted life. But looking at him, I can't help but see again that bewildered, frightened but ultimately brave little boy in the playground, fighting his corner against all comers, however much bigger and stronger they were. So I nod, meet his eye, try to give him something, some sense that there's somebody in this life who gives a fraction of a damn about his plight.

'Okay. Leave them with me. But, Terry, seriously? Fucking drop this, yes?'

Terry looks at me. 'Yes,' he says. And I know he doesn't mean it.

*

I leave the office early, my mind taken up with how a father's influence can shape our lives for decades even after they stop being a real, tangible threat to our day-to-day existence. My premises are on a tired parade of shops, pizza delivery and letting agents and cheap furniture stores, outside the tangle of commuter towns of Chadwell Heath, Collier Row, Seven Kings, Romford; outside London, outside civilised society, an almost laughable climb down from my previous office in the heart of the City, sixteen floors up. Terry, I think, we've all got problems. I lock the door, check my watch and figure it's about time I went to see my father.

2

I FIND HIM in his garden, already half-drunk, no doubt just back from the pub. He is garrulous, good-humoured in his usual unpleasant way, stretched out on a lounger, drink on the tidy grass of the lawn.

'Oh look, it's Perry fucking Mason,' he says, waving a hand at the garden table, which holds a bottle of gin, a bottle of tonic. 'Help yourself.' He holds up his glass. 'And help your old man too.'

I take his glass, pour, not as generously as he would have judging by the look he gives me as he takes a drink. 'Forgot the fucking gin, son,' he says.

'Garden's looking good.'

My father grunts, doesn't answer. Incongruously, for a man to whom sentiment is an aberration, he has a passion for flowers, for chrysanthemums and gerberas and roses, so many roses, neatly cut back every winter, proudly displayed every summer. Ornaments are scattered every-where, faux-stone windmills, a hedgehog pushing a wheelbarrow from which bursts a spray of peonies. The garden has a sense of peace, or would have if my father wasn't in the middle of it. Relaxing on the lounger, he looks like a burglar taking five on his victim's lawn before going back inside to finish the job.

My father lives in a drab house, the same small place I grew up in, pebble-dashed and crazy-paved and unchanged since the seventies. It is on the outskirts of town, lonely, isolated, surrounded by fly-tipped washing machines and failing farmland, a twenty-minute walk to the centre. It is a walk I know well as my father is a far more diligent gardener than he was a parent, and a lift in to school was out of the question. Don't even think about money for school uniform. Keep out of the way, especially during drinking hours. Disappear.

'You remember TJ Campion?' I say.

'Who?' He remembers, but you don't get anything easily from my father, he'd make you grovel for the time of day.

'TJ Campion, sold cars. His place burned down, everybody said it was an insurance job.'

'Short little prick, had a heart attack, couldn't keep off the booze? Yeah, I remember. You making any money?'

'Met his son today. Know he's a copper?'

'Fuck me, is he now? That what gave his old man the heart attack?' He laughs, a hacking cough, feet jerking up from the lounger with each exhalation, gin and tonic slopping over his open shirt, over his belly. My father is not a tall man but, if he'd been a boxer, would have made cruiserweight comfortably. His forearms are massive, something I have inherited from him, tattoo-covered hams, you'd need two hands to encircle each one. I've seen him laugh a lot, a head-back full-throated malicious bark, but I've never in all my life seen his eyes smile. I've seen people leave pubs as he walks in.

'Anyway, what about him?'

'Nothing. Just a face from the past.' I look over the garden, my father's downed tools. 'Do anything for you?'

'Dressed like that?'

'What do you want?'

He nods across the garden, to a stump, a spade next to it.

'Wasn't that the willow?'

'Diseased. Got to come out.'

I cross the lawn, pick up the spade, start digging around the roots. My father watches me as I work, bleak and unblinking, like an overseer debating when to start flogging. The roots are deep and I know that I will not get it all out today, that I have been set an impossible task; I work for forty-five minutes until I can feel blisters forming on the fleshy bottom of my thumbs and the stump is beginning to rock, the roots on one side excavated and broken, showing bright white where the spade has cut through them. It needs a digger but my father would not spend the money, or let its tracks cut up his lawn. I know that he will not be satisfied, that he will have some comment to make, but I am accustomed to these hopeless situations; heads I win, tails you lose is a game my father has been playing with me ever since I was a child. In trouble at school, I was warned he didn't want me turning out like him. When I graduated with a degree in law, he supposed I was something special, too good for him. When I lost my job in the City, narrowly escaping being struck off, he couldn't believe I'd thrown it all away, what was wrong with me, after all he'd given me?

I put the spade down and cross the lawn to get a glass of water; I think my father is asleep but as I pass him he grunts out, 'Giving up, are you? Lazy cunt.'

I sit back down next to him, sweat dripping off my forehead. My shirt is stuck to my back and the muscles in my shoulders and arms are humming. I press the glass to my face. My father belches loudly, a growling, meaty sound, teeth bared like a baboon, then levers himself up on to his elbows and looks at me. Here it comes.

'Got any money?'

'How much do you want?'

'Fucking never have enough, so whatever you can spare I'll take.'

I knew that he would ask, and I know he'll take whatever I have whether it's offered or not, so I pass him my wallet, which I filled with exactly what I can spare before I left to see him, a sum that won't be anywhere near as much as he'll want. I have never properly known how my father made what little money he has; but I do know that there are limited opportunities for stertorous sixty-five-year-old ex-wannabe gangsters, and that he would never demean himself by working a regular job. He takes out the £200, looks at me, sneers.

'And there I was, thinking the legal profession was a licence to print money. The fuck's wrong with you, son?'

I do not answer, there is no point; as far as he is concerned, being born was my one unforgivable sin, the wrong that can never be righted. It was my father's misfortune, and of course mine, that my mother disappeared days after she gave birth to me. I often wonder what our life would have been like, had she stayed around. It could hardly have been worse.

We sit in silence, listening to the buzz of insects, my father slurping occasionally. I can hear his breathing; it is heavy, and I wonder about his health, his heart, wonder if there is any force on earth that could kill him.

'Talking to you.'

I shake myself out of my thoughts. 'What?'

'Derek's granddaughter. Been missing nearly a week.'

'Yeah. I heard.'

'D'you know her?'

'Not really. To speak to. No news?'

'Not even eighteen.'

I know her by sight, a small girl, dark hair, quick words and a disarming smile, somebody I instinctively liked the few times I met her. Derek is a drinking friend of my father's, someone to share war stories with from the days when they were, if not respected, at least feared.

'Fucking nonces. Only got to open the paper. Know what we used to do with them?'

I tune out, not keen on hearing my father's creative methods for dealing with sexual deviants, a subject he's made very much his own in recent years. So much unrealised violence lives within him, continually on the lookout for a suitable outlet. His reserves astonish me; would impress me, probably, if I hadn't lived with them for so long.

'Be seeing you, Dad.'

'Stump's still in the ground.'

'Call me if you can't manage it.'

'Saying I can't manage it?'

I do not answer, know from experience which questions to avoid. I walk into the house, through the patio doors, pull them closed after me. I stand at the window watching my father, the back of his head, his tanned body lying on the lounger, old blue tattoos showing through the bronze. He's still got all his hair, stiff grey brushed back in rigid waxy waves, a vain man underneath the careless exterior. Lost in my thoughts, I don't notice him turn in the lounger, struggle around and look back over his shoulder at the house, the patio doors, at me. Some strange sixth sense, the predator's instinct. He arcs his glass at me and it smashes against the window, liquid streaming down and making my father's face, seen through it, unreadable. Why would any father react like that, at the sight of his own son?

3

BILLY'S GOT ONE leg in traction and he tells me that the worst of it is that he can't lean to one side, part a cheek, break wind discreetly. He says there are one or two pretty nurses and the last thing he wants is a reputation for uncontrolled flatulence. What he actually says is: 'You don't let one go around the fanny, Danny. Trust me, they don't like it.'

I assure him I'll take it on board, take his word for it. I even make a note on a pad I've brought, the kind of thing any proper lawyer should carry. Billy watches me in fascination, his jaw worrying a piece of gum agitatedly, his whole body a tightly wound coil of enforced inactivity almost humming with frustrated movement. This is probably the most still Billy has ever been. Anybody who questions whether hyperactivity is a real disorder, all they need do is meet Billy. He would make a cat with a firework tied to its tail look lethargic.

Much of my work involves what society would disparagingly call ambulance chasing, though I can't claim to do a lot of chasing. Any personal injury work I do walks through my office door. Or, in the case of Billy Morrison, calls my office line, as even hyper Billy would struggle to walk with a broken spine, broken femur, two fractured tibiae and a collarbone that is, apparently, 'utterly fucked'. He was hit by a car at a pedestrian crossing, in front of witnesses, at eleven o'clock the night before last. And now, rather than dead, he's potentially in line to win a lot of money in compensation, thousands, perhaps hundreds of thousands. Less my ten per cent, naturally.

That he's not in the morgue, that he was lucky enough to be mown down in front of witnesses who gave a description of the car, even caught a partial registration, sits in stark contrast to the Billy I know. A ubiquitous, if not popular, face in the local bars, Billy has a reputation for bad luck and worse judgement. He once stole a television from a house, then went to a pub later in the day and unwittingly attempted to sell it back to its owner. The television had a sticker on it, Billy told me after he was discharged, which read 'I ♥ Alicante', a strange decoration for a television but a stone-cold clincher for the angry and inebriated scaffolder whose television it turned out to be. Billy still carries the scar from where the man snapped apart his glass in Billy's cheek; they had him laid out on the bar, ran out of beer towels to staunch the flow of blood, had to get new carpets after he'd been carried away. In hindsight, Billy told me, he perhaps ought to have taken the sticker off. Billy deals almost exclusively in hindsight, foresight being something he appears to have been born without, like some children lack an arm.

Billy is grinning at me happily. 'How much, do you reckon?'

'Depends,' I say.

'Right,' says Billy, nodding wisely, not an idea in his head.

'First we need to find the car. The police have spoken to the witnesses, got a description, a partial registration. But we're not there yet. You say you don't remember anything about the accident?'

I already know he doesn't, want to check his story for inconsistencies on the off chance we go to court and a lawyer tries to find holes in his account, catch him in a lie. Though the eye witnesses we've got make anything Billy says largely irrelevant, all three of them sure that the crossing signal hadn't even begun to flash its warning at the point Billy went over the car's roof. Anyway, Billy isn't listening, his mind jumping ahead to the point when he's got a pocket full of money, revelling in the swagger and authority he imagines any significant sum will automatically bestow upon him.

'You know how big the biggest plasma screen they make is? Like, I'm talking, I'm going to hit up the store, get the biggest ass screen, just walk up, say yeah, I'll take that one. Gimme that one, I'm not even joking.' He looks at me. 'You got Blu-ray?'

I shake my head.

'Like, it makes things so real, you don't even know you watching TV. Seriously, you're like...' He opens his wide, mimes astonishment. 'You think you're there mad.'

'We've got to find the car first, Billy,' I say. 'Let's n carried away just yet.'

He shakes his head. 'Nah. They'll find it.'

I wish I shared Billy's childlike confidence, but the truth is I've had little joy pressing the police for a result so far. A partial registration involves man hours of follow up, which they've told me they can't spare at the moment, particularly given the search for the missing girl. I picture the worst-case scenario, an unrepentant sinner matter-of-factly scraping Billy's blood from his headlights, washing his hair off the windscreen, arranging an alibi, getting away with it. Not that I really believe that will happen; in my experience, it is more likely that the driver is holed up at home, missing work, downing booze to deaden the dread he, or she, feels at having hit a man and run, more than ready to confess all to ease the maggot of guilt burrowing into their staid, suburban psyche. Whichever, the car needs to be found before we can begin any litigation. And in this particular case, the case of Mr W. Morrison of no fixed abode, I suspect the police – and part of me, sadly, understands their point of view perfectly – really aren't that fucked.

Billy nods at me, winking, jerking his head towards the other side of the room where a nurse with limp greasy black hair and acne scarring reaches up tiredly to adjust a tube above a grey-faced man's bed.

'She's who you've been holding it in for, is it, Billy?'

'Gloria. She's from Brazil. Want to guess how many brothers and sisters she's got?'

I shake my head.

'Twelve,' says Billy in satisfaction. 'Fucking twelve. All same parents. You believe that? Same mum, same dad. Un-fucking-lievable.'

I recall some details of Billy's home life, his feckless mother whose eventual dependence on narcotics led her to prison and Billy into a care home, allegations of abuse by a stepfather, or uncle, or casual interloper, these distinctions unrecognised within the human chaos that habitually orbited the Morrison family home. It strikes me as amazing that Billy can for ever wear that sunny face, present that breezy smile to a world that has shown him nothing but disdain.

'I know you'll do the right thing, Danny,' he says, looking at me shyly, unused to any declarations of trust. Why do people keep saying that to me? I'm a lawyer, not a priest. I smile at Billy, give his shoulder a squeeze, tell him I'll be in touch. He nods vaguely, gone, lost once again to blissful dreams of easy affluence and the unfathomable wonders of Blu-ray discs.

I leave the hospital, pass worried relatives and sickly pensioners in dressing gowns smoking guilty cigarettes, happy for the sun on my face after the chemical yellow fizz of the hospital's neon strips. At my house, Sophie will be packing her things, filling bags as quickly as she can, possibly checking the windows as she empties wardrobes, praying I don't come back while she's there. Three nights ago, I reacted to a petty provocation, an offhand comment on my upbringing and the chip on my shoulder, by kicking over the coffee table as we watched I cannot now remember what. What I can recall, and what shames me as I think about it, are her eyes wide in her face as the rest of her diminished, toes pushing her shrinking body into the corner of the sofa; I could almost see her reduce in size from the sudden exodus of her trust in me. Her brother, a self-righteous colour sergeant in the Rifles, will also be there to lend his muscle and I know too well what will happen confronted by him, how I will react at the slightest rebuke or the merest hint of a sneer as he helps shift the wreckage of another failed relationship. I can't go there.

The unlovely concrete of my hastily built town is bathed in late-afternoon light by now, softening edges and reflecting warmth, uniform grey taking on subtle pastel shades of yellow, pink, orange; even the shadows are a cool blue. Every pub spills out into the street and laughter is, for now, winning the battle over traffic noise, delighted shrieks overwhelming the hiss of air brakes at red lights; close your eyes and you could almost believe you were somewhere else, a busy Spanish resort, a seafront bar. An evening like this is not one to spend alone, dissecting the ineptitudes and failings of my life, taunted by the sounds of friendship and intimacy. An evening like this calls for the company of the one person in this life I regard as family.

4

'I LIKED SOPHIE,' says Gabe. 'There you are. Should have known.'

'She was frightened of me.'

'Who isn't?'

Gabe isn't. Gabe never has been. Our friendship, I am sure, owes almost everything to this one simple fact.

'What did you do?'

'Fuck all.' Honest pause. 'Well.'

'Hate it when you say "Well".'

'Well, kicked over the coffee table.'

'Hard?'

'Enough. Enough to frighten her. Took something she said the wrong way.'

'Danny. You silly bastard.' Gabe looks at me, concerned, not afraid to hold my gaze, challenge me. He has eyes that are a pale unwavering blue, like a husky's, and seem to have an almost clairvoyant power. Next to my bulk he is whip-thin, lean and muscular; a man with an easy, almost loping animal physicality. He sighs, shakes his head, and when he looks back at me his eyes are bright and crinkled. 'Just the table, was it?'

We are sitting outside the Branfield Road Lawn Tennis Club, a place that, while I was growing up, became as much a home to me as my own; more, if a home is somewhere you feel welcome and valued. Strangely, it was my father who introduced me here, tennis becoming a fad that he and his socially ambitious cashed-up friends wanted to buy into. His presence at the tennis club did not last long, a combination of his own lack of co-ordination and, though he'd never admit it, too many sideways glances from the fascinated-yet-petrified respectable middle-class members. I, on the other hand, soon discovered that I had a serviceable forehand and an instinctive, explosive backhand, which could punish any serve from the juniors upwards, and was asked, practically begged, by the club's committee to keep coming back.

Gabe and I played doubles together for years, had success on a county level before my backhand came up against serves that even it didn't know how to reply to, and I could no longer cover for Gabe's unreliable volley. And while disappointing, the stability and generosity that the club showed me during those years of success opened my eyes to a way of thinking, a philosophy not exclusively governed by self-interest, which previously I could never have imagined existed.

I seem to be surrounded by people, and in that number I count myself, for whom something is always missing, lacking, for whom disappointment is the default state. But Gabe has always radiated the air of a man whose life is complete, who could not want for more. During a tour of Afghanistan with the 1st Royal Tank Regiment two years ago, he was patrolling behind a Challenger main battle tank when an IED disguised as a pile of camel shit exploded, shrapnel shearing his left leg off just below the knee, the surgeons taking more so that it now ends just beneath where his kneecap starts. From the day I saw him back in the country, attached to a drip at Selly Oak, he has given the impression that this minor inconvenience has utterly failed to exert any influence on his life, or diminish him in any way. But recently I have noticed a distance in him, a lack of focus in those unnervingly clear eyes, as if he needs dragging back from some other, unknowable place. He has been gone too long, and seen too many things, for me to know where to start in reaching out to him; and besides, I am sure that he can look after himself.

I am in awe of Gabe, always have been. I consider him remarkable. The fact that he was accepted into the Cavalry tells its own story about his class background, orders of magnitude above my aspiring working-class origins, but this was never an issue for him and soon became irrelevant to me, too.

One of the courts has stopped playing, four men in tennis whites passing our table, glowing with the satisfied aura of health and not inconsiderable wealth. 'All right, Hopalong?' one of the men, whom I know by sight but not name, says, laughing and clapping Gabe a little too hard on the shoulder. He has wiry black hair on his tanned forearm and a Breitling on his wrist that must have cost more than my car; possibly a lawyer, one who's doing infinitely better than I am. His group stops at our table.

Gabe smiles but I see his lean frame stiffen; still, discipline is discipline and he does not let the jibe, whether meant well or spitefully, provoke him. I, on the other hand, cannot accept this casual arrogance so equably. I look the man in the eyes, my dead fuck-off stare. He attempts to meet my look, his pleased smile faltering like a birthday boy who's just been told his dog's died.

'What?' he asks, a braver man than I had given him credit for.

'I hear you say something like that again and I'll put you on the floor,' I say.

Gabe reaches over and places a hand on my forearm, tendons raised from my closed fist. 'Excuse my friend,' he says to the man, who now will not look at me. 'I'm sure you didn't mean anything by it. Right?' An edge to his voice.

'Right,' says the man. He turns to his friends. 'Let's go.'

'Christ's sake, Danny,' says Gabe, watching them walk away, their backs a little less straight, their strides a little more diffident. 'This is a tennis club, not a nightclub. Behave yourself.'

'You think a man like that would take a medal home from war?' I ask. 'Fuck him.'

Gabe laughs softly. 'He'll be looking in the rear view of his Merc all the way home. You've done enough.'

We sit in silence, watching bats flutter like tossed scraps of black cloth through the glare of the court floodlights, the soft murmur of members on the veranda around the corner. Peace is something I have known little of, but, whenever I do imagine it, this is where I place myself, always with Gabe opposite me.

My mobile has been vibrating and I've been ignoring it, unwilling to let the real world intrude into this temporary oasis. Eventually, though, I pick it up and call through to my voicemail, aware that it could be urgent, though why someone would be calling me in an emergency I can't imagine.

'Danny, it's Terry. Just wanted to say, look, I know what you're saying, I hear you, but I'm not going to let this go. I can't. I...' His voice pauses, comes back louder, outraged. 'You saw my face, what they did to me. I'll call you.'

Terry Campion, undiluted piss and vinegar even after all these years. I couldn't blame him, knew that if I were in the same situation I'd want to exact my revenge, too. I am enough of a hypocrite, though, to still curse him for not taking my advice and leaving it alone.

'Problem?' says Gabe.

'Work.' I explain to him about Terry, somebody Gabe won't know; when we were young, we moved in two very separate worlds. I am aware that it is a disgraceful breach of client confidentiality to discuss Terry's case but the normal rules have never applied in my friendship with Gabe.

'Police,' he says contemptuously. 'Let them shake hands and make up, promise to play nicely. Storm in a bloody teacup.'

I describe Terry's face, the stitches, the bruising, and can see Gabe's eyes slide away, uninterested in the detail. I imagine Gabe in Afghanistan, hauling screaming drip-fed soldiers into helicopters, watching them take off and clatter away, leaving him with another man's blood clotting on his dusty battledress; I stop talking. Perhaps he has a point. I decide I'll wait until tomorrow to call Terry back.

'Been upsetting our esteemed members again?' asks George, seventy-three but you'd be lucky to return his forehand unless you hit your approach within a foot of the baseline, and hard at that. He leans over our table, shakes my hand. 'Hello, Danny, how've you been?' George is one of the original members to have seen my potential, both on and off court, and is a man to whom I owe an unpayable debt of gratitude. 'Hear about that young girl?'

I nod, don't answer. It is hard to avoid the story, a media sensation mostly due, I suspect, to the fact that she is white and comes from a respectable background. I do not wish to sound uncharitable but, if she had been black, or impoverished, her disappearance would be as unremarkable to most people as a lost cat.

'Bar's closing, might not have noticed but every other bugger's fucked off,' George tells us. 'Haven't you got homes to go to?'

Now there's a good question.

When I get back to my house, it is empty and I am surprised by just how much of its warmth had been provided by Sophie and her possessions, how little of me there is to fill the space. She has left no note. I promise myself that I will forget about her entirely within a month.

5

THE NEIGHBOURHOOD HAS begun to wither under the heat we've had over the past two weeks, dry yellow grass rising in motes as it's scuffed by feet, days only coming alive after four o'clock when the temperature starts to dip under thirty. But the sun is working its tonic on me, Sophie behind me and a case I stand a chance of winning waiting, possibilities opening up like a parched flower after watering. Looking up at the blue sky, I can appreciate its warmth, any clouds for the moment vanished.

My office doesn't have air conditioning; no great surprise, neither does it have a carpet, windows that open or a photocopier. I spent money on the exterior, a painted sign the width of the building bearing my name and occupation, Solicitor, in a script that I was assured by a lady named Tanya with a Y looked both modern and traditional, appealing to all. It wasn't cheap, but after the sudden ejection from my previous job I did not lack for money, at least not immediately. From outside my office on a clear day, you can just make out the tops of the City's tallest buildings, but where I am now feels infinitely far from the office I occupied at my last place of work. There, on the sixteenth floor of an imperious glass building on Bishopsgate, I looked down on streets and people from a panelled room with a desk and two easy chairs designed by a Dutchman in the twenties whose name I forget; I am not a proud person but it is no boast to say that I was close to the top and ascending rapidly, to the point where I had already earmarked my potential future office up on the eighteenth, the partners', floor.

I open the mail myself; I am a thirty-seven-year-old lawyer and cannot afford a secretary and, in any case, I have no space for one. Back in the City I had my own PA, a pretty lady called Allie who was permanently amazed, and often scandalised, by everything she read, heard or watched on the television. Indirectly, it was Allie who caused my steep decline, although that does her an injustice; as so often with open, kind and trusting people, she was an unwitting pawn in a much larger and more sinister game.

The firm I worked for, and which I was expected to count myself lucky to belong to, was one of the City's major players, experts in dispute resolution in the fields of construction, engineering and real estate, and past masters at wielding intellectual superiority like others would a rubber hose. I suspect that, as well as my outstanding degree and track record, the board members who lobbied for me to join secretly enjoyed the notion that I would add a rougher texture to their customary silk.

My father is a bully, but he is also a man who is honest about his motivations, which are, generally, money, women and drink. Nor is he unrealistic; he has always accepted that, just as he metes out violence, sooner or later he'll have the same indignity visited on him, something that has happened on far more than one occasion. In the haughty marble corridors of Steinman Hall, the firm I worked for, bullying was a strictly one-way transaction, and it was carried out on a daily basis without mercy or second thought. The victims were the weak in general and women in particular; the board was a boys' club in which sexual equality was considered a delightful joke. I would not join in this bullying, but people's perception of me as some kind of dormant brute meant that it wasn't remarked upon; they all assumed I'd do something heinous sooner or later. And in a way, I suppose, they were right.

Asking a harassed PA with three children waiting at home to pick a pen up from the floor so that a millionaire partner can steal a glance at the top of her G-string is one thing; morally unacceptable but not something I felt strongly enough about to risk a six-figure salary by confronting. That was my feeling at the time, shameful though it is. But then one day Martin Andersen, a slope-shouldered specialist in commercial real estate and also the intimidation of women, asked Allie if she wouldn't mind tucking his shirt into his trousers for him as his hands were still wet from when he'd washed them after urinating. I do not think he knew I was in my office; perhaps he assumed that, as the door was open, I had left. Allie, a bubbly personality with people she knew but a tongue-tied wallflower in the company of strangers and those she regarded as her social betters, did not know how to respond.

'I don't want to, thank you,' she said, her voice cracking with uncertainty.

'I mustn't get these trousers wet, you see,' said Andersen stridently. 'Any idea how much they cost?'

'I could fetch you a serviette.'

'Serviette? Oh, you mean a hand towel. Well, if it's all the same to you, just hurry on and do what I asked, could you? Come on.'

There was a pause during which, behind my desk but already beginning to rise, I could almost hear Allie swallowing back her shame and discomfort.

'I really don't want to,' she said. 'Please?'

It was that 'please' that did it for me, plaintive and followed by an exasperated grunt from Andersen. In dispute resolution, because it was business and conducted on at least a notionally level playing field, I never lost my temper. But right then, listening to Andersen's petulant voice, I experienced the tunnel vision that is always the precursor to something dramatic and regrettable. I left my office, picked him up by his shirtfront and laid him on Allie's desk, Allie scurrying away as if she'd just discovered a mouse. Andersen didn't fight back, wore a shocked half smile like he thought this was probably just rough play and he'd soon understand the joke. I pulled down his trousers and underpants and walked him, holding him by the collar, into the area that held the secretaries, ten of them listening to Dictaphones through earphones, typing letters. They looked up at the sight of one of the senior partners waddling along, expensive trousers and striped boxer shorts bunched around his ankles, wide eyes taking a

32

second or two to process the surreality of the scene. I then, and I do not pretend that this does me any credit, whispered in Andersen's ear that if he didn't lift his shirt to expose whatever he was hiding to the nice ladies then I'd snap his fucking spine.

Ultimately, I suspect I'm not really cut out for the corporate world; at least that is what I've told myself in my subsequent darker moments as I realised word of mouth had made me all but unemployable in the higher echelons of the London legal profession. But there is some truth to it; I often feel that I am somebody who has had education and refinement poured into a body entirely unsuited to the task. As I think about this inherent contradiction, I thumb in Terry's number again. Since I ignored his call three days ago, I have tried him continually but he has never picked up, something which is beginning to cause me worry. This time, though, he answers.

'Hello?'

'Terry.'

'Who's this?'

'Daniel. Danny.'

'Oh, right, Danny? How you doing?'

His innocent bonhomie is about as convincing as a wet Rembrandt; underneath the bluster there's an edge of anxiety, maybe fear. Over the phone in the background I can hear an indistinct burst of Tannoy, a terse announcement.

'Where are you?'

'Yeah, I'm... Look, I'm at the airport, Danny. I'm getting the fuck out of this country.'

Terry tells me that he is on his way to Spain where he knows 'a couple of faces' who'll look after him until things have quietened down, letting me into half the story without explaining what has prompted this flight, a desperate one judging by the catch in his voice. I tell him to calm down, tell him that, as his lawyer, I am going to need a little more information than he's giving me, what's going on?

'I told him. Baldwin. Told him I'd copied the CCTV, told him I'd take it up high if he didn't put his hand up. He's a fucking animal, Danny, he's off the scale.'

'Yeah, take a breath. You, what, you expected Baldwin to turn himself in?'

'I told him, you tell the brass what you did, say it was a fuck up. I ain't gonna make a fuss, press for any disciplinary action, all you'll get's a rap on the knuckles. I said I'll even say I provoked you if you want. But you need to put your hand up.'

'You thought he'd take that?'

Terry doesn't say anything. Thinking about his naivety causes me to close my eyes, breathe deeply to centre myself. Terry.

'What did Baldwin do?'

What Baldwin did, Terry tells me as emotion gradually tightens his vocal cords and reduces his voice to an indignant whine, was to gather up his complicit colleagues and follow Terry's sister's car from her place of work, a dental clinic I know on a busy crossroads, back to her home. As she put her key in her door, one of them, she doesn't know who, doesn't know how many there were, put a sack over her head and pushed her through into her living room. Men

34

held her down, while one, he told her that Terry would know who he was, put his hand into her knickers and roughly abused her with his knuckles. She said that she could smell stagnant breath through the sack as he did it, told Terry that it was like being electrocuted, the point of contact devastating her entire body. The man told her to give Terry a message, to tell him that he was to drop it or he was dead. And then they left, leaving his sister in a state so traumatised that she had not spoken a word since, had not moved from the foetal position Terry had found her in.

And now Terry is leaving the country, with no plans to return as long as Baldwin remains a policeman.

There's little for me to say. I tell Terry that I am sorry, that if he or his sister wishes to report the crime then I will do anything I can to lend support and credence. But the fight has left Terry and all he wants to do is get angrily drunk on a beach in Marbella. He chokes out a 'Bye, Danny' and hangs up.

I spend the rest of the day in a pointless chase, trying to speak to somebody in a uniform who can tell me of any progress in Billy Morrison's case, but after being shunted from desk to indifferent desk I succeed only in persuading somebody to leave a message for somebody else who is nominally in charge of the investigation, such as it is. Billy's Blu-ray wonderland is looking farther away with each passing day.

6

IT FEELS STRANGE, attending a funeral in glorious sunlight, a further fuck you to the dear departed consigned to the damp sod. Shouldn't we be pondering the measure of our loss under cold dark blustery skies filled with the threat of rain? The cemetery is as flat as a snooker table, green baize punctured by gravestones and the gaggle of stooped figures surrounding Rachael's grave, trees billowing with leaves the backdrop under an enormous, indifferent blue sky. I stand on the periphery of the crowd around the grave, that should-I-be-here feeling of the loosely connected, unsure whether my presence is appropriate or merely an intrusion, making me unwilling to meet the eyes of those surely experiencing grief far keener than mine. As soon as people start turning to one another, the coffin descended and commiserations being gently offered, I turn to leave. Five steps away and I hear my name.

'Danny.'

I turn. 'Hi. Sue. I'm, yeah.' Sue's nodding at me, smiling, sparing me the empty words. From where does she, a recent widow to breast cancer who should be pitying herself, find kindness for me? 'Nice weather for it,' my attempt at levity.

'She'd have been glad you came. Really.'

'I hope so. She was a bit special, Rachael. Drove me mental to be fair, but I loved her.'

'She'd have said the same about you. I'd say don't be a stranger, but...' She shrugs, knowing me, knowing our different worlds, accepting the inevitability of our diverging orbits. Another thing I thank her for, her lack-of-fuss honesty. I am sweating underneath my black suit, part heat, part discomfort.

'Thanks for taking the time. To talk to me. Makes me glad I came. Less... awkward.'

'She'd hate you to think that. She talked about you a lot.'

I know she probably did.

'But you're okay?' In her eyes I can see the same concern Rachael used to show for me.

I smile as warmly, as confidently, as I can. 'Yes. Absolutely blinding.'

I knew Rachael a quarter of a decade ago as Ms Dawson, my English teacher, a tough woman who children with their surgeon's eye for abnormality singled out for ridicule for the fact that she habitually wore trousers and could be seen on weekends selling a left-wing newspaper on the High Street. She noticed with a far more generous eye that I was brighter than my combative exterior suggested. She encouraged me to apply for a scholarship, not because she was an advocate of private education but because she didn't see why the privileged should be born to advantage and wanted me to even up the balance. I sailed through the entrance exam and, almost before I had considered the implications, found myself in a revered Regency institution surrounded by strangely uniformed children of an entirely different class from my own.

Needless to say, my clothes, accent and origins were ridiculed with delighted fascination, a wild beast in a cultivated cage. Soon, however, and this is a gift I think only children truly have, I entirely reinvented myself in the image of my peers. I learned how to speak differently, my diction based on how I believed an over-privileged and brilliant child should sound. It worked, and at the same time it didn't; I was young enough to convince other children that I was one of them; it was a trick I never managed to pull on myself.

I know, though she never told me, that Rachael felt ambivalent about her decision to help me better myself; that she often wondered what she had helped create. I had had a first-class education, earned a distinguished degree, found a job at the pinnacle of the legal profession. But there is an expression I once heard, I cannot recall where, that you cannot put lipstick on a pig. I am an articulate savage, a gentleman thug. A sociological experiment gone dangerously awry.

As I'm about to drive away, my mobile rings.

'Connell.'

'Daniel Connell?'

'Help you?'

'I'm investigating the hit and run incident involving an,

ah…' I hear the flipping of pages '…William Morrison. Night of the seventeenth of July. I understand you're acting on his behalf and want an update. With me?'

I'm with him. 'Yeah. Be nice. To know you're doing something to apprehend the driver responsible for my client's injuries. Anything at all.'

He's sharp, the officer on the other end, a man not accustomed to letting barbs sink in unchallenged. 'Anything at all, right. Well, Mr Connell… Daniel… I've fucking picked up the phone and called you, haven't I?'

I'll give him that, he has. And his manner doesn't ruffle me; I look at my eyes in the rear view and allow myself a smile. This sounds interesting. 'Congratulations on finding the telephone, officer,' I say. 'Now, what can you tell me?'

'What I can tell you I'll tell you in your office,' says the man. 'When are you –' imitating the manner of a sycophantic menial '– available for visits?'

'Don't know,' I say. I am a lawyer. Here is a policeman looking to get under my skin, putting on voices, looking for a rise. I have to ask: why? 'I'll have to check my diary. Got a number?'

I pick up a pad and pen, phone clamped under my jaw.

'I'll see you at midday tomorrow,' says the man. 'Your office. Be there.'

'Got a name?'

'Baldwin.' He waits. I can hear him breathing, waiting for a reaction.

'Look forward to it,' I say.

*

My radio is on, the traffic gridlocked, the news fixed on the missing girl, Rosie O'Shaughnessy, unseen now for ten days. The breaking story is that her boyfriend, who witnesses claim had had a violent argument with her just before she disappeared, is about to be arrested. In an eerie demonstration of synchronicity I see that the traffic I am in is being held up by a policeman, behind him a battery of cars with flashing blue lights surrounding a building which I realise is the home of the under-suspicion boyfriend.

Rosie's mother's voice fills my car as I watch an indifferent policeman hold up his hand to a passer-by. 'Just, she wouldn't, she'd never just *disappear*,' the word spoken with a puzzled mystery as if she suspects her daughter has been magicked into another world, rather than that which everybody is merely waiting to have confirmed: that she's had her life prosaically taken away from her by a man who wanted something from her she was not prepared to give. For the first time, I feel the weight of her vanishing; I have to blink to blot away the mental image of her tearful mother talking inexpertly into a microphone at a press conference she never imagined she'd have to attend, a shot of her daughter's face behind her. Poor blameless woman.

I look out of my windscreen at the blank red-brick repetition of the block where Rosie's boyfriend lives. Can evil fester in a place so utterly ordinary, so unremarkable? I turn off the radio, spooked, even in the heat hunching my shoulders against a shiver. I have been exposed to too much death for one day.

Still trapped in the traffic, I call Terry's number, not expecting him to answer but intrigued by the call from

Baldwin and not convinced Terry has been completely open with me. From what he's told me, I can't see an Alpha-male like Baldwin knocking on doors for the likes of Billy Morrison. He picks up on the second ring.

'Hello?' He sounds as if he's in a bar, noise in the background and a lazy imprecision in his speech.

'Terry? It's Daniel.'

'Danny, mate, yeah, fuckin', as it happens you've, yeah...' He fades out, a hacking laugh in the background, a shout of 'Oi-oi'. 'Just it's... not a good time.' Underneath the boozy wandering of his speech, I can tell he is cagy, on his guard.

'Anything you need to tell me?'

'Tell you? Yeah, tell you, the weather's fuckin' blinding, it's three o'clock and I'm half-cut in my mate's bar, and, Danny, son, listen to me you should check out the fanny, I ain't being funny but it's shooting fuckin' fish in a tin can. Awesome.'

This is not the Terry I spoke to in my office, scared yet still righteously outraged by Baldwin's betrayal of their, the police's, collective moral values. I have cut my teeth at the top tables of dispute resolution; I can pick up on bluster like a doorman can spot a drunk.

'Just got a call from Baldwin. So how about you sober up for a second and tell me something I don't know?'

There's a long silence and then Terry is back, bluster replaced with apprehension. 'What's he want?'

'Didn't say. He's coming to see me. So, again. Anything you need to tell me?'

What Terry hadn't told me and what he now admits as emotion shakes his voice and, towards the end, causes him to weep unashamedly, is that while Baldwin's knuckles were violating his sister another man compelled her to tell them Terry's number. Her head still covered and a phone pushing the rough material of the sack against her cheek, she begged him in her own private darkness, her voice rising to muffled panicked shrieks, to tell Baldwin where the discs with the copied footage from the station were. Which Terry did, he tells me through his tears, and I cannot blame him for it.

'You should have heard her, Danny. You imagine? My own sister, she's, she's not like us. Not... She works at a fucking dentist. So yeah I told them, Christ, Danny I'm sorry it's not like I thought... You're a lawyer, you'll be all right.'

The traffic starts to move, the policeman waving cars, vans through. Terry stops, steadies himself, I hear him take a drink. 'Just, be careful. Cunt's not fucking human.' Click. Terry's gone, and my guess is that he'll be too busy with the bottle to be accepting my calls for a while.

Rachael, Rosie, Terry and his sister; it has been a day of troubled souls. It is dark when I finish at the office and pull up on the gravel driveway outside Gabe's house, unannounced because I crave the bright warmth of a spontaneous welcome. Gabe lives in a brick-and-timber house, which must be worth nearly a million, its architecture a haphazard collection of sloping tiled roofs and chimneys and gables and small square-paned windows, an inheritance from his old-money parents, an oddity in this area of nouveau-riche criminality where most houses are bought or built on the proceeds of dubious property dealings and the trade in controlled substances. Lights are on down-stairs as I knock; I have to wait some time before Gabe comes to the door. His eyes, normally so focused, drift across me and down, snap back, fall away. I have never before seen Gabe slump but now his forearm is taking his weight against the doorframe, chin dropping to his shoulder. The diffuse light coming from the room behind him blurs his edges, softens him; this is the first time it has ever occurred to me that Gabe could be vulnerable.

'Daniel.' He talks clumsily like his mouth is full of dry rags. 'Wasn't expecting you.'

I look past him into the house, smell the marijuana. 'Having a party?'

'Just me.' He smiles stupidly. 'Neil Young night.' In the background I can hear *Harvest* playing, Young's melancholy voice. I look down, see that Gabe is holding a gun limply in the hand not propped against the doorframe, its black barrel reflecting dimly in the light. This is not what I came for.

'You all right?'

'Brilliant. Fucking top drawer. Why wouldn't I be?' He dares me to respond, straightens up, sways belligerently. Fuck sake, Gabe.

'Yeah, no reason. Want company?'

Gabe looks at me for the first time with precision. Under-neath his uncoordinated and hostile gaze, I believe I can see sadness. He shakes his head. 'Not tonight.'

I nod, turn away, conscious that I am leaving a friend in need but unsure what I can offer, suddenly aware that the scars he brought back with him from Afghanistan may run deeper than I had imagined. I drive away, Gabe still standing in his doorway. My thoughts are confused by the shock of being confronted by a man I believed I knew completely, behaving like an irrational stranger. He holds his hand up in a swaying farewell and as I turn into the street I can see the silhouette of his gun pointing up into the night sky.

7

BY MIDDAY, MY hangover has abated, three cans of Coke undoing the ill effects of the bottle of Burgundy and three glasses of rum I'd emptied the night before after getting back from Gabe's, soothing my murderous and culpable mood in front of banal late-night television. I am ready for Baldwin's visit now, infused with that warm, charged, delicious anticipation I always feel before the threat of confrontation and violence; it is the feeling I imagine an addict experiences walking home to his flat with his score in his pocket, about to sate an urge that can never be fully mastered.

Baldwin keeps me waiting, but I would not have expected anything less. Twenty minutes late, I hear the bell ring and walk to my small lobby, let him in. He walks past me without a word, looking at the tiny entranceway with the deliberately unimpressed air of a man taking a look about a vacant house he knows he can well afford. Although I have to admit that what he sees is not in the least impressive: two metres of mismatched floor tiles and a bulb that wants a lightshade.

'Through here?' he asks, opening the only door, into my office. I do not bother to reply, follow him in, already furious that he has taken control of my space. If he sits behind my desk, I promise myself emptily, I will break his jaw. All policemen are the same, I know, years of state-backed authority washing out any vestiges of human manners; they no longer have any need of them, do not have to ask permission to act as they please. Yet Baldwin takes this arrogance and somehow makes it personal; I feel as if he has my arm up behind my back. I push past him, get behind my desk, stake my claim. He looks at me, amused, and lowers himself into the chair facing the desk. I am surprised it is big enough for his bulk. Baldwin is massive; perhaps eighteen stone, perhaps forty-five years old, his face loose and pouchy but beneath the soft exterior he gives the impression of immense solidity, uncooked pastry draped over granite. He has grey hair cut short and flat on top like a marine sergeant's and flat incurious eyes which regard the world as a dentist would a loose tooth. Just as, by outraged consent, we will no longer suffer predatory paedophiles to act as priests, so too I believe we should not allow violent sadists to join the police force. His presence makes me want to take a shower.

'Sit down,' he says. He is in my place of work, giving me orders. It is as if, as I step into the ring for a much awaited title fight, my opponent attacks me from behind with a baseball bat. How can I have been psychologically ambushed in my own office?

'You want to talk about Billy Morrison,' I say, my voice level, trying to regain the initiative. Baldwin pats his jacket, retrieves a notepad from his inside pocket, takes his time.

'I'll ask the fucking questions,' he says calmly. 'If you don't mind.' He looks down at his notepad then looks up, smiles at me. But his eyes remain flat and expressionless; he has the unassailable air of a predator who long ago took his place at the top of the food chain for granted. I am not easily intimidated but Baldwin makes me wish we had an ocean between us. 'Francis Connell, that's your old man. Right?'

'That has nothing to do with the investigation at hand,' I say. 'Let's keep to the script, shall we?'

'Just saying,' he says. 'You in the law, him the wrong side of it. Wonder what he thinks. Of all this.' He gestures with his hand at my little office. 'All this,' he repeats, allowing himself a soft wet chuckle.

'Billy Morrison,' I say. 'We discuss him or this conversation is over.'

'Right. Down to business. I've got some information on young William Morrison, something you might find useful. Save you some of your no doubt valuable time.' He looks around, looks at me.

'Go on.'

'Don't fucking *go on* me, pal,' he says. 'First things first. I help you, I'm going to need something from you.'

'As an officer of the law, any information you might have pertinent to my client's case, you are obliged to share with me,' I say. 'You know that.'

Baldwin closes his notepad, pokes it back in his jacket pocket. He leans forward, the chair creaks ominously. 'See that? That's me going off the record. Right?'

'Not right,' I say. 'This meeting is finished.'

'Hold up,' says Baldwin. 'Let's see if we can't help each other. Now, I've got a confession to make. I made my mistakes, with Terry. Used the stick, not the carrot. Bad psychology. Didn't work.'

'Who's Terry?'

'Right, yeah. Nice try. Fucker's skipped off, someone tells me he's in Spain but nothing I can do about that now. He did pass on some useful information though. See, I want what he gave you. You give it to me, I'll help you out with Billy Morrison. The carrot.' He looks at me, head to one side as if he's inspecting a suspect mole. 'I think I'd need a bigger stick for you.'

'So tell me what you know about Billy Morrison's case,' I say. 'It'd better be some carrot.'

'And you'll hand over the discs?'

'What would I want with them?' I say.

It turns out Billy, as Baldwin explains it, doesn't quite fit the role of innocent victim he has been playing in his hospital bed. Ten nights ago, he and three friends piled into a Transit van, drove up an isolated farm track five miles from junction 28 of the M25 and cut their way through a link of quarter-inch chain securing the gates of a wire fence that ringed a corrugated iron-sided barn. They used an angle grinder to cut through the lock on the barn door and loaded up twenty thousand pounds' worth of Japanese stereo equipment, which, in turn, had vanished from a shipping container in Tilbury Docks a week earlier.

In Billy's world, the perfect crime constitutes one you are not caught at the scene of, and Billy made it back to his house unscathed. As far as he was concerned, he had got away with it; having got away with it, he could not help but boast of it. And this boasting inevitably reached the ears of the aggrieved party, in this case, Baldwin told me, his jowls wobbling with spiteful mirth, a serious character called Vincent Halliday, a local underworld name I am familiar with myself and who had arranged the initial robbery from Tilbury Docks. I can easily imagine his reaction on being informed that not only had he been ripped off by Billy bloody Morrison, but also that Billy was telling anybody who would listen about what a piece of piss it had been.

Billy's hit and run was no accident. The hit that Halliday put out on him in retribution, Baldwin tells me, is the worst-kept secret since Prince Harry was born with ginger hair. He doesn't know who drove the car, doesn't particularly care; this is one investigation that's going nowhere fast.

'Spare you the trouble,' he says. 'Fuck that Billy Morrison off, he's a mug and he's a fucking dead man. Yes?'

Oh, Billy. I busy myself with arranging the pens on my desk, unwilling to meet Baldwin's eyes, which I know will be relishing this moment. Knowledge is power, and right now Baldwin is making me look like a primary-school child playing at lawyers.

'So, quid pro whatever. The discs, sunshine. Now would be good.'

'I don't know what I can do with that information,' I say, looking up at him. 'Do you have any evidence?'

'Very funny. The discs.'

'Because, this is my problem. If what you say is true, and if there is no evidence of this crime, then how am I going to prosecute this Halliday and get significant criminal damages for my client? And if I can't get him damages, then how am I going to get paid?' I frown at Baldwin, an expression of bafflement. 'I thought you were going to help me?'

Baldwin looks at me in surprise. The penny is dropping; he begins to understand that I'm not going to hand over those discs. Even if it wasn't for Terry and his sister, I would keep them on principle; anybody who comes to my territory and acts in the manner he has acted will get nothing from me.

'Oh,' says Baldwin. 'You're going to make me fetch my big stick.'

'You found the door all on your own on the way in,' I say. He doesn't reply. I meet his eyes, regard him coolly. 'So go on,' I say. 'Fuck off.'

Visiting hours start at four o'clock, and the two-hour wait to see Billy feels like an age, which I try to occupy with casework but cannot concentrate. The electric buzz from my meeting with Baldwin has me wired like a come down from a night out clubbing. Despite winning the closing round, I cannot shake the feeling that from the bell Baldwin had the upper hand; I replay the moment he walked into my office obsessively, trying different tactics, taking different shots, trying to work out how I could have taken him on points.

At five minutes past four, I walk up to Billy's bed where he is talking on his mobile, laughing the exaggerated bark of an Essex wide boy on the make. I would like to force his phone into his mouth, down his throat, the thought of his strangled surprise making my hands become fists. I stand over his bed and he looks up at me, sees something in my face; I have never been adept at hiding my feelings. He says a quick 'Ta-da,' hangs up.

'All right, Danny son?' he says.

'If your legs weren't already broken,' I say, 'I'd be doing them now.'

As far as Billy is concerned, the crime that put him in his hospital bed is an event as distant as his own birth; he is intellectually incapable of making the link between his petty criminality and his present situation. But my gloves are off; I will not pull my punches.

'Heard of a man named Vincent Halliday?' I ask him. Billy's eyes glance guiltily across the room, down, anywhere but at me, like a dog that's been caught eating the Sunday joint. 'Because he knows all about you. And while I'm making a mug of myself calling the police five times a day, he's drinking fucking Martinis in his swimming pool wishing whoever it was he paid to have you offed did a better fucking job of it.'

But I am not a cruel man; my words have hit home and I have no interest in punishing Billy unnecessarily. I stop, watch him process what I have told him.

'Halliday?'

'Remember those stereos you stole? They were his.' Of course, this isn't entirely accurate; but Halliday did steal them first, which, in the criminal world I have more than a passing acquaintance with, does confer some extra-legal rights. 'He had you taken out, Billy. I'm sorry.'

Billy may be simple, but he too has an instinctive knowledge of the rules his world is governed by and he immediately knows, with a sudden clarity he is unused to, that by crossing a man like Halliday his life is now forfeit; that this temporary sanctuary in a hospital ward is as transient as a summer's day. Quietly he begins to weep. Again, oh, Billy. He looks up at me like a baby looks up at a bottle of milk.

'Danny? You can sort this, right?' A small tear rolls down his thin, unloved and unshaved cheek. 'Right?'

8

GABE'S VOLLEY HAS never been as reliable as his baseline game but, now that he is playing off one leg and a prosthetic limb, a cup on one end attached to his knee and a Nike Air trainer on the other, he has no choice but to stay up at the net; he lacks the speed to chase a wide, deep ball down a tramline. Perhaps I am being harsh on his volley; since his accident he has worked on his net game and right now is putting away angled balls with a casual contempt. Our opponents, two lean investment bankers who sauntered on to court and dumped their expensive tennis bags with a complacent authority, are now running with sweat and wondering how these two men, one with a false leg and the other a meaty thug as wide as he is tall, can be beating them quite so viciously.

I am serving, thirty–love up in the third game of the second set, one set and two games up in the match. These men are not used to losing, either in tennis or, I suspect, judging by their top-line equipment and the Porsche they arrived in, life; they do not appear to be enjoying the experience. My serve has seventeen stone of well-drilled bulk behind it and the man I am serving to, his once-immaculate blond hair plastered to his scalp and eyes dark with exhaustion, can only watch the ball hiss past him down the T and thud into the green screens hanging on the fence behind. He takes a deep ragged breath and goes for his towel. Gabe turns around, looks at me, winks.

'Serve.'

I nod, grin, bounce the ball, toss it up and cream a flat serve wide to my opponent's backhand. He doesn't get within two metres of it, flailing flat-footed, his racket waving clumsily like a drunk wielding a broken bottle. He is absolutely finished. If it had not been for the graceless air of privilege they arrived with, I might feel pity for our opponents.

Gabe has been given, by the local tennis authority, special dispensation to remain exclusively a net player except on his serve, not swapping after every point as the rules stipulate. It is an allowance that he did not ask for and argued strenuously against, until the pain I felt watching him forlornly chase passing shots caused me to deliver an ultimatum: stay at the net or I would no longer play with him. As a war hero, there has been little muttering; besides, Gabe is a popular and well-liked man. Of course, there will always be exceptions.

'This is bullshit,' says the man who has just watched my serve go by, tanned with close-shaved black hair and a razor-sharp goatee. 'I stayed at the net all game I'd have energy to burn.'

'Return a serve. Wear him out,' I suggest. 'Not his fault he's a spectator.'

'It speaks,' says the blond-haired man.

'What did you say?' asks Gabe.

'Nobody told us we'd be playing care in the community.'

'That why you're losing? Out of charity?' I ask coolly.

'Let's just fucking play, can we?' says the close-shaved man. He can't get off court fast enough.

It is the blond-haired man's serve; he is wiping sweat out of his eyes, bouncing the ball. He tosses the ball high; I have to give him credit, his serve is a thing of beauty, an easy wind-up and explosive follow-through. It comes at me a little wide and I hustle to it, returning it sweetly, a fast looping cross-court forehand, though a little high and short. It sits up a shade too invitingly on the server's forehand; he steps into it and hits through it, a vicious flat bomb down the line, the other side of the court from me. I have no chance of making it. Gabe takes the awkward, fast jump step he has learned with his prosthetic leg and reaches out a backhand, takes the ball low at arm's length with a magnificent touch and punches it back over the net, past the close-shaved volleyer and into the open backhand court of the blond-haired man who is still standing admiring the forehand he would have bet his house was a clear winner.

'Bollocks,' the blond-haired man says. I cannot help but laugh, my heart full of pride and admiration for Gabe who, on one leg, has just hit one of the finest volleys I have ever seen.

I put a beer down in front of Gabe, back at our outside table of five nights ago, watching a foursome of retirement-age ladies gently lob balls over the net, trot after them, miss them. My body is still hot and buzzing from our win, the memory of the two men angrily stalking off court as they declined the offer of a third set still exhilarating me.

'They'll be worrying at that for a month,' I say. 'We took some of their pride away there.'

Gabe doesn't respond, watches a sixty-year-old hit a tennis ball vertically up in the air. She giggles like a child, hand over her mouth. He seemed well this morning, his eyes dancing with anticipation. Now he looks up at me with his pale eyes radiating scorn. It is a hard gaze to meet for any length of time.

'Problem?'

'You think we took their pride away from them? Never happen, never in a million years. They're back in the Porsche right now, back to their six-figure jobs, they'll be taking it out on their secretaries within the hour, making themselves feel better. People like that don't stay down for long.' He takes a drink, turns away from me. 'But, if it makes you feel all good and strong inside, fucking press on, Dan.'

This isn't fair. 'So, what, beating two good players doesn't mean anything any more?'

Gabe turns back to me. 'You talk about taking something away from them. You know what they've still got, which'll keep them sleeping happily in their beds tonight? Two fucking legs each, that's what they've got. They got beaten by a cripple. So what? They'd still rather be them, not me. Call that a victory?' He shakes his head, disgusted by my naivety.

I do not know what to say, trapped, wanting to offer something to help but conscious that I do not have the first idea what Gabe has been through, what he feels now. For this most bitter and testing part of my best friend's life, I am no more than a spectator. Anything I do say he will treat with contempt, the empty words of a civilian. But as in tennis, so in life; when in doubt, go on the attack.

'So you're smoking weed now,' I say. 'Didn't know that was what tank commanders did.'

'Well, Dan,' he replies evenly, 'I'm not a tank commander any more, am I? So I can do what the fuck I want.'

It was the wrong thing to say, I know. But I also realise that, whatever I say, Gabe will not connect with me, will rise above. He is the most self-reliant and capable man I have ever met; trying to break through to him with confrontational words is like throwing gravel at a head-stone. I sit back, out of his space, drink my beer. On court the ladies string a five-shot rally together and react with delight, dropping their rackets and applauding as if they, not us, have emerged the winners today.

The heat seems, over the weeks, to have lowered, settled so that we are now living in a stagnant pool of hot air that smells of dry grass, petrol, melting tarmac. I do not go back to the office but do not wish to head home; I am loath to admit it, but Baldwin's visit is playing on my mind. I refuse to allow him to have his hand over me and am in danger of becoming consumed by fantasies of vengeance. He is a policeman, backed up and protected by the law; I run an unsuccessful one-man down-at-heel lawyer's firm. How can I take him on?

I take a drive out on to the three-lane concrete A-roads that encircle the area where I live, the air superheated by articulated lorries heading to the Channel, my window open and a dirty breeze blowing through my hair, tearing at my shirtsleeve. It is nearly evening but the weather is so still I cannot gauge any change in temperature. I pass Tilbury Docks looking for a cooling breeze from the river and drive by mile upon mile of corrugated-steel shipping containers, giant battered Lego blocks stacked by some clumsy, soulless giant. Looking at them, I cannot help but think of Billy Morrison, still in his hospital bed but his problems started here, at these docks, with a stolen consignment of stereo equipment. I would like to wash my hands of him, throw him to the sharks; whatever fate has in store for him, it is of his own making. But Billy's problems are too close to home, and our histories are, to an extent, intertwined; we have both had unhappy upbringings and I am not arrogant enough to pretend that, but for the intervention of kind and generous people like Rachael, I could not have turned out like him. I am his lawyer. I feel that I need to do something for him, or the advantage I have been given in life will be worth nothing. But, heading back for my home and certain trouble, I am able to admit to myself that I do not relish the prospect of getting involved with a man like Halliday.

9

WHEN I WAS young, the building was the clubhouse of a chapter of the Outlaws, the pavement outside blocked by chopped-down Harley-Davidsons and men in leather waist-coats over heavy guts, beards obscuring their black Jack Daniel's T-shirts. Along with a boy called Gary Kostas, I once, for a dare, emptied a can of black paint over the seat of one of the parked tilted bikes before running as if death was at my back, Gary by my side sobbing and snivelling and gasping in fear. We were never caught, but I did not walk down this street for years afterwards.

The bikers eventually moved on and now the building, part of a row of shopfronts on a busy street just off the centre, is a bar owned by Vincent Halliday. It has been part of his property and entertainment empire for years but tonight it is being relaunched as Karma, refitted and aimed at a modern and fashionable crowd. I am not a betting man, but I would be happy to stake my car that Vincent has no idea what karma means. My background means that I am still sufficiently well connected to the local semi-legitimate business world that I warrant an invitation, and I am curious to see what Vincent Halliday looks like nowadays; I knew him vaguely when I was young as one of the men my father looked up to and occasionally did work for. Nowadays, I know him only by reputation, though it is some reputation.

Halliday began his professional life as a boxer, a big-hearted middleweight who could go the distance but soon got the reputation of a slapper; in all his fights, he never once put a man on the canvas. After he hung up his gloves, he used the connections he had built up with men who were not averse to a fight, and began running security for clubs in the area. But naturally, with such a wealth of muscle at his disposal, he found other uses for it, and soon he was controlling the drugs trade within those clubs; then, when he had cornered that market, expanding out so that he ran the distribution and the importation of whatever that day's narcotic of choice was, across the whole of south Essex.

Since those days, Halliday has diversified, owning strip clubs, bars, property. But everybody knows that these outward signs of wealth are only the tip of the iceberg and that the real money comes from the dirty worlds of drugs, gambling, women. Despite the superficial appearance of legitimacy, Halliday has always carried with him the whiff of villainy; his chances of assimilating into decent society are about as good as a mongrel winning at Crufts. He is surrounded by stories of violence done, rivals terrorised, enemies found dead; but his network of influence is so diffuse that the trail is always broken before it reaches his door. In the late-eighties, he was almost put away for the murder of two men, Michael Connor and Gavin O'Dwyer, rivals in the door trade who vanished and who were last seen in the company of Halliday. Despite blood being found in his car and a recently fired gun buried at his home, their bodies were never found and the case against him fell apart. You have to give him credit, he has never been caught, done only minor time. And he is a far richer, and possibly happier, man than I will ever be.

I nod to the men on the door, grey camel-hair coats and bald heads, show them my invitation. They look at me with the curious, appraising air I attract from hard men as they assess my threat level. Inside, the bar is full, the crowd separated into its usual constituent parts: middle-aged men talking quietly together, used to getting by without the need to raise their voices; brash young wannabes with chunky silver and hair they have spent too long over, competing to see who can talk loudest, trying to make their mark; and overly made-up skinny women wearing expensive clothes, young and old alike, treading a very thin line between skimpy and indecent and, I think unkindly, more often than not finding themselves on the wrong side. This is the Essex I grew up in, as delineated and hierarchical as any public school, bound by its own laws and expectations and dress code. And it is true that I feel more at home here than I ever did on golf weekends in the company of soft and successful lawyers.

'Danny! Hello, son, where've you crawled from?' A man named Jimmy, whom I have known since we were small children, has separated himself from a group of men and joined me standing at the bar. I am trying to attract the eye of a sullen girl in a crop top who appears to believe that serving drinks is beneath her, and Jimmy reaches over and closes my fist over the note I am holding. 'On me, Danny, put your money away. Here, darling, you serving or just looking pretty?' The girl looks up at Jimmy's cheerful shout, comes over. 'Whatchoo having?' he asks me.

'Get me a beer then,' I say. 'Thanks.'

'Nah, pleasure, Danny.' To the girl, 'Two beers, and if you can manage a smile you can have one yourself.' She twitches a small, sarcastic effort at Jimmy and turns away to handle our order. ''Sa matter with her?' he says. 'Face on her like her fanny's healed up.' He grins at me lopsidedly. He was born with a cleft palate which was perfunctorily reconstructed by a surgeon who perhaps had half a mind on the golf course; it gives Jimmy a perpetual sneer that his irrepressibly cheery character robs of any malice. His father left his family when Jimmy was a young child and he and his two sisters were brought up single-handedly by their mother, a proud, honest and hard-working woman who watched in dismay as Jimmy became involved in petty criminality. But whatever misdemeanours Jimmy gets up to in his life, he is always a welcome face in mine. He is a man it is impossible to dislike and I often wonder how he handles the more unpleasant aspects of his business; I cannot imagine him putting the frighteners on anybody. Perhaps he waits outside in the van.

'How've you been, Jimmy? Your mum?'

'Yeah, she's good. She's well. Still working, you know what she's like. I try to tell her, "Listen, gel," I say, "you need to take it easy, slow down." Says she'll have plenty of time to rest when she's dead.'

'Sounds about right.' The girl comes back with our beers, holds up a third in meek enquiry.

'Go on then, seeing as you asked.' He pays her, takes a swallow. 'You? Still doing all that lawyering?'

'Yeah, still doing the lawyering.'

'You done well there, Danny,' says Jimmy. 'Me and Mum, we always say that. Proud of you, what you done, how you got out.' He points the bottom of his bottle at the crowd. 'Made summink of yourself.'

This isn't an area I want to discuss. Got out? Then what am I doing here, my mind full of thoughts of Vincent Halliday? I change the subject. 'So, Karma. That your idea, Jimmy?'

'My idea? You think…?' He looks at me, sees that I am joking. 'Cheeky cunt. Nah, weren't me, Halliday's new piece, it was her idea. You probably know her.' He stands on tiptoe, looks across the bar. 'Sat there in that gold dress. Debbie, used to follow her brother around, Paul Chance. Remember?'

I follow his gaze, see a pretty blonde woman sitting on her own. I do, vaguely, a grubby girl in dirty white socks and sandals trailing a cloth doll. Looks like she's come a long way since then. 'Yeah, Karma, it was her idea. Reckons it's classy. Eastern or summink.'

'Right.'

Jimmy takes a swig, looks at me. 'Shit, ain't it?' He grins, slightly nervously; though he's talking with me who has no vested interest, mocking any decision Halliday has okayed is dangerously seditious.

'I'm nearly forty,' I tell Jimmy. 'What do I know?'

65

'Tell me about it. I need someone like Debbie meself, keep me young.' He casts a speculative look at the available candidates in the bar, comes up empty, turns back to me. 'You seeing anybody?'

I think of Sophie, gone from my life now as if she had never existed. 'Nah. More trouble than it's worth.'

A man from the group Jimmy left is jerking his head in our direction. Jimmy notices, rolling his eyes at me but making sure his back is turned so the man cannot see. 'Gotta go.' He puts his hand on my arm, gives it a squeeze, says honestly, 'Good seeing you, Danny.' He swaggers off to the group and I watch him go wondering at the decisions we make at a young age and how they trap us for life; me and my schooling, Jimmy and his early immersion in the local underworld.

I talk to some more people I know, my status as lawyer not causing any suspicion in this gathering of men who habitually live on the wrong side of the law. In this social stratum, lawyers are seen as neutral entities, their allegiances to either side, crooked or straight, merely a matter of which is willing to pay the most. I consider myself a basically honest man; but out here I am a long way away from the black-and-white certainties of law school, and my day-to-day work often reflects that. Cash deals off the books for house purchases, properties put in the names of geriatric Alzheimer's grandparents babbling to themselves obliviously in nursing homes; I am upholding no cherished ideals. I often ask myself whether I am on a slippery slope. I like to believe that I am not, that my moral underpinnings are still strong. But I am also aware that, so far, they have not been seriously tested.

Debbie recognises me, I don't know how; but, living in the goldfish bowl of my town, everybody knows somebody who knows somebody. I am passing her, heading for the exit and home, when she calls my name. She is alone, texting on her phone, bored. She must be eight, nine years younger than me; she is dressed, even for this place, in an outfit that suggests an equal lack of taste and modesty. I already know, from conversations I have had tonight, that she was a dancer at one of Halliday's gentlemen's clubs, the current euphemistic term for a dark room with an expensive bar and a pole in the middle. She caught his eye and it did not take much persuading to tempt her off the stage and into his mansion where she took her place next to him in bed, still warm from the departed body of wife number four.

'Hello, Debs,' I say. 'It's been a while. Surprised you remember me.'

'You ain't changed so much,' she says. She has the uninterested vacuous eyes of somebody who is not only ignorant but who believes that having a vanishingly small frame of reference is in itself a strength, something to be proud of. 'Besides, I used to fancy you, didn't I.'

I do not know what to say in response. I smile down at her; despite her being near enough my age to make a relationship unremarkable, I cannot help but treat her in an avuncular fashion. She is still just a girl.

'You're like a lawyer now, intcha?'

'Yes.' Again I am stuck for anything more. Everything she says is a statement, a brash declaration that smothers any answer. Debbie is looking back at her phone. I am about to say goodbye when she looks up again.

'Ask you a question?'

''Course.'

'How comes they let that boyfriend out when he must've killed that girl?'

'Who?'

'Rosie O'Shaughnessy. They nicked her boyfriend but now they've let him go. Says here.' She holds up her phone, which is connected to a news site. 'On bail.'

'They can only keep him so long without charging him. They can't have enough evidence. They still haven't found a body, have they? No evidence of any crime.' Like Halliday, I cannot help thinking. Connor and O'Dwyer; no bodies, no case.

She looks at me blankly for a second, two, three. 'She weren't that much younger than me, you know.' I nod, do not reply. She was about a decade younger than Debbie but it would be unkind to point this out. I notice her eyes focus on something behind my shoulder, something she's not entirely happy to see. I hear an abrupt voice. 'Know you, son?'

I turn to see Vincent Halliday, a man with a face over which the skin is stretched tight, his bone structure underneath creating ugly lumps around his cheekbones and eye sockets, his jawbone easily visible. His skin is shiny and smooth and seems thin, his hair is cut close to his scalp. He is shorter than me and stands back on his heels, his chin thrust forward. His eyes dart about, from Debbie to me and back again.

'Vince, this is Danny. Frankie's boy.'

Halliday doesn't react, keeps looking at the two of us, waiting for more. He reminds me of a snake; he could strike at any time.

'Yeah, Frankie Connell. You know. This is Daniel, his son. The lawyer.' Debbie looks at me. 'I think he's going senile.'

Halliday turns to her, doesn't say anything but the sparkle dies in her eyes like she's received bad news. He turns back to me.

'Yeah, I know Frank. Bit of a mug but no harm to him. You his boy, are you?' He speaks quickly, as if he can't wait to get to the end of his sentence, move on. Tension runs through him like a pulse. He looks at me, challenging me to be quick with my answer. I take my time to respond. I am no admirer of my father but I can no more let this calculated insult go unanswered than I can close my eyes and vanish.

'I think your daughter's ready to go home,' I say. I regret saying the words even as I speak them and experience a dizzy feeling as if I'm taking a leap off a cliff into a deep black gaping unknown. Halliday's jaw tightens and his eyes flick all over my face, as if looking for some physical clue as to why I've just said something so utterly suicidal. I think he is going to go for me, his body tensed for attack; then he masters himself and the moment passes. He smiles distractedly, turns, chins two men towards him.

'This man's just leaving,' he says to them. He looks at me. 'Go on, piss off. We'll meet again.'

'I hope so,' I say. 'I want to talk to you about Billy Morrison.'

'Who?' he says.

'You know who he is,' I say. 'Otherwise, why would you want to have him killed?'

10

I AM AT home and drinking a beer in my living room, trying not to think about what I have just done, what I have just said. The news on the television is talking about the missing girl and I try to gain perspective on my situation by imagining the pain and fear her parents must be experiencing right now, but I cannot shake the sense of menace that seems to lurk all around me.

My telephone rings and I do not wish to pick it up, do not want to invite further problems into my life right now; but it does not stop ringing and eventually I cross to the counter and answer it.

'Danny?'

'Gabe.'

'Yeah, Danny, spot of bother. Wondered if you could bail me out. Sorry to have to ask.'

His voice is imprecise, a little too loud, not the disciplined delivery he learned in the Army where not a word was wasted. He has been drinking.

'As in, the legal sense of provide money to secure your release?'

'That sense, yeah.'

'Where are you?'

'Station on Main Road.'

I know it; I have spent more time there, waiting for clients and, on occasion, my father, than I care to remember. 'Be there in ten. You kill anyone?'

'Don't think so. Nearly, but not quite.'

At the custody desk, I speak with a young woman behind glass who would be pretty if not for the expression of weary suspicion she wears like it's part of the uniform. I explain who I am, that I am representing my client, a Mr Gabriel McBride. She taps some keys on her computer, tells me to take a seat, she'll try to find the officer in charge. I sit down on a moulded plastic chair and read the notices on the wall opposite, posters advising on how to deal with domestic abuse, what to do if you witness suspicious behaviour that could be linked, in some tenuous fashion, to terrorism, the number to call.

An old couple are across from me, sitting slumped in an attitude of defeat. The man's phone rings, he answers, tells whoever is on the other end that Dean's been picked up again, that they've been waiting for hours to see him. The man on the other end, who I guess is Dean's father, swears fluently and audibly down the phone; the gist of his tirade is that his son, Dean, is a cunt and if he thinks he's coming down to get him out he can fucking well think again. The old man catches me watching and tells Dean's father to hold on, he'll go outside, calm down, son, don't get excited. But, watching the collapse of the old woman's shoulders, I suspect that this is a road they've been down many times before and that Dean's story will have, ultimately, an unhappy ending. Some people are not destined to be saved.

Clearly, my status as lawyer wields more clout than that of two pensioners with a troubled grandson; the woman at the desk calls my name, shows me to a door behind which is waiting a uniformed sergeant, a good-humoured man in his late-forties, perhaps early-fifties, short hair and a trim moustache and broken veins on his cheeks. The woman buzzes me through.

'Mr Connell?'

'And you are?'

'Sergeant Hicklin. Follow me please.'

Sergeant Hicklin has an amused glint in his eye, which immediately tells me that, whatever it is Gabe has done, it is not too serious. 'Know your client well?' he asks over his shoulder as I follow him down a neon-lit corridor.

'Well enough.'

He opens a blue door, a card on it reading *Interview Room 4*. He holds it open, waits for me to pass, follows me in.

'Sit down. Young Mr McBride is on his way.'

I sit down at a wooden table, tape player on one side. The walls of the room are some kind of textured concrete, pale mottled green. Hicklin passes me, sits opposite, facing the door.

'What's he done?'

Sergeant Hicklin examines my face, looking for I don't know what. 'Where'd he learn to fight?'

'Iraq, Afghanistan, Aldershot, take your pick.'

Hicklin nods. 'Know him well, right? Friend of yours.'

'Let's keep this on a professional footing.' This man is nobody's fool; he has already guessed that our relationship goes deeper than simply lawyer–client.

'As you like.' Hicklin leans back in his chair, looks me over. 'Well, professionally speaking, your client, Mr Gabriel Bruce-bloody-Lee McBride has, tonight, started a small war of his own, outside Liquid nightclub.'

'Doesn't sound like him.'

'No?'

'He's a soldier, not a hooligan.'

'Ex-soldier. Yes, well. At the moment I've got two confirmed hospital cases, and numerous cuts and bruises. A lot of pissed-off people. Two or three fairly impressed bouncers.'

'I'll give you ten to one he didn't start it.'

Hicklin picks up a pen, holds it between two hands, nods. 'And I wouldn't take those odds. Because I'd agree. Got a witness, see. Tells me a group of lads found it amusing he was missing a leg. They'd been drinking, thought they'd have some fun with him. You can probably guess the rest.'

The Gabe I know, trained though he is in numerous, creative methods of disabling opponents, would have let any insult ride. Things would not have escalated into a brawl; he would have walked away. But, not for the first time this week, I have to question just how well I know Gabe nowadays.

'I'll be honest, I'd hate to see what he's capable of on two legs. I watched the CCTV.' Hicklin chuckles. 'The whole nick watched it. Could have sold tickets. Man's an overnight celebrity.'

There's a twinkle in Hicklin's eye and I instinctively know he is on Gabe's side; that here is a policeman who goes by his experience and gut rather than the book. I relax.

'So he banged a few heads together,' I say. 'Got that established. You going to charge him?'

Hicklin nods, gets down to business. 'We've got the witness. We've had a look at your friend's war record. We've got no axe to grind. My youngest is in the Paratroopers.'

'Which leaves us where?'

'We'll bind him over, if you'll agree to keep an eye on him. Keep him out of trouble.'

There's a knock on the door.

'Ah, that must be Rambo now,' says Sergeant Hicklin.

Apart from a minute sway, Gabe looks as fresh and sober as if he's appearing for a job interview. He grins at me, nods to Sergeant Hicklin. Behind him is a young constable with the come-on swagger of the young and power happy. Gabe pauses in the doorway and the constable shoves him from behind. I get up from my chair.

'Tell your constable he touches my client once more and I'll be filing a complaint before his shift is finished.'

Hicklin sighs. 'Sit down, sit down. Constable Dawson here's got a lot to learn. Hormones, the latter stages of puberty. I apologise on his behalf. Happy?'

I sit down, push out a chair for Gabe.

'I'll stand,' he says.

'At ease,' says Hicklin, first signs of irritation. 'Christ's sake. We're not nicking you. Got those papers, Dawson?'

Dawson hands him a stack of sheets, kicks my chair leg as he passes. I frown at Hicklin, who shakes his head, looks

75

to the ceiling: God help me. He flicks through pages, then shoves two sheets across the table to me.

'Sign these, get your friend's signature, then do me a favour. Foxtrot Oscar, as they say in the Army.'

Gabe doesn't talk much on the way home, and I cannot tell whether it is because he is still too drunk to talk or simply too ashamed. We drive through the dark streets, empty apart from one or two swaying shirtsleeved men unwilling to admit that the night is over and that tomorrow is already upon them. Yellow streetlights paint Gabe's face as we drive.

'Couldn't have just walked away?'

'He says. When's the last time you turned the other cheek?'

He's got a point.

'You need to talk to somebody.'

'We're talking.'

'You know what I mean. This isn't you.'

Gabe rouses himself, reaches forward and turns on the radio, finds a station, scans for another one. I do not know how to speak to him, how to reach him. In our history, there has never been awkwardness, no subject has been taboo. How can he have become so distant?

'It's about the leg, isn't it?' I say. But even as I say the words I sense how hollow, how amateurish and clumsy they are. Gabe is one of the most complex and intelligent men I have ever met. I have no idea what he is going through; I have no idea where to begin. Gabe looks across at me and I cannot meet his eye.

'Daniel?'

'Yes?'

'Let's not.'

We spend the rest of the journey in silence, like a couple who've been out to a restaurant and left in a hurry after a spiteful argument. I pull up outside his house and get out of the car with him, follow him to his front door, walk in after him without waiting for an invitation. Gabe doesn't seem to care, disappears upstairs. I wait for him in his kitchen, put the kettle on, do the things we're taught to do in circumstances such as these. The kettle has boiled and tea is made and I am beginning to think that he has gone to bed, passed out, when I hear his uneven steps on the stairs. I am still rehearsing what to say to him when he appears in the doorway holding something in his hand.

'Remember this?' he says.

I look at it. It is our trophy, our defining moment, Essex Junior County doubles champions. Of course I remember it. Just looking at its silver form of two boys, one serving one crouching, brings back the memories of that time, perhaps the finest of my life; a time when Gabe and I believed ourselves indestructible, blowing opponents off the court with an ease that, at times, felt pre-ordained, as if we had been divinely chosen. Sixteen years old and favoured by the gods. I remember the smell of barbecues, endless conversations about women, late nights and too much beer, the delicious challenge of girls' bras, parties in strangers' houses held while their parents were away. Endless blue skies and limitless possibilities. And Gabe, always Gabe, my constant partner.

'I remember. 'Course I do.'

'I want you to have it.'

'Why?'

He looks at me and I notice how unsteady he still is on his feet, how he is wavering subtly, constantly regaining his balance. He is still far from sobering up; or perhaps he has just been tapping some secret stash upstairs. But Gabe is no ordinary person and, drunk or not, he is still capable of unmanning me with his gaze; I struggle to keep eye contact. But for once he breaks off first, sighs, puts the trophy on the kitchen counter. He walks away, back upstairs, and I wonder, while simultaneously hating the cliché, whether he is likely to do anything stupid.

At the stairs he turns back to me, one hand on the banister. 'Because, Danny, I can't bear to look at the fucking thing any more.'

11

I DO NOT sleep well and wake up early, listening to the sound of birds outside my window and wishing that I did not have to open the curtains, let the real world intrude into the sanctity of my home. As I eat breakfast, trying to keep my mind off the events of the night before, I hear the news over the radio of the discovery of Rosie O'Shaughnessy's body in the dense woodland of Epping Forest. A broken neck, no evidence of sexual assault. I have a mental image from my childhood, of a blackbird that flew into the French windows of our living room; it lay, dead, on the patio, its head bent away from its body at an acute angle, its yellow eye gazing sightlessly up into the sky. Rosie must have lain there for days. She was not even twenty years old; she never had the opportunity to at least make her own life-changing mistakes.

I look about my kitchen. I live in an airy Victorian four-bed, constructed over a century ago when houses were built to a quality rather than a cost; it has high ceilings, period features, and is as close to luxury as I will ever need. But this morning listening to the news of Rosie's death, for the first time I see it in a different light, my own comfort in such sharp contrast to the squalid end of her life. The white walls bathed in early-morning sunlight seem a splendour I do not deserve, in fact feel guilty for enjoying. When did my life become so safe, so comfortable? This thought naturally leads me to my next, which hits me with such sudden force that I lay my spoon down on the table and stare blankly out of the window, unable to move until I have processed the implications. What the hell was I thinking challenging, no, worse, insulting a known gangster and murderer in his own bar?

I do not have long to worry; Halliday is clearly not a man to allow an insult to go unanswered for long. Later that morning, I am at my office and considering a long-running case, an elderly couple who had the chimney and part of the roof of their six-hundred-year-old converted coach house demolished by a wrecking ball supposed to be razing their neighbour's garage. The neighbour is a footballer and apparently needed somewhere bigger to park his Hummer; he is South American from an impoverished background and is finding it hard to accept the cost and bureaucracy involved in the repair of a Grade I-listed building, despite his astronomical weekly wage. But dispute resolution is my area of expertise and I believe I am making progress towards a satisfactory outcome, his histrionic Latin outrage an act I am becoming familiar with and beginning to enjoy.

I am disturbed from this modern and tabloid-friendly tale by my bell ringing. I put my papers together, place them to one side and walk into the lobby. Standing outside my door is Vincent Halliday in a grey suit with two of his men, both bigger than he is and dead-eyeing me through the glass from behind him with the nonchalant air of those practised in brutality. I pause, steady myself, realise that I have little choice. I open the door and nod them in. I dealt this hand; now I must see how it plays out.

If anything, Halliday's reaction to my place of work is even less impressed than Baldwin's. I momentarily question whether a colour scheme of white, black and chrome would convey a more professional ambience or would come across as too masculine; I have heard that condemned men are plagued with inane thoughts on the walk to the execution chamber. Halliday takes in my meagre office in several agitated and disgusted glances and I wonder about his blood pressure. He is wound up as tightly as anybody I have ever met. His men take their places at the door to the lobby, one either side, and I realise with a sick suddenness that this is a scene that the three of them have played out, with variations, many times in the past.

'We'll start,' says Halliday without any preamble, 'with what you said to me last night.' We are all still standing in front of my desk; I would like to invite him to sit down but feel the volatility in the air and worry that it might be the last thing I ever get to suggest. My office is not big and our combined presence, so close together, is oppressive; we are like four dogs in the back of a van that have not yet decided who will be the first to launch. Halliday meets my eyes and I am surprised by the amount of rage in his; he is barely in control of himself, his hands squeezed into fists at his sides.

I wonder what is keeping him from attacking me, or giving the nod to have his men do it for him. 'What have you got to say for yourself?'

His choice of words is oddly paternal, as if he has caught me cheating at school. I need to choose my next words very carefully.

'I was reacting to what I saw as a provocation,' I say slowly. 'My father might not be successful or come with a reputation, but I could not and cannot understand why you would call him a mug to my face.' Halliday is watching me intently and so far he doesn't react. I take a deep breath. 'I should not have said what I said, and I am willing to apologise. But I still believe that I was provoked.' There. I cannot be any more contrite; I have offered Halliday everything that my pride will allow. He stands still, as still as he can, but his entire body somehow betrays his thought processes, as if the violence of his internal deliberations is causing his body to minutely vibrate. He blinks, his eyes once again search my face.

'Fuck me you've got a pair on you,' he says, a flat statement that implies no warmth or admiration. 'I dunno.' He unbunches his fists, puts his hands together, wraps one with the other. There is silence, and I cannot help but wonder at the assurance this man carries with him; he is deciding my fate in front of me, in my own office, reaching his decision in his own sweet time. 'I dunno,' he says again.

But like anybody there is a limit to my patience. I walk behind my desk, sit down and pull my papers towards me. 'Don't let me rush you,' I say, looking down.

I do not know if my actions prompt his decision but Halliday sits in the chair in front of my desk and pulls his suit jacket apart, crosses his legs, makes himself comfortable. Although he has not said anything, the feeling in my office lifts like sun emerging from behind a cloud. One of the men by the door takes out his mobile and checks for messages. Halliday looks about my office with less agitation than during his first appraisal, takes his time, then looks back at me.

'Fucking horrible place you've got here.'

'Thanks,' I say. 'I like it too.'

Halliday cannot help the suspicion of a smile appearing on his thin lips. 'You've got more mouth than a cow's got tits,' he says. 'You know that?'

I do not reply, try to keep my expression neutral. I do not have the merest idea how this man thinks.

'Here's what's going to happen,' Halliday says. 'I'm looking to buy some properties for rental purposes. You are going to deal with the purchase, tenancy, all that paperwork shit. Spare me the trouble. Be the man in charge. Right?'

'How many properties?' I ask. He has caught me off guard but I am attempting to roll with his punches, keep up with his relentless onslaught. I may, and I believe I do, appear calm, but it is an act. Though I am not a wealthy man and I am trying to grow my practice, Vincent Halliday would not be top of my list of prospective clients. Anything he is involved in is going to be toxic and I do not want to touch it.

'One. A conversion. Old convent into flats. Apartments.'

'All right, well, if you'd like to engage me as your solicitor I will need some details. I'll need to see your passport.'

'You what, son? Do me a favour. This ain't your everyday fucking transaction. This'll be done through a company I'm setting up, is all you need to know for now. And you –' Halliday leans further forward '– you'll be our representative. Any correspondence, it comes to you. I don't want nothing to do with it.'

'Not really my area,' I say. 'I can do the conveyancing...'

He continues as if I have not spoken. 'So if and when Revenue and Customs come sniffing about, this is where they come first. With me?'

His energy is unstoppable; already for him this discussion is finished, the deal is struck and he is ready to leave, move on to his next piece of business. But I am not done. I believe I can see where this is heading and I want to know more.

'You'll expect me to vet any prospective tenants.'

Halliday is halfway out of his seat; he sits back down. 'Tenants.' He looks at the two men he came in with; they smile, one of them laughs. Halliday looks back at me. 'We'll take care of all that. Less questions you ask the better.'

'Right.' I think I see.

'With me?' he says again.

'I think so.'

So there it is. I am going to be fronting a property scam for Vincent Halliday and I am being given no choice in the matter. My profession is often slandered by people and it is true that there are plenty of lawyers who will cut corners; but it is not easy to find a lawyer who will willingly act as an accessory to major-league money laundering, which I suspect is the case here. I look at Halliday. His suit is expensive, probably cost him close to a thousand pounds, he drives a Bentley, he lives in a twelve-bedroom mansion. For a criminal with few visible means of support, this is a perennial problem: how to explain away your manifest wealth when the tax office comes knocking. One answer is to buy a string of properties, fill them with fictitious tenants and use your own illegal profits as rent. Your bank account fills up with money that looks whiter than white, washed through your property; all you need is a lawyer to give it the appearance of legitimacy. For Halliday, I am a gift from heaven.

Halliday stands up. 'I'll be in touch.'

'Hold on, I've got something to say.'

Halliday raises his eyebrows patronisingly. 'Yes?'

'Nothing happens to Billy Morrison. You leave him alone. He's not a bad kid, just, what was it? A bit of a mug.'

'I don't know who you're talking about.'

'I'm sure you don't. I'd still like your assurance.'

I meet his eye with a direct stare. Now I know that he needs something from me I feel less fear. Halliday stares back, eyes flickering over my face, then shakes his head, amused. 'Christ, you're like your mother, d'you know that?'

'My mother? You knew my mother?' I cannot stop my words; I have said it before I realise I am going to, a shameful display of weakness. But Halliday's reaction is curious; he looks away from me, busies himself with his phone, turns to the door. His manner is suddenly as furtive as a guilty child distancing itself from a broken vase.

'Not really, son, no. Can't say I did.' He nods to his men and, without waiting for them, abruptly leaves; they peel away from the wall and follow him, fighters in formation. After they have gone I stand behind my desk and wonder about what just happened. How did Halliday know my mother? And why did he all but run away when I asked him about her?

Forgiveness comes at a price from men like Halliday; I accept that I have, compared to some other men who have crossed him, got off lightly. What he has asked me to do I will deal with; what he has asked me to do is not my first concern right now. I sit down, pick up a pen from my desk, click it open, closed. Events and revelations have occurred too quickly for the implications to coalesce and make sense in my mind and I need to take some time to work things through. I am thirty-seven years old. In all of my life I have never been able, though I have tried and cajoled and demanded, to persuade my father to discuss my mother; worse, to even acknowledge her as more than a bitter accusation. She went. She left us. She didn't care. She was nobody. A bitch. Now a man I barely know has looked me in the eye and seen something in me that reminded him of her. For the first time, I sense my mother as more than simply an absence, an untraceable, foreign name on a birth certificate; for the first time, she is a person who contributed some genetic substance to my existence, who, according to Halliday, I am 'just like'. Just like a disbeliever who discovers faith in God, I suddenly see my mother as more than a mundane act of betrayal; she is a person and a part of me. I cannot let this go. I will find out the truth, though I know that delving into the secrets of the past rarely unearths answers that we like.

12

EVERY SATURDAY MORNING, I coach juniors in tennis, at the same club I was coached at myself nearly thirty years ago. My mind will not stop worrying at what Halliday said, and I know that to get to the truth I must visit my father, today. But Saturday mornings are untouchable, the one part of my week I will not allow to be tainted by the tawdry events of real life; so I finish my breakfast, pack my rackets and head for the courts. It is cooler this morning with a breeze that feels like a reassuring murmur on my skin, and in the summer light the events of the last days feel distant, unreal. As I step between the high hedges that surround the club, I get the feeling that I have always had walking on to the courts; that ordinary life is far away, and that nothing matters now except for the geometry of the game, the trajectory of the balls, positions of the players, angles of approach. It is a simple and fine feeling, and I would not exchange it for anything.

At the court, the juniors are dutifully lined up against the fence outside the courts, waiting to be invited in. They are dressed mostly in white, their parents gathered around the picnic tables outside the clubhouse, raised eyebrows nodding encouragement to their skinny children who, they hope, will be Britain's next great hope for an Open victory. I enjoy these mornings, coaching young people who believe anything is possible, who have not yet been corrupted by the real world outside the false lines and rules of a tennis court.

'Morning, young man,' says George. He takes the youngest group, his legs being, he claims, 'absolutely buggered'. He has an instant rapport with the kids, which I do not; they love him, they are a little scared of me. Not that I am a tyrant, but I give praise sparingly and am critical when I see a child playing a lazy stroke I know he or she can hit sweetly. Perhaps I take it too seriously. But when I do praise a child's shot their face will light up like they're blowing out their birthday candles, so I guess I am not doing anything too wrong.

I am helped every week by Maria, a tall, dark lady who is a teacher at the local primary school and who represented Essex until university took her away to the North East for five years. She is lively, irreverent, and she always lingers in my mind for some time after the end of the lessons. She is far, far too good for me.

'Oh,' she says, looking at me with concern and dropping her racket bag. She is a knockout in a white skirt. 'Did Daniel climb out of the wrong side of bed this morning?' I shake my head, trying not to smile, failing. 'Seven,' she says, her head cocked as she scrutinises me. 'Out of ten. Your hangover. Am I right?'

'No hangover,' I say.

'Just not quite your normal sunny self.' She nods. 'Uh-huh. Just do what I do. Take it out on the kids.' She steps in close, whispers. 'They're more resilient than they look.'

We split the kids into two groups, one group per court, and each play a revolving rally; two lines of children queue on each side of the net and after each kid hits a shot they scoot round the other side, join the other queue, wait for their turn again. If they miss a shot they leave the rally. It is amazing how peer pressure and the fear of humiliation can improve a seven-year-old's ground strokes. We move on to drills, volleys, and finish, as always, by warming up their serves. No match play; my tennis club does not believe in forcing competition at too young an age. My instincts tell me that this is wrong but every other country does the same and their tennis players win Grand Slams, so I am happy to keep my opinion to myself. By the end, the children are tired but happy; I invite them into a huddle and tell them that they have done well and that they should remember that it's not how hard you can hit the ball, it's where you can hit it and how consistently. They look at me with big eyes, nod seriously as if I'm the keeper of some mystical truth. How can some people take that kind of trust and abuse it?

After the kids leave, their parents full of praise for the shots they have witnessed, the effort their child put in, I sit on my own in the sun drinking a Coke. They are lucky, these children; many others could never have dreamed of such affection, of such interest being taken in their lives as they grew up.

Maria sits down opposite me, flushed from her work; she smiles at me happily. I wonder what it would be like to hold her and lay my forehead in the perspiration which films the tan skin of her neck. She has long, black wavy hair, which she has let out of the ponytail she wore during the lesson and she is stunning. I look down at my big blunt hands.

'Penny for them,' she says.

'Oh, nothing,' I say. 'Just my usual existential crisis.'

'Oh, that,' she says. 'Take two Aspirin. If that doesn't work there's always suicide.'

I laugh, which feels good.

'I heard about Sophie,' she says. 'Gabe told me. I'm sorry.'

'Didn't work out,' I say. 'No big tragedy.'

'She was too good for you anyway.' It is Maria's attempt at a joke and I know I shouldn't but I cannot help but take it the wrong way. She sees that her attempt at levity has missed the mark and she instinctively reaches out and places her hand on mine. 'I'm sorry. Stupid. Take it back.'

'Kids enjoyed it today,' I say, changing the subject to help her forget her embarrassment, her touch making me unsure of my voice. 'You're good with them.'

'I get enough practice,' she says. 'Some adult company wouldn't hurt now and then.'

I do not answer, hope this conversation isn't going in the direction I fear. Maria smiles at me. 'We could always, if you thought it might help… We could maybe go out.'

I look at Maria. She is a good person, genuinely good, which may sound mawkish but is a rare enough quality that I find it remarkable. But I have just invited trouble into my life and do not want her anywhere near it. This is the wrong time, and I am the wrong man for her.

'I don't think so,' I say abruptly. It sounds rude, ungracious, and I can see that I have hurt her. She notices she still has her hand on mine and she takes it back awkwardly.

'Okay, no big deal,' she says.

'I'm not your type,' I say, trying to make up for my reaction. 'Believe me.'

'Maybe I could decide that.'

'No.' This is getting worse. 'Really, just...' What? 'Please, forget it,' I say tersely.

Maria's face closes up and I know that one door has shut, one opportunity gone for ever. It makes me feel desperately sad and I wish I could reach out, could go back and handle this conversation better. But really how else could it have ended? I will not ask this woman into my life, however much I would like to. It is better this way. Maria gets up, turns away. 'See you next week,' she says formally and goes. I crush my can of Coke in my hand and a sharp piece of metal cuts the inside joint of my index finger, makes it bleed.

As I leave, George stops me. Does he live here? 'Did you hear about that girl?' he asks me. 'They found her, poor kid.' I nod, nothing to say. 'Who would do something like that? How could they?' George seems genuinely distressed and I wonder with a grudging admiration how somebody can live over seventy years and still retain their belief in the essential goodness of people; how he can be so surprised that they often act in hideous ways. He clasps his hands together as if in prayer, pauses a second as if he is about to deliver bad news.

'Listen, Daniel, look out for that friend of yours, could you?'

'Gabe?'

'He behaved rather badly here a few nights ago. One too many light ales I'm sure and, really, who hasn't made an arse of himself once or twice?' I'm willing to bet George hasn't. 'But perhaps you could have a word? See how he is. Losing a leg, it's never going to be plain sailing, if you know what I mean.'

'He's going through a rough patch,' I say. 'I'll keep an eye on him.' I do not tell him about last night, about Gabe's recent brush with the law. George is a close friend to both of us but a tennis club is, in many ways, no more discreet than a sewing circle. Gabe does not need his problems publicised.

'All that post-traumatic what-have-you. He's a fine young man. We all think so.'

I nod, tell George that I'll handle it, exude a confidence in dealing with him that I do not feel. I have now not one but three men, all dangerous men in their own ways, to worry about. Gabe, Baldwin, Halliday. I try to think of them as cases and wonder which, if any, I will be able to resolve happily. Or if not happily, at least without anyone getting hurt. If I am to be honest with myself, I have no idea.

I leave the club and head to my car, past a group of builders standing outside a half-constructed mock-Tudor house that must have at least eight bedrooms. I need to visit my father; I know that I am putting it off, delaying the moment I have to confront him about my mother. I can predict how it will go, the silence, the resentment, the sudden switch to rage; it is a cycle I have been experiencing since I was a child. One of the builders has his thumb in a mug, looks like he is in pain. Another builder offers him a plaster, but the builder with his thumb dipped in the mug says no, he needs gauze, there's too much blood. Seeing them makes me think, perhaps because of his wound, of Gabe; I have a feeling of guilt, made worse by what George has just told me. I have not spoken to Gabe since he went upstairs in his house, leaving me holding our trophy from so many years ago. He has not answered his phone since and I cannot help but worry, while telling myself that I am being melodramatic, that it may already be too late to help him. Before I get to my father, I need to know how Gabe is, and see whether there is anything in our friendship that I can offer him.

13

GABE INHERITED HIS house from his parents several years ago, both of them having died within months of each other of two different forms of cancer, any fight his father was putting up against his rotting lungs vanishing when his wife lost her battle. Gabe's father was, like me, a lawyer; but after that bland comparison all similarities end. He was a gentle and principled man who took the train every morning into Temple where he was the co-founder of a small set of chambers dedicated to defending the civil and human rights of the underprivileged and oppressed. He worked hard but his weekends were sacrosanct, dedicated to Gabe and his two sisters and, as Gabe and I became friends, to me too. He never attempted to play a fatherly role with me, but he did set a quiet example, which had a profound influence. He was slight and unimposing, a man of books and reasoned conversation. I often wonder where Gabe got his steel and adventure from. He must have had one hell of a grandfather.

Since his parents' death, Gabe has done little to the house and in the dining room the walls are still covered with a history of Gabe's life; as a baby, school photos, an action shot of both of us in a county final, then another of us in tennis whites holding up a trophy, each with a hand on a handle. Then Gabe in his first uniform, more Army shots, a group photo of him and his platoon sitting nonchalantly on a tank. That must have been taken in Desert Storm, before he was posted to Afghanistan. Seeing myself in those early shots only makes me realise how little I know of Gabe's life after he left for the Army; I do not feature in any of the photographs after he puts on his uniform.

Gabe eventually answered the door after I had rung three times and started to check out the windows, looking for easy ways in. I had disturbed him from his physiotherapy; he answered the door flushed and sweating and seemed embarrassed for me to see him in that state. I do not think he noticed the relief in my face, just seeing him alive. Now from where I have cloistered myself in the dining room I hear the physiotherapist leave. Why am I hiding from my best friend? A barrier seems to have invisibly and mysteriously appeared between us and I am not sure how to address it. But I do not wish to politely ignore it; not with Gabe.

He walks in, still in his workout clothes. The back of his grey T-shirt is dark with sweat. 'Coffee?'

I follow his lurching walk into the kitchen, although I cannot help but still think of it as his mother's kitchen where she would allow me to sit for hours rather than go home, whether Gabe was there or not. My throat briefly swells and aches at the thought of her busy kindness. Gabe flaps a sleeping cat from the top of the Aga, which stretches resentfully before ambling off. I sit down, take a breath, try to find a voice that sounds natural.

'How've you been?'

'Yeah, not bad,' Gabe says, his back to me. Doesn't give me anything more. Silence. I try again.

'Spoke to George today. He said something about…' This is no good; why dance around it? 'And the other night, with the police. I'm just worried, you know. That you might be losing the plot.'

Gabe's back stiffens and I wonder if he will go on the attack. Then he relaxes and laughs gently. He turns around and his pale eyes are amused. 'Yeah,' he says. 'Yeah, you could say that. You could say that.'

He sees that I am not laughing and something like compassion appears on his face. He hobbles over and sits down awkwardly opposite me at the kitchen table. I am pinned by his fathomless eyes. He picks up a salt cellar, looks at it, puts it down. 'Dan,' he says. 'What did you think would happen? Did you think I'd tough it out and come out the other side stronger? I'm not fighting a disease here. I'm facing the fact that I'm going to be a cripple for ever.' He shakes his head. 'I'm not going to win, Dan, because I've already lost.'

Of course my instinct is to reassure, refute, find the positive. But I know that he is right; he is far wiser than me and I can do nothing but nod. 'Can't blame me for worrying. It's just, this, it isn't you.'

Gabe smiles. 'Yes it is. It's just not who I was.'

'That's…'

'I was a captain. On my way to becoming a major. I was

97

heading for a place on the world stage, if I played my cards right, ten, fifteen years I'd be a brigadier. It's what I joined the Army for. Now, Dan, I'm irrelevant. I will never have influence again, never save another man's life, never shoot an enemy. Never.'

'I thought you were angry with me.'

'Why would I be?' Gabe struggles up, walks to a cupboard, reaches down coffee, filters. 'Look, yeah, okay, I'm angry. You're here, you want me to make it easier for you, to tell you I'll be okay, set your fucking mind at ease.' He puts water into the machine, switches it on. 'But I can't. Maybe I'll kill myself... I don't think I will. But sometimes it gets so hard that it's a possibility. My life is awful and it isn't going to get better because my leg, Dan, isn't going to fucking grow back.'

I do not know if Gabe is suffering from mental illness; I suspect that he is, that he is in the grip of a depression so profound and encircling that he has assumed it is his permanent reality. But perhaps this is just what I am telling myself; his argument has a ring of rationality about it. The loss of his leg has ruined his life and I am not about to patronise him with empty words about how he can turn it into a strength, how he cannot let it beat him. As he says, he's not engaged in a battle; he has already lost. It is typical of Gabe to want to cope with the aftermath alone, in his own way. This self-sufficiency is what made him officer material, what allowed him to lead a Cavalry company into action. There is nothing I can do to help him.

We sit and drink our coffee and I tell Gabe about Halliday. He laughs when I tell him what I said to Halliday in the bar, a delighted and honest chuckle that sounds like the Gabe I grew up with. He has always been amused by tales of my wayward aggression; I think he is the only person I have ever met who is, maybe because he has always known that I will never turn it on him, and perhaps also because he is a man who is comfortable with brutality. I know that he loved war.

I do not mention my mother, it is too soon; if my search for her is a dead end then I would prefer to deal with the disappointment alone. We are not so different, he and I.

I say goodbye, swallow back the 'If there's anything I can do...' We arrange a game of tennis and I leave, knowing that, if I thought the conversation we've just had was difficult, it will seem like nothing compared to what is coming next.

It is early afternoon when I arrive at my father's house and I am apprehensive that he might already be drunk. It is hard to connect with him at the best of times, but when he has been drinking he is as unpredictable as a pit bull. I ring the bell but there is no answer so I walk around the side and open the gate to the garden.

He is working on his flowerbeds, his back to me, wearing a white singlet and shorts, and as he squats down I can see the massive muscles in his calves before they are covered by his thighs. He is dead heading his roses and he has not noticed me. I am ready to confront him and have my words chosen and ready. But as I approach him he hears me and turns, and as so often with my father he sucker punches me before I can get my words away.

'Fuck you doing here? Dontchoo work for a living? Here, go get that bag of fertiliser for me.'

He turns back to his roses and I walk to the house, pick up the sack and lift it on to my shoulder. My father has been told what to do by more successful and powerful men his entire life. The resentment he has felt he has always taken out on me, by treating me as if I am an indentured servant rather than a son. I dump the sack next to him and he grunts, doesn't say anything. It is hot and I sit down, watch my father work.

'I spoke to Vincent Halliday earlier,' I say after a minute has passed, tossing the statement into the bright summer's day like an unsuspected grenade. My father stops, rigid. That's done it.

'Halliday,' he eventually says through a cough. 'Oh yeah?'

'You know him?'

'Me and him, we, yeah. Yeah I know him.'

You and him don't live on the same planet, I think. You are as insignificant to him as a starling. I don't say anything, see how long it will take until my father sacrifices his pride to his curiosity and asks me to tell him more. I hear the distant rhythmic beat of a train going over points, the sound carrying over the stunned silence of the hot day. I do not have long to wait.

'So what's he want with you?'

'Just a bit of business. Client confidentiality, couldn't tell you more if I wanted.' I am aware that I am being childish, withholding information to goad a man for no other reason than I can. I stop. It is not what I came for. 'Anyway, he said something to me, wanted to ask you about it.'

'Yeah?'

This is it. I feel as apprehensive as a boy about to ask his first girl out on a date. 'He mentioned, said, that I was like my mother.'

My father doesn't reply, busies himself with a rosebush. After he is satisfied with his work, he says, back still turned, 'He did, did he?'

'So he knew her?'

'Well, I guess he must've fucking done. Or why would he say it?' An edge has entered my father's voice, never a good sign.

'Yeah, well, go on then,' I say, meeting his impatience with my own. 'How did he know her?'

At last my father lays down his secateurs, turns and looks at me. A vicious sneer disfigures his face. 'Fuck knows. Probably one of his bits on the side. I ever tell you she was a slag?'

'I want to know more about her.'

My father doesn't answer, just regards me with hostility. He is breathing heavily. He is having difficulty controlling himself.

'What did she look like?'

Still no answer. There is a spade stuck into the earth next to him and he takes it in his hands. He is still looking at me. I can see his flanks moving, in, out, his breathing laboured from the emotions he is dealing with.

I can feel myself losing control. I cannot feel my legs. 'What was she like? Funny? Pretty? What fucking colour was her hair?'

My father's knuckles whiten underneath his tan. I know that things have now gone too far, that my questions and his silence must now lead to something, that we have reached a point of no return. I am throwing questions at him like I'm throwing stones at an angry bull.

'Is she even alive?'

My father lifts the spade and hurls it at me, blade first like a two-handed javelin. I step aside and it misses me but there is no doubt that he meant to hit me with it, inflict serious damage. I feel the buzzing in my ears and experience the clouded vision that can overwhelm my reason and cause me to act with unthinking rage. He is an old man, I say to myself, he is a sick old man. I know that one more provocation will tip me over the edge into the freefall of violence; I have never before raised a hand against my father but all of a sudden the inevitability of this confrontation hits me. There is too much latent resentment, too much unspoken anger between us. It must come out.

'I wanted to have you aborted,' my father says. 'Stupid bitch wouldn't let me.'

He is an old man but he is still strong and as I step towards him he throws a punch that I try to avoid and it hits me on the shoulder, nearly turning me. I can feel the heft of his arm behind it; he is immensely solid. I grab his wrist and with all my strength I pull him towards me. He resists but I am too strong and, as I pull him off balance, I step past him and pull his arm with me, turn it up behind his back, wrapping my other arm around his throat and pulling his whole body close to mine so that my head is over his shoulder and my mouth is at his ear. I can smell his sweat and feel his breathing and it occurs to me that this is the most physically intimate I have ever been with him.

I can feel his bulk and it surprises me that at his age he can still be so powerful. I want to say something irredeemably hurtful, obscene, whisper it gently so that he feels violated and it turns in his mind for months as he seeks sleep. Yet at the same time I realise that, powerful as he is, he is no longer a match for me and that I must let him go and walk away. I am not, like he is, a bully.

'I will find out,' I say. I take my hand from around his neck, let go of his wrist and walk away. My back feels as if it is covered with a faint electrical charge and I have to use all of my will not to turn around, see if my father is coming at me. I keep my eyes on the grass beneath me and have to admire its condition; my father has never let a ban on using hosepipes get in the way of a beautiful lawn. As I open the gate, I hesitate.

'Cunt,' says my father far behind me.

14

THAT NIGHT, THE police reconstructed the disappearance of Rosie O'Shaughnessy, to show her last movements on local television. A young woman, little more than a girl, played the part of Rosie and she was filmed drinking with friends in a local bar before receiving a text from her boyfriend and quickly drinking up and saying goodbye. From there she left the bar and walked along a busy street, crossed over, walked into a McDonald's where her boyfriend was waiting. She was not in McDonald's long before she left, followed by her boyfriend. He pulled her by the arm, tried to stop her, but she shook him off, yelled at him. She headed off up a side road, her boyfriend following her and shouting insults. That was the last time Rosie was seen alive by any witness, apart from her killer. She entered a park and walked into darkness.

The reconstruction attracted a crowd of bystanders, the same people who rush to throw flowers at the spot where someone they do not know has died. Rosie's boyfriend had agreed to play himself in the reconstruction, a fact that I would imagine counted in his favour. However, one member of the public clearly did not share my view. As the filming ended, he ran at the boyfriend, assaulting him; the police were on the scene already but it took them several seconds to understand what was happening and come to the boyfriend's aid, by which point he had been stabbed in the back seven times with a kitchen knife. The man who assaulted him was wrestled to the ground, handcuffed and led away through the watching crowd to the police car; along the way, people patted him on the back, told him, 'Well done, mate, did the right thing, spot on.' As the police car pulled away, several people applauded.

While the assailant was being charged with attempted murder and Rosie's boyfriend was fighting for his life in hospital, I was trying to get to sleep, my mind drowsily flitting between two states: imagining what my mother might be like, and worrying about what might have happened to her. My father's reaction had been extreme even by his standards; it felt as if there had been fear behind his aggression. But why? What was he afraid of, or trying to hide? No matter how many times I told myself that I was being overly dramatic, I could not help but think that perhaps my mother did not leave us; perhaps, like Rosie, she disappeared into a blackness she would never leave. Was my father capable of that, of murder? I did not have to consider for long; he was an angry and embittered man and I had no doubt that he hated women. With thoughts like these, I gradually drifted off; it was a warm night and I had left the window open in the hope of a breeze.

*

My dreams were punctuated by strange noises and filled with convoluted tales of being hunted by faceless enemies, the dreams of a man with a fever. I woke up around three and saw a black shape next to my bed, felt breath on my face. Not sure whether I was still dreaming, I did not feel any fear, instead simply grunted a disorientated 'Yes?' The shape retreated, turned and left and the sound of footsteps down my stairs brought me back to sudden clarity and I swung out of bed and on to my landing, finding a switch and throwing the light on to I think two people who were leaving through my front door. I followed and ran down the stairs through the open door into the night and saw two, maybe three figures running down the street. I ran out after them but as they turned the corner I knew that in bare feet I had no chance of catching them. As I realised this, I also realised that I was yelling enraged threats and vulgarities at their departing backs, sounding like an inebriated man in a pub brandishing a pool cue. Across the street a light came on, a window opened; it was Ronald, a diffident man with three children and a pushy wife, who works in the City for, I believe, a major insurance firm. He peered out, skinny arms braced on the windowsill; he did not have his glasses and I imagined he had been ordered out of bed by his wife, outraged that scenes like this had the temerity to play out in her street.

'Is everything okay?' he half spoke, half hissed, nervously.

'Go to bed, Ronald,' I said, dismissing him. I was suddenly aware that I was in the middle of my street wearing only boxer shorts. The sight must have been frightening for anyone who did not know me, maybe frightening for anybody who did. With a suit on I can pass for a civilised man; half-naked I am a different proposition. But with Ronald it does not matter much, I lost his family's good opinion long ago. Last summer, I was leaving my house when a man drove past my car, clipping the wing mirror and breaking it. He paused, considered, then drove on so I ran out and stood in front of his car, then walked to his door, pulled him out through the open window and pinned him with one hand to his bonnet as I went through his wallet with the other, pulling out notes. Ronald's wife witnessed this and since then every time she has seen me she has shepherded her children close to her with one arm and quickened her walk. If I am honest, I can't really blame her.

I got back in my house exhilarated at having caught men in my own home and at the thought that I could have inflicted damage on them, frustrated that they got away and intrigued by what they wanted. I put on a dressing gown and sat and watched rolling news for hours, making irrational connections between the different stories to reinforce my view that the world is essentially a dangerous and inhuman place with little to redeem it. Around six o'clock, I dozed off and woke up at nine, hot from the blazing sunlight pouring through my living-room window on to the sofa where I lay. I had sweated on to the leather and in my dressing gown must have looked like a wrestler fallen on hard times, sleeping off the previous evening's shameful defeat on a borrowed couch. Not the finest night of my life.

Now I am standing in my office, looking at the wreckage of my professional life and thinking that the day isn't shaping up to be an unqualified winner either. When I arrived, my glass door was smashed and walking into my office I saw that somebody had gone through every drawer and file, lifted the carpet tiles, taken out the polystyrene squares of the false ceiling and looked into the cavity above. There are only two possible culprits, Halliday or Baldwin. And Halliday has just engaged me as his pet crooked lawyer, which narrows the shortlist down to one. Baldwin, it seems, won't stop until he's got his hands on the discs Terry Campion asked me to look after for him. This thought does not bother me; I took a dislike to Baldwin when he tried to intimidate me in my own office and I remind myself that I have got something he wants. As a lawyer, you never know when a bit of influence with the police is going to come in useful. Of course I have not kept the discs on my premises, or at home; Baldwin has either underestimated me woefully or he is simply desperate. One thing I do know for sure: I will cross paths again with Baldwin, and soon.

'Redecorating? Thought this place needed a bit of love.'

I turn and see one of the men who had accompanied Halliday when he came to put the screws on me standing at my office door. He is holding a pile of paperwork and wearing an amused smile.

'Who are you?'

'Eddie,' he says. 'Brought you this, from Mr Halliday.' *Mr* Halliday. Please. 'Should be everything you need.' He looks about, takes in the mess. 'Where'd I put it?'

Every surface is covered with my scattered work, my filing cabinets on their sides, my desk buried under paper. 'For the moment,' I say, 'you can stick it up your arse.'

'Not very nice,' Eddie says, unruffled. 'He's keen for you to get to work soon as. I'll stick it on the desk.' He makes some space and puts the files down. I right one of my filing cabinets, grunting with the effort, and when I look up Eddie is standing against the wall, legs apart and hands clasped over his crotch like a doorman outside a nightclub.

'Anything else?' I say.

'Mr Halliday wants me to keep an eye on you.'

'So you thought you'd take him literally.'

Eddie doesn't answer; I suspect he is having difficulty getting to the bottom of that last sentence. He leans his shoulders against my office wall, making himself as comfortable as he can in a room with only one intact chair. This is too much.

'You realise this kind of thing can take weeks? You going to stand there all that time?'

Eddie shrugs. 'If I have to.'

I look around the devastation in my office and can feel my pulse hurrying. I have not slept well and have a lot of work to do and Eddie has picked the wrong time to be pressuring me, irrespective of who his boss is.

'Look,' I say. 'This is my office. I have client confidentialities to respect, other cases to take care of. No offence, but it's going to be hard to do that with some hired goon standing in the corner.' Eddie frowns. 'By hired goon, Eddie, I mean you.'

Eddie smiles. 'Not going anywhere.'

'Yes, Eddie, you are. If Halliday wants me to work for him, I'll do it my way, in my own time. He doesn't like it, he can find another lawyer. That what he wants?'

Eddie looks conflicted, his mouth slightly open as he works out the best thing to do. Even he knows that bent lawyers are a little thin on the ground, and that Halliday won't be keen on finding another. He has his orders, but I am not going to budge. What to do? It cannot be easy, being Eddie.

He comes to a decision, crosses to the desk, finds a pen and writes on top of the pile of paperwork.

'Here's my number. Give me a call if you need anything.' He writes slowly, forming the numbers with difficulty, his tongue held between his teeth. I wonder whether Eddie still points at aeroplanes. He finishes, stands up. I hold the door to the entrance hall open. Eddie stops as he passes me.

'Be back tomorrow. Better be progress, sunshine.' For a second I believe he considers patting me on the cheek, there's a good boy, but he sees the look in my eyes and reconsiders. Perhaps he isn't as stupid as I thought. Instead, he leaves quietly and I close the door behind him, breathe deeply, try to calm down. My life seems to be full of uninvited and malign presences right now and I have the feeling that I am losing control, that my existence is being co-opted by outside forces. I look over at the pile of papers Eddie has left for me and have to fight down an urge to kick it all across the chaos of my office.

After Eddie has gone, I spend several hours rebuilding my files, matching paperwork, putting it into piles and eventually into folders, which I place back into my filing cabinets. This process does little to improve my mood as I realise just how paltry and mundane my caseload is. Never before has my previous life as a successful City lawyer seemed so far away and for the first time the thought of what my previous colleagues are now doing and achieving bothers me enormously, makes me question myself.

To escape from these existential doubts, I get into my car and drive to the hospital where Billy Morrison is still lying with his leg in traction. At least here I can make some kind of difference, unconventional as it may be from a legal perspective. I walk into his ward where he is reading a magazine with a picture of a girl on the front wearing only a pair of bikini bottoms, the word 'Philippa!' splashed across the cover and the dots on the 'i's of her name covering her nipples. He is absorbed and does not see me approach so I bat the cover against him and he looks up. I can see a brief panic in his eyes and I regret frightening him; he is clearly haunted by the spectre of Halliday. Billy recovers and gives me a cocksure smile.

'Danny! 'Choo doing here?'

'How are you, Billy?'

'Good, blinding. They give me a bed bath the other day, right, all sponges like, everywhere. You ever had one?'

'No.'

'Coupla sorts, nurses, should've seen them. So halfway through...' Billy lowers his voice to what he probably believes is a discreet whisper. 'I get, you know. Aroused.'

There's no preamble, no nicety with Billy; he just dives straight in. 'I'm sure they've seen it all before,' I say.

'You reckon? Know what they did? Only milked me, din't they? Said it was a shame I was NHS, else they'd've given me the works. Their words.'

Billy beams up at me, expecting me to be impressed by his immature fibs. I shake my head at him, admonishing a child. 'I spoke to Halliday. Looks like you're in the clear.'

He sits up, looks at me with wide eyes. 'Yeah? Really?'

'Just, Billy? Keep out of his way.'

'Yeah, no problem, brilliant. Really? He's letting it drop?'

'Reckons you'll have learned your lesson.'

'Oh fuck yeah. Yeah, I mean, definitely.' Billy sinks back down into his pillow, his mind released from the fear he's been feeling these past few days, racing forward to plans for the future now that he has one. I can see his lips move faintly as he tells himself stories with happy endings. He rouses himself.

'Danny, listen, thanks, man. Dunno what to say. I knew you'd come through.'

'Don't worry about it. Just stay safe.'

'Yeah. Yeah, I will.' He smiles and I pat his good leg and turn to go. As I do so, a thought strikes Billy.

'Danny?'

'Yes, Billy?'

'I still getting that money? For the Blu-ray?'

15

THE NEXT MORNING, I am taking a shower when I hear the doorbell ring. Thinking it might be a delivery, I hustle down the stairs and open the door in my towel, ready to sign. Instead, I am shown a warrant card held by one of two policemen and I recognise Sergeant Hicklin from the other night, when I had gone to the station to bail out Gabe. Next to him is his over-enthusiastic constable, Dawson. I instinctively think of Gabe and wonder what trouble he is in now; whether he has inflicted it on others, or on himself. I open the door wider, gripping the edge, tense with anxiety.

'Get you out of the shower, sir?' asks Hicklin. His voice lacks the good humour of the last time we met; it is all business today. I gaze at him levelly, not bothering to answer such a redundant question. Instead, I ask, 'This about Mr McBride?'

'Not this time, sir. No.' He pauses, looks around, takes his time. It is interesting to see him in tough copper mode; he is good at it, a natural, authoritative without being heavy-handed. I wonder why he is still a sergeant. 'Are you the son of a Francis Connell?' He strokes his moustache with an index finger and thumb. I relax my grip on the door.

'What's he done?'

'Done?' says Hicklin. His colleague, Dawson, is eye fucking me from behind him. In the morning sun, I notice, with a practised eye, that he's a good four stone lighter than me. 'He's not done anything.' Hicklin sniffs. 'Were you at his house at around three o'clock, two days ago?' He looks up at me. 'That would be the twenty-third.'

'Yes.' I wonder what this is about. If my father has not done anything, then something must have happened to him. 'Is he all right?'

Hicklin ignores me. 'I have a witness who saw you arguing with your father.' I am about to speak when he holds up a hand, takes out a notepad, turns a page. He will not be hurried. 'This witness claims that you had your father in a choke hold, in his garden. Would you deny this?'

'Would I? We're in the here and now, Sergeant. Do you mean do I?'

Hicklin looks at me blankly. 'Did you have your father in a choke hold?'

'Yes.'

'Mind explaining why? I might remind you that there are laws against assault.' He smiles blandly, robbing the statement of any force or threat.

'I'm a lawyer,' I say. 'But thanks for the heads up.'

'So you do not deny that you had an altercation with your father?'

'No. What I'd like to know is why you are interested. And unless you tell me right now, this conversation is finished.'

Hicklin looks me up and down and I am suddenly aware of how I appear. It is hard to achieve a psychological advantage when one of your hands is holding together a purple towel and water is cooling on your shoulders, pooling at your feet.

'At approximately ten o'clock last night, he was admitted to Queens General suffering from a suspected heart attack. He had also been beaten. Savagely.'

'Is he going to be all right?'

Hicklin consults his pad. 'Suspected heart attack. Beaten, savagely.' He takes a deep breath, puffs it out, shrugs. 'Christ knows.'

That is below the belt, I cannot help thinking. 'Well then, Sergeant Hicklin, let's stop dancing, shall we? Are you here to inform me of my father's heart attack, or are you charging me with some kind of crime?' I look over his shoulder at Dawson, give him a do-you-want-some look. *'What?'* Dawson doesn't know how to respond and drops his gaze. I look back at Hicklin.

'No need for hostility, sir,' he says. I have to give him his due, he is not easily riled. 'We're here to take a look at you, ask you some questions. We're not here to inform you of your father's heart attack. Do we look like the Red bloody Cross?' He smiles without malice and I almost laugh; he's got me there.

The sight of my father, fed with a drip and with a machine breathing for him, his face slack in his sleep and looking like the spent force I suddenly realise he is, gives me pause. He is no longer a monster, merely an old man who has been on the receiving end of a ferocious beating; and, while one part of me believes that it was almost certainly merited, I cannot get past the fact that he is still my father. It may sound atavistic but I am the only person who can avenge him and, despite all he has done to me, I believe I must.

The doctor told me that, although he looks unscathed, his heart attack was almost certainly caused by a sustained physical attack; underneath his hospital-issue gown he has severe bruising around his kidneys, ribs and thighs caused by a blunt instrument, possibly a baseball bat. Or a police baton.

According to the policemen who visited my home, my father had been drinking in the Good Friends, a pub I know, narrow and dirty and panelled in dark wood. It is unwelcoming to strangers, full of alcoholics who, together, make believe that their lifestyle is no worse than anybody else's but would still prefer to get on with their serious drinking away from judging eyes. He left at around ten o'clock and made his way home, a distance of half a mile. Along the way he passed a park, little more than a stand of trees and a kids' playground. It was there that he was found just before midnight, sullenly unconscious and sat up against a little elephant fixed on a heavy-duty spring that kids can ride, bathed in moonlight and looking like an evil visitation in a child's dream. He was found by two teenagers out for some al fresco petting; the girl said she was so freaked out by the sight that she screamed, almost had a heart attack herself.

It is fortunate that the teenagers did find him; any longer without medical treatment, the doctor told me, and he would have died. My father's heart has been weakened by a lifetime of alcohol abuse and poor diet and, if some alternative therapists are to be believed, too much hatred and far too little laughter. The doctor needs to perform an emergency bypass and asks me to give my consent, my father unlikely to regain consciousness before the operation. I give the form a quick scribble, then leave the hospital. There is nothing I can do there and I am happy to let my father recover, or not, on his own. I am sure he would do the same for me.

The Good Friends opens at eleven, by which time there is already a queue of men outside, some old, some who merely look it, all waiting to nurse beers until the afternoon when they can begin drinking in earnest. Even drunks have some standards, and they do not wish to be legless before lunchtime. I am also in the queue when the bolts slam open and Dean pushes the door from the inside. I know Dean a little; he is close to my age and, although we did not attend the same school, our social backgrounds are close enough that our paths sometimes crossed, often waiting together outside pubs like this one for our fathers to eventually emerge. He sees me and frowns; he may own this pub, but that does not mean that he wishes to see acquaintances, people he likes, drinking in it. He would hope they have higher standards. To drink in the Good Friends is as much a declaration as it is to stand up in an AA meeting and say, 'Hello, my name is Francis and I am an alcoholic.'

Dean nods greetings to the men who pass him into the pub, suffering their tired witticisms with a patient smile.

It occurs to me that he is running a community service every bit as vital to these men as home visits from a nurse are to the elderly and I feel sorry for him; it must be a bleak kind of life. Dean looks at me and smiles.

'Danny. How've you been? Got a call from the Old Bill, sorry to hear about your dad.'

'Yeah. Well.' It is hard to know what to say. Am I sorry? Does it matter all that much to me? I suppose it must, otherwise why would I be at a place like this at eleven in the morning?

'Want to come in?'

'Okay.'

I follow Dean inside and smell that old pub odour of sour beer, wood polish and musty upholstery. The pub is dark and every surface looks tacky, as if it, like its clientele, is limned with an ancient veneer of sweat and dirt. Dean walks behind the bar, says, 'Drink?'

'No thanks,' I say and I can see relief in his eyes.

'So then, what can I do you for?' he asks.

'You know what the police are like,' I say. 'They won't want to waste their time on the likes of my father. They been by?'

'Joking. Quick phone call I got, some geezer with an attitude, asked me what time Frank left, if he left with anyone. Sounded like he had his dinner on the table, couldn't get off the phone fast enough.'

'Sounds right. So thing is, Dean, what d'you reckon? Know anyone who'd have wanted to do him?'

Dean thinks for a moment. 'You know, Danny, he's in hospital and I'm sorry for him, but I have to say I saw you growing up and how he treated you, and yeah he drinks in my boozer and I'm happy to take his money but, not being funny, Danny, your dad, he's a right nasty cunt.' He looks at me, worried about how I'm going to take his little speech, but I just smile.

'Can't argue with you there, Dean,' I say. 'So what, did you do it?'

'No, no fuck, Danny,' he says. ''Course not.'

'Winding you up,' I say. 'But he pissed anyone off especially, that you know?'

'Oi, oi, Bern, that's enough of that.' I look over and see an old man hitting another man over the head with a rolled-up copy of the *Racing Post*. 'You want to be barred again?' Dean turns back to me. 'Fucking want to be in homes, telling you,' he says. 'You know he asks me to help him to the loo? Like, seriously, look at me, do I look like Florence fucking Nightingale?' He doesn't, he looks like what he is, a pub landlord knocking forty who wants a bit more sun and wants to drink less of his profits.

'Sorry, what... Oh, yeah, right, who'd want to bash him. Can't think of no one in particular, Danny, he weren't little Mr Sunshine but he kept himself to himself, didn't make no fuss. Probably just kids, thought they'd have a go at a pissed-up old fart.' He looks at me anxiously again. 'No offence.'

'None taken.' I hand Dean my card, tell him to let me know if he hears anything. He tells me he will, tells me to take care of myself. As I walk towards the door, he flicks a switch and a jukebox comes on, playing Ultravox. He claps his hand together, says in the brightest voice he can muster, 'Right then, gents, what will you all be having?' My professional life may not be all it once was; but it could be a lot worse.

16

MY MOTHER IS beautiful.

I am in the attic of my father's house, a low close cave of heavy insulation and overwhelming heat so that I feel as if I have been slid into a pizza oven, the thirty-year-old dust-blown fluorescent strip giving off a dull malignant glow. Clean light pours up from the house through the open hatch like a distant promise of sanctity from this baking hell. I have been crabbing around from box to box, opening them up in the hope of finding some evidence of my mother and, after worrying a few last crates out from under the eaves, I have at last hit pay dirt. At the bottom of a box is an A3 envelope, card-backed, and inside are a stack of Polaroid photos held by a near-perished rubber band, the photos having survived the passage of time unfaded because they have never been permitted to see the light of day. My mother, banished to the farthest reaches of my father's existence for over thirty years.

Now I am looking through them, a meagre fourteen photos of the woman who brought me into this world. But fourteen is infinitely better than zero and these amateur shots have an odd effect on me; at once a throat-tightening sense of wonder that my mother lived, that she had a face and a physical reality, and also a deep pain that this lovely woman never stayed to smile at me as she smiles at whoever took these photographs. Because she is lovely, a tall dark-haired woman with a wide generous mouth and lively, laughing eyes. Wearing a garish flowered too-tight dress, she is anchored in the seventies but her expression is vibrant enough that it can reach through the decades into the here and now. Or am I simply being sentimental, caught in these novel moments, laying eyes on my mother for the first time?

I place the photos back into the envelope and lower myself back down through the hatch, down the ladder and on to my father's landing. I am sweating through my T-shirt and, even though my father's house does not have air conditioning, the contrast between the attic and his landing is like coming out of a sauna. I walk downstairs, sit down on my father's sofa and lay the shots out on the coffee table. I cannot help but feel guilty as I do this; I check the door despite my father lying unconscious in a hospital five miles away, like a schoolboy would who is in possession of his father's pornography.

Five of the shots were taken on the same day; a trip to the coast, although I cannot tell to which seaside town. She wears a yellow mini-dress and a wide-brimmed straw sun hat which she always has one hand clamped on; she clearly picked a windy day to visit the sea. I assume that it is my father behind the camera because he is not present in any of the shots; he is not the type of man to kindly ask a stranger to take a photo of the two of them. The sky is a pure blue and framed against it my mother seems to be laughing at some private joke; I smile as I look at her, try to imagine what that laughter would sound like.

I know without a doubt that she is my mother because of one photo in which she and my father are standing together in front of a caravan, she quite visibly pregnant and my father with a proprietorial hand over her belly, a fuck-off expression on his face I would recognise anywhere. How like my father to see the glorious prospect of welcoming a child into the world as yet another excuse to flex his muscles, to invite the world to try it on should it dare. Yet my mother does not appear to notice; she is wearing an expression as blissful as a leading lady on closing night clutching a bouquet of flowers flung by a head of state.

The other shots are a mixture of portraits of my mother on her own and the two of them together, always outdoors, my father in every instance wearing the territorial scowl of an Alpha-male protecting his property. But what I notice above all about them is the absence of other people; in only one or two of the photos are my mother and father joined by others. The overall impression is one of a relationship carried out clandestinely or, alternatively, between the last two people left on earth. Perhaps they simply did not have friends; perhaps they did not have any need of them, they were complete on their own. But knowing my father as I do, surely he would want to have been seen with a woman as lovely as my mother on his arm; he would have wanted, not to show her off, but to flaunt her, to goad other men with her. Look, here, look what I've managed to land. Want a piece? 'Cos she's not fucking available. That would be my father's style. He would not have wanted to keep her to himself. What would have been the point in that?

I toss the last photo on to the table, lean back on the sofa as if to give myself physical distance from them. I rub my face, feel the stubble. Rather than give me some grounding, some sense of provenance, these pictures serve only to mock my existence further. A woman with a face as warm, as loving as this; even she was not interested in me.

But these thoughts are not going to help so I rouse myself, get up and pick up my father's telephone directory. I know the name I am looking for, though I fear she might have changed it; she has been divorced from her husband for years and I do not know her maiden name. In all the shots of my mother, there were only two that also showed other people; and, from them, there was only one other face I recognised. My blunt finger works down a list of names and stops; this must be her. She is, as far as I know, the only person in Essex whose name begins with X. Xynthia Halliday. Looks like she never got around to changing it.

I do not call ahead; Xynthia lives close by and, if there is any murkiness about my mother's disappearance, I would rather not give her time to get her story straight. I am in my car, the envelope of photographs on the passenger seat next to me, a drab packet almost humming with signifi-cance such that I am tempted to pull over and look through the photographs again, examine them, search them for meaning.

The traffic is slow and when I turn a corner into the main shopping street I can see why; the town has stopped to witness a procession of people, young and old, and their passage is being treated with a reverence which, to begin with, I cannot fathom. The group at the front are all wearing white T-shirts. When one of them turns I see that there is a photograph of a face printed on the T-shirt, and then I recognise with a jolt that the face is Rosie O'Shaughnessy's. Some of the group are holding flowers and some are holding candles, shielding the flame with their hands although it is so bright the flames are barely visible; each line of the group has their arms interlocked as if they are marching in protest at some invisible oppressor. The silence of the onlookers is profound, an almost shamed quiet; collective guilt at what was done to Rosie, at what was allowed to happen, here, in their town. The group passes by slowly and I guess that they are on their way to the park gates, to the last place Rosie was seen alive.

To be confronted so suddenly with the fact of a murdered young woman gives me pause. The photos next to me seem no longer to be proof of my mother's existence but rather grisly artefacts of a life cut brutally short. My father will not speak of her, will not acknowledge her; everything about her has been sucked into the black hole of his silence. I realise with sudden finality that, whatever I discover about my mother, it will not be good news. Why would she leave me voluntarily when, as my father claimed, she refused to have me aborted? Whichever way I look at it, her disappearance now strikes me as sinister, a malignant secret at the heart of my life. Yet I cannot turn away from it; I must know the truth.

Xynthia Halliday lives in a third-storey flat in a geometric seventies block, which must have been built around the time of my mother's disappearance, a concrete box wearing a Mondrian grid of windows and coloured squares of cladding. I climb the outside stairwell and pass along the walkway, stop outside number eleven with the envelope of photographs in my hand. I am nervous and sweating from the climb and the heat and I pause before ringing the bell as if something dangerous and evil lurks behind the door.

I know Xynthia Halliday from years before when she would help out at my school, teaching dance and theatre to children whose parents were pushy and rich enough to afford the extra expense; of course I never attended. But her presence around the school was hard to ignore whether or not you were lucky enough to be taught by her, a bird of paradise amongst starlings. In the past, she had been an actress, never successful but well enough known in local repertory theatre to have caught the eye of Vincent Halliday. It did not take long for her to turn her back on her career and assume the responsibilities of full-time villain's wife, hanging off his arm wherever he needed to be seen. After he traded her in for a younger beauty, she found herself without a career or a future, which was when she started touring schools, offering her meagre acting experience in return for meagre money. But I never thought of her as down on her luck; she always seemed to carry with her an irrepressible air of glamour and excitement, her flamboyant clothes and astounding hairstyles lighting up my school's monochromatic corridors.

So I am shocked when she opens the door to me. It has taken a long time for her to answer and I am just about to ring the bell again when I hear soft footsteps approach.

'Who is it?'

'Daniel. Daniel Connell.'

'Who?'

'Frankie's son.'

After some fumbling with the chain, she opens the door and I wonder whether I have got the wrong place. But looking at her carefully I can see that, underneath the tired grey skin and sparse hair, this is the same Xynthia Halliday from a quarter of a century ago. It is as if some ancient succubus has taken over her body, causing it to decay and atrophy but leaving her essence somehow still present, there in her eyes and the turn of her lips. The reason she has taken so long to get to the door is that she is dragging an oxygen cylinder on a trolley, a clear tube snaking up from it to her face, two smaller tubes invading her nostrils as the tube bridges her top lip.

'You're Frankie's boy?' Her voice belies her appearance, as clear as a bell.

'Daniel. I remember you from school.'

'How is Frankie?' She asks it offhandedly and I get the feeling she is enquiring more out of politeness than interest. 'He well, is he?'

'In hospital. He had a heart attack yesterday.'

'Frankie's had a heart attack,' she says to herself. I lose

her for a few seconds, wait for her to come back to the present. 'So what can I do for you?'

'I want to ask you about my mother.'

Xynthia sighs sadly, as if this visit is something she's been expecting for decades. She looks me in the eye and I can see a level of sympathy, pity even, which takes me aback.

'Come in, son,' she says quietly and steps aside. 'Into the living room, sit yourself down. I won't be a minute. We'll want a cup of tea.'

Xynthia's living room is a museum to her past, her pre-Halliday past when she still believed that her life would become something extraordinary. Framed photographs of her in various roles, all black-and-white, are ranged on every available surface like an entrenched army facing one last battle. I sit down on her sofa, another relic from the past, and wait for her, listening to the soft tick of a carriage clock on the mantelpiece over her gas fire. She takes so long I worry that something may have happened but eventually she reappears. Her manner has changed and her eyes seem brighter and I can now recognise the Xynthia I remember from way back. She has put on make-up and, though she is still attached to the oxygen cylinder, she seems to have miraculously shed a decade. It occurs to me that perhaps she could have been a very fine actress, if she had managed to escape Halliday's clutches.

'Tea's ready, doll,' she says. 'In the kitchen. Be a good boy and fetch it, could you?' I put down the envelope of photos I have been holding and go into the kitchen, where there are two cups on the counter. When I get back to the living room, Xynthia is looking through the photographs, rotating each to the back of the set in a way that I can only describe as loving. She looks up when I come back with no hint of apology for having taken them without permission; instead, she smiles up at me kindly.

'Lovely-looking girl, weren't she?'

'She's my mother?'

'Yes, my darling, yes she's your mother.'

'You knew her.'

'Not well but, yes, I suppose I knew her. As well as anyone.'

'Is she dead?'

Xynthia puts down the photos. I am still standing and she pats the sofa beside her, a strangely coquettish gesture that could only have been made by somebody who was used to getting her way with men. I sit down next to her and she takes one of my hands.

'You know, you look like your father but there's something of Marcela in you too. You're darker than Frankie. You like him in other ways?'

'I hope not,' I say. She likes this; her eyes crinkle.

'I used to see you, in school,' Xynthia says. 'I used to watch you, see how you were getting on.' She squeezes my hand harder. 'Was he terrible to you?'

I do not reply immediately, look down at my hands, try to think of the right reply. 'Not terrible, no,' I say. 'But he never wanted me. I always wished that he would. It's hard for a kid, knowing that.'

'Daniel.' She lets go of my hand, leans forward with difficulty and picks up the photos again. She breathes heavily.

'Emphysema,' she says. 'Smoking. It's an absolute fucker, I don't mind saying.'

I smile at her casual profanity. 'I only know her name,' I say. 'What was she like? Where was she from? What can you tell me about her?'

'Whatever you want to know,' Xynthia says. 'The question is, do you really want to know? Because it's a story as bad as any I ever heard.'

My mother's full name was Marcela Cosma and she came from a small village in Romania. One day an advertisement appeared on her school's noticeboard, advertising university courses in England, offering them free as part of a British-Romanian exchange programme. My mother was a promising student but came from a poor family, which could never have afforded to send her to college; her future was mapped out, dedicated to helping her mother and father. It was the reason she'd been conceived in the first place, a purely expedient decision on her parents' part to ensure there would be somebody to look after them when they grew old. So she didn't tell her parents about the programme, applied for it in secret. To her very great delight, she was accepted and she left, again in secret, for her new life studying English Literature at a university in London.

That there was no university place, and that there had never been a university place, was something that, Xynthia tells me, my mother never truly believed. She clung to the belief that she had been driven across Europe in the back of a van by men entirely unconnected to the original advertisement and that, on a campus somewhere in London, a room was still patiently waiting for her. Regardless, the reality was that she'd been sold into the sex trade and that was where she was trapped. But my mother had an unshakable belief in the ultimate goodness of humanity, something she held on to throughout her terrible ordeal. She always expected that something would happen to make it stop, this awful nightmare she'd found herself in. So, when my father fell for her, that was it. The fairytale ending she had been waiting for had arrived.

'I never had my father pegged for a knight on a white charger,' I say.

'That's because he fucking wasn't,' Xynthia says, her sudden vehemence causing her to cough. I wait for her to finish, listen to her sucking in breaths. 'Sorry,' she says. 'But it's true. Oh, listen, he liked her enough. Maybe even loved her, I don't know. But a knight? Fucking joking, aren't you?'

'So how did you know her?'

'Vincent.' She almost spits the word, like it tastes bad and she doesn't want it in her mouth. 'Your mum, she was one of his girls.'

Halliday had stood in my office and threatened me, forced me into a humiliating position in which I have to do his dirty work, and all the time he knew that he had been the master of my mother, had forced her into infinitely more depraved and humiliating situations. My hand holding my cup of tea begins to shake; Xynthia notices and calmly takes it from me.

'I'm sorry, my darling,' she says. 'It isn't what you came to hear. But you do have a right to know.'

'So…' I grasp for words. 'How did it happen? What did Halliday think, about one of his girls, and my father?'

'He was inside at the time. Six months for aggravated assault, somebody owed him money and Vincent broke his arm. Your father and Marcela got together while he was inside. By the time he got out, it was too late for you to be…' Here Xynthia's composure falters, the brutal realities of the situation too much for her to comfortably articulate. 'Got rid of,' she manages. 'Thank sweet heaven. But Vincent weren't happy. See, your father was working for him at the time, doing fuck knows what, but what he definitely shouldn't have been doing was knocking up one of Vincent's girls. Vincent was not best pleased.'

'So I was born. Then what? What happened to my mother?'

'Oh, Daniel. I am so sorry.'

'Did he kill her? Did he have her killed?'

'Killed? No, no, Vincent didn't kill girls. Did a lot of other things, but not that. No, he didn't kill her. He sold her. While your father stood by and did nothing.'

'Sold her?' For a moment, Xynthia's words do not make sense. How can you sell a person? I look at her in shock; she is rubbing her forehead, pinching her eyes, shaking her head in sadness. But it is not grief I feel. Halliday sold my mother, and I feel nothing but rage.

17

THE WOODCUTTER WILL come. The woodcutter will come and he will slay the wolf. He is approaching, stealthily. He makes no sound. The wolf will not hear, he is too intent on eating, his head is buried in Red Riding Hood's stomach, nosing through her entrails, snuffling at her innards. The woodcutter must come. I believe I can smell him. I know I can smell him. The wolf raises his face and looks at me and his jaws drip blood that has the texture of treacle falling in long unctuous lines from his teeth. He tilts his head to one side and regards me. I do not see him speak but I can hear his voice.

'You're awake, I know you're awake.'

I cannot open my eyes but I know that the woodcutter is coming. I know that Red Riding Hood has a face like a dead girl I have seen, and I know that the woodcutter is coming and I know that he will slaughter the wolf with his axe and that I will be safe, that I will no longer have to watch the wolf snapping at a poor dead girl's guts.

'You're awake, cunt. Open your eyes.'

I inhale the smell of the woodcutter but his image is fading from my mind and I can see light. I open my eyes and the glare is too bright and I close them again but the light has extinguished my dream and, although I try to fight it, I cannot escape reality taking my dream's place and I know that I am somewhere every bit as bad as that of my dream.

'Cunt's awake. All right, lift him up, lock him to that.'

I feel hands gripping me and pulling one of my arms and a noise like the snapping of a lock and now my arm will not drop back down, something is holding it up. I open my eyes and see my wrist is handcuffed to the handle of a lathe. My head is in a pile of sawdust and small offcuts of wood. I lift my head and see three men standing above me. One of them is Baldwin. He is gazing down at me with a look of petulant annoyance on his massive, sagging face. The other two I do not know; I assume that they are policemen, though this does not give me any reassurance. I do not know how I got here or even where this is apart from it looks like a carpenter's workshop. There is a workbench next to me, the lathe and a bandsaw next to that. The ceiling is made of brick and is curved and I suspect that this workshop is underneath railway arches. It is brightly lit with fluorescent strips and the walls are hung with tools.

'Back with us? Wakey-wakey, rise and shine.' I have closed my eyes and drifted away again and Baldwin's voice sounds as if he is speaking to me from within a box, muffled and distant. Somebody kicks me in the ribs making me wince, and I am back in the here and now and the workshop I am in comes into sharp focus as if the lens on a camera has been tightened, the sounds clearer as if I have surfaced from underwater. Baldwin is leaning close

136

enough to my face that I can smell his breath, the sharp tang of a recently smoked cigarette. I look at him and will myself not to show fear.

'Now I'm going to ask you again, and this time why don't you make it easy on yourself?' He stands tall and sighs as if I am a recalcitrant schoolboy who is wasting nobody's time but my own. 'You've only got so many fingers, son.'

I feel a quick stab of panic in my chest, the feeling you get when you are walking blithely along the street and remember something dreadful, like you have forgotten you should be at a job interview, or left a gas hob burning. I hardly dare to look at the hand that is still lying in the pile of sawdust. But even as I summon the courage the memories come back and all of a sudden I know where I am, I know how I got here, and I know what has happened in the time since I arrived. I dare not look. I must look. Like a mother asked to identify her child I will myself to look, to look down at my hand.

It is missing its little finger. They have cut it off. These men have cut off my finger and now I am scared, more scared than I have ever felt before. Because I know that this is just the start. They will not finish here. They can never let me go, not now.

After I left Xynthia's, I had gone back to my office to finish the clear-up from my break-in, needing something to keep my mind from obsessing over what I had just learned. She had tried to comfort me, to describe to me my mother's character and how much she had looked forward to having a child, how she would have loved me given the chance. But

Xynthia knew even as she said the words how inadequate they were. In the end, she begged me not to do anything stupid, to leave Halliday alone, telling me that he was evil and that my mother would not have wanted me to put myself in danger. I could not help but notice how Xynthia always referred to my mother in the past tense. Despite her reassurances that my mother had been sold rather than killed, if she held out so little hope for her life, what did I have to cling to?

By the time I left my office, it was growing dark. I got into my car and headed for home, agitated and driving with a murderous recklessness. So I was not surprised when I saw flashing blue lights in my rear-view mirror and I pulled over immediately. Perhaps I should have been surprised that the officers who approached my car and requested that I turn off my engine were in plain clothes, but I turned the key and got out without a second thought. There were two of them and they told me that I had been speeding, that I had been doing forty in a thirty zone. I did not argue but they asked that I join them in their car so that I could review the footage of my driving that they had recorded on their camera. I asked them if it was necessary and they said no but by then I had walked with them to their car. One of them was behind me and as I stopped and reconsidered he must have hit me with a baton because that was the last thing I remember, before waking up in the workshop underneath the arches.

I have been knocked unconscious before, though not recently; my father once hit me with his fist after I had taken £10 from his pocket to take a girl to the cinema and when I came to on the kitchen floor he had left for the pub and taken the money with him. I recognised the headache and disorientation and the nausea when I woke up, instinctively going to rub the back of my head and being brought up short, my hands shackled in front of me around the leg of a workbench. I was sitting on a chair, my head resting on the top of the workbench as if I was snatching a quick nap in a quiet library. I lifted my head and saw Baldwin and the other two policemen who had stopped me in my car standing at the other end of the bench; they weren't paying any attention to me, engrossed in a game where they tried to knock a nail into a piece of wood in one hammer stroke. One of them, a short man with a moustache and the puffed face of a drinker, missed the nail and the wood jumped and skittered across the floor next to me. They followed its progress, laughing and calling him a cunt, and noticed me watching them.

'Oh look, Sleeping Beauty's woken up,' said Baldwin. 'Let's get this over with, shall we?' The other men leered, wolf-like.

'Fuck's going on?' I said, trying to put some force into my voice. Trying not to show fear.

'We asked you, didn't we? Nicely. But you wouldn't play ball, so now here we are.' Baldwin indicated the workshop around him as if he was showing me his own private kingdom. 'So I'm going to ask you one last time. Where are those discs?'

He approached me, the other two men slightly behind. The short man with the moustache was one side. On the other was a tall balding man with a pinched face that made him look like he was sucking something bitter. They were men you could meet anywhere, unremarkable in every regard. I would never have believed I could be afraid of men like this.

'I'm not going to tell you where they are,' I told Baldwin. 'You must be out of your fucking mind.'

Baldwin smiled reasonably. 'If you don't tell me,' he said, 'I'm going to cut your finger off.' He raised his eyebrows, as if a thought had just struck him. 'On that bandsaw.' He nodded over at a large, green machine made of metal, hunched over like a robot praying mantis with a thin blade pointing down like a steel tongue.

'How you going to manage that?' I asked.

'Do what?'

'Cut my finger off, dickhead.'

'Turn on the saw, run your finger through it. What do you think?' said the man with the moustache as if explaining it to a child.

'Undo those handcuffs and I'll tear your fucking ears off,' I said.

Baldwin chuckled. 'Probably would, too,' he said. 'You must've had one fucked-up childhood. Keep you in a kennel, your old man, did he? How is he, by the way? Heart, wasn't it?'

I thought of a response, but looking up at Baldwin's blank eyes I felt my bravado leave me. I was powerless, utterly at the mercy of these men. Fear took over. Fear of what they could do. How they could hurt me. My muscles were tensed, ready to flinch away from the first punch, the first kick. I had a fleeting, shameful impulse to capitulate.

Say please. Please don't, it's okay. I'll give you what you want. Offer my hand, all a misunderstanding. Anything to get out of this terrible place. He must have seen the shame in my eyes because he smiled, nodded. Like he understood.

'So, you got something to tell us?'

But no. Not yet. I had survived my upbringing. My father had not broken me. I had reserves of strength, deposited over many years. I was not beaten yet. I took a deep breath. Coughed to test my voice. Looked him in the eyes. Tried to speak firmly.

'No. Nothing.'

He held my gaze, sighed. 'Get the bottle,' he said to the balding man. He shook his head at me, disappointed. 'Fuck's the matter with you?'

The balding man crossed the room to a sports bag, kneeled and unzipped it and took out a clear glass bottle with a pharmaceutical label on it.

'Should be a flannel in the bag too,' Baldwin called. The man came back holding the bottle and a rag, handed it to him. Baldwin unscrewed the bottle, inhaled from a distance and made a pantomime woozy face. He upturned the bottle into the rag in his palm, soaking it. Handed the rag to the balding man.

'I'll hold his head,' said Baldwin. 'Might be too much for you.' He walked behind me and put one arm round my neck, the other crossing my forehead. He was so strong, stronger than I would have believed. A Frankenstein's monster, a freak, not of this world. I felt the fingers of the hand that held my forehead caress the side of my face, the skin around my eyes. I could hear my breath coming out in fast ragged pitiful snorts. While he held me firm, the balding man pressed the rag up to my mouth and I breathed in a smell like paint thinner, which made my eyes tear. The balding man's eyes were focused and intent on keeping the rag covering my mouth and nose, and those eyes were the last thing I remembered.

Now Baldwin's phone rings and he takes it out of his trouser pocket, looks at it in irritation. He walks away and hits a button.

'Yes? Yes I'm on duty... No, I don't... Well for fuck's sake can't somebody else do it?' He paces up and down the work-shop. 'He still there? Yeah I'll come in... Is he off his head? No? That's something I suppose... Don't let him see his brief 'til I get there. Yeah. 'Bye.' Baldwin walks back to us. 'They've picked up Francesco.'

'Fucking Francesco,' says the thin-faced man.

'Stupid prick. Who's he stabbed this time?'

'They've got him back at the nick. Guv'nor wants me to have a crack at him.' Baldwin pauses, frustrated. He looks at me with dislike and exasperation, as if I'm a kid who has vomited in the back seat. He has put his phone away and he pulls it out again, in two minds, not sure what to do.

'Gary, you stay here with this fucking... We'll be back. See if you can't get something out of him.' Baldwin snaps his fingers like he's calling a dog and the puffy-faced man with the moustache obediently follows. They walk out of the workshop through a small door in a bigger set of double doors and the silence they leave is like that silence you remember as a child when your father switches off the ignition of the car and just sits there, you don't know why. I realise that I am trembling and I cannot stop. The workshop is still and the tools are arranged neatly on pegs on the walls, saws and vices and chisels and planes all hanging innocently. But I know what Baldwin is capable of and I fear his return; all of these tools can easily be used against me and one of them could be responsible for my death. I am aware of a pain in my finger, or what is left of it; it is a throb with a sharp undercurrent, a rough edge which makes me think of a saw's teeth and which I suspect is going to get worse and worse.

But now that Baldwin has gone, the menace of my situation seems less. I can think straight, or at least without panic. Gary does not seem keen on torturing me on his own; he has casually worked his way to the other side of the workshop where he is fiddling intently with his mobile. He looks like a middle-aged dad worrying about where his daughter is and when she's getting home. But I'd like him closer because I want to lay my hands on him, or at least the hand which isn't shackled to the handle of the lathe. And I know policemen; they do not respond well to insults and taunts, inculcated as they are with a sense of institutional omniscience.

'Pussy. Reading text messages from your boyfriend?'

Gary looks up at me amused; he's heard it all before from behind the doors of the cells, or from piss heads banged up in the back of the van.

'You're supposed to be finding out where those discs are. Right? But instead you're reading text messages from your fucking boyfriend. And when your daddy comes back, that's what I'm going to tell him. Sorry, Baldwin, I haven't spilled my guts yet because your little streak of piss, your little drink of water here didn't want to ask me because...' I look Gary in the eyes, across the workshop; he shouldn't be looking back at me, not if he knows what's good for him. 'Because, Baldwin, your little boy is fucking scared of me.'

'Keep talking,' says Gary but he's got a quaver in his voice. He quickly clears his throat, betrayed by his vocal cords.

'Scared of me because I'm a big macho man even though I'm chained to a piece of heavy machinery.' I laugh. 'Hey!' I call, a note of hysteria in my voice. I want to wrongfoot him so that he doesn't know whether I'm angry, compliant or simply unhinged. 'I do know where those discs are. And I'll tell you where, if you make it worth my while. You think I want another finger cut off?'

Gary's been leaning against a chest of drawers but he straightens up, slowly, reluctantly interested. 'Yeah? How's that?'

'I've got a case. Pending. Need it looked at. Charges are going to be brought.' I take a deep breath, sigh. 'I hit someone. Driving. I was pissed.'

Gary frowns, confused. 'That's it? You've, you've...' He runs out of words, pauses, lost. 'Why didn't you say that before? You know, before Baldwin cut your fucking finger off?'

'Because I don't like Baldwin. But I can do business with you.'

Gary pushes himself off the chest of drawers, walks towards me. Here you come. He stays out of range. I have pulled myself towards the lathe. There is slack in the chain of the handcuffs, though Gary cannot see that.

'Go on,' he says. 'Don't worry, I can make a DUI disap-pear like –' he clicks his fingers weakly, nothing compared to Baldwin's authoritative snap '– that.'

'Sure?'

'Sure.'

'And I can trust you why?'

Gary's face has been open and inviting but it closes suddenly at my question. Policemen don't like being challenged. I retreat.

'Okay, fine,' I say. 'You can sort me out, okay, I get it. I'll tell you. Fuck.' I take a deep breath and it catches and becomes a retch, a sequence of liquid bubbling heaves that make my eyes roll up and then close and my legs twitch as if I am being electrocuted. I thrash and throw myself up against the lathe and crack my head against one of its huge metal legs, the world shuttering as my eyes close. I lie still, unmoving, my breaths coming irregularly.

I watch the bricks of the curved roof through the veil of my eyelashes. Concentrate on my erratic breathing. It seems an age I lie there. Breathe. Breathe. Where is he? Eventually, I see a dark shape, Gary, corner of my eye. He's getting closer. He approaches slowly, looks worried, doesn't want me to die. Doesn't want me to take my secret, the whereabouts of the discs, to my grave. Closer still. Peering down at me. Doesn't know how to play this. I wait. Breathe raggedly. He bends his knees to get a better look, reaches out a hand, slowly. So close now. I open my eyes. See his eyes widen in shock. I sit upright and take him by the throat and squeeze and there is no way in the world that he is going to wriggle away. His neck feels like I am holding a closed umbrella, he is so insubstantial. His eyes widen further still as he suddenly understands that his strength is nothing compared to mine and that it is no use; he might as well be an eleven-year-old boy again, so weak is he.

I have been at the mercy of these men for hours; I have never before, apart from at the hands of my father, been at the mercy of anyone for so much as a minute. I am angry, furious, livid; no words can adequately describe the feelings I am experiencing, which make my enraged body vibrate like a just-plucked guitar string. Still, I do not believe that my feelings excuse what I do next; explain them, perhaps, but nobody deserves what I next visit on Gary.

He is now lying on his back on the floor where I have forced him down. I am squatting above him, hampered by having one hand still latched to the lathe. I let go of his neck, quickly punch him as hard as I can in the throat. He gasps for breath, struggles to fill his lungs. I worry I have broken his windpipe and he will die. Eventually, he gets his breathing under control, to the point where he can hear what I say.

'Keys,' I say and I put my index finger into Gary's eye and scrape across it as hard as I can. His eyeball gives and I am surprised that it does not burst. It has the texture and firmness of a pickled onion. He screams and his legs kick wildly. I wait for him to calm down, ask him again.

'Here, here in my fucking pocket,' he shouts. His world is upside down and he has no idea what I am capable of. He is in pain, hysterical. He starts to sob.

'Take them out then,' I say. He reaches spastically into his pocket, jerkily pulls out coins, a screwed-up receipt, a key. I take it and reach over and unlock the handcuffs. I stand up and feel the pain in my knees from crouching too long, which makes me think about my finger that has been cut off and I feel like a shark finning through dark water. I crouch back down again and hit Gary in the side of his head where his jaw meets, once, twice, three times until I feel it break under my knuckles like a bigger piece of wood in a bag of kindling. The feeling sickens me suddenly and makes me stop; I may be enraged but I am not a murderer.

As I stand up, I worry that already I may have gone too far; Gary is quiet and still but he is breathing and I again think about my finger and decide he can take his own chances. I walk towards the door that Baldwin left by, passing the ranged tools on the walls along the way, and as I reach the door I feel as if I am passing from some dark fantasyland of pain and torture and monsters back into the real world. I see orange streetlights and breathe the clean night air deeply and close the door gently behind me.

18

MAJOR BUTLER TELLS me that my finger is nothing, that he once tried to resuscitate a corporal who had had an arm blown off by an IED, performing CPR in a chopper flying away from Basra chased by tracer-fire. He tells me that they took a round in the tail rotor and the pilot nearly lost it, the chopper rocking crazily as, in the back, he worked away trying to get the corporal's heart started again, his hands slipping on the corporal's chest as he pushed down, fingers made greasy from all the blood. Despite his best efforts, the corporal's heart stopped and he was about to give him up for dead when the chopper crashed on landing, throwing Butler out of the door and on to the dusty ground of the British Army base. By the time he crawled back to the helicopter, the corporal was sitting up; the impact of the crash had brought him back to life and he wanted to know what had happened to his rifle, he couldn't be without his rifle.

He laughs softly as he tells me this but I know it is only a strategy to take my mind off the fact that he has just brushed the top of what is left of my finger vigorously because, he explained, it's no good splashing on antiseptic to clean a wound, you need soap and abrasion just like you're washing dishes. He has injected me with anaesthetic and I cannot really feel it; but in some strange way the sight of my red-raw stump being torn open again by the brush makes my brain imagine the pain anyway.

I am in Gabe's kitchen; I headed for his house when I left the workshop underneath the arches, recognised that I was close enough to stumble there, took back streets in case Baldwin came out looking for me. Gabe opened the door and I was relieved to see that he was not drunk or stoned; he saw my finger and pushed the door wide and watched me in. I told him I had nowhere else to go, that I was paranoid enough that I did not want to visit a hospital, worried that Baldwin might find me out. He poured me a Scotch and told me to keep calm, sit tight, said he knew someone who could sort me out. He made a phone call and left, and half an hour later he came back with Major Butler. The man was carrying a bag and his introductions were brief; he obviously did not want to tell me his first name and, anyway, I suspected that he wasn't really called Butler and that his rank was higher than major. He was a tall man with grey hair and a pair of half-moon glasses; he could have been the owner of a rare book shop except for his eyes, which seemed to be constantly evaluating, assessing, making decisions.

He worked with Gabe to sterilise the kitchen table, laid a green sheet over it, set up an Anglepoise light that Gabe had brought down from his study and told me that this might hurt a little, and that it might not be something I wanted to watch. He said this in the offhand way of a man well used to performing unpleasant operations in difficult settings and his unflappable manner set me at some kind of ease. He did not ask me what had happened, except to ask how clean the blade had been and how long it was since the finger had been cut off. He did not bother asking whether I had the rest of my finger; battlefield surgeons, I suspect, aren't very interested in reattaching fingertips. In any case, I hadn't got it; it was back in that workshop and I did not wish to go looking for it. I had been refilling my Scotch glass while I waited for Gabe to come back and by the time Major Butler was ready to work on me I was half-cut, giving me a feeling of giddy detachment. Fuck it, I said. Just do what you have to do.

As he tells me about the corporal's miraculous recovery in the back of the downed chopper, he cuts the skin into four triangles around and down from the tip of the stump and pulls the flaps over to seal the end. He is wearing glasses with magnifying lenses and he stitches with a finesse that astounds me. The reason he is doing this, he tells me, is so that the tip retains sensation when it is healed.

'Five-star treatment, this,' he says. 'Usually, I'd give you a couple of Aspirin and tell you to stop your moaning. Now your thumb, that would be a different matter. The British Army takes thumbs seriously. Thumbs and trigger fingers. There.' He puts down his needle, takes off his glasses and stands up.

'Thank you, sir,' says Gabe. 'I owe you.'

'No drama,' says Major Butler or whatever his real name is. 'How's the leg?'

'Spot on.'

'Still doing the physio?'

'Yep.'

'Any depression?'

'Please.'

'Suicidal thoughts?'

'As if.'

Major Butler examines Gabe with those see-all eyes of his. 'Bollocks,' he says. 'Remember, get some help before you do anything stupid. Psychs don't do their best work at funerals.' He turns to me. 'Keep it bandaged and keep it clean,' he says. 'Try not to lose any more.' He packs up his bag quickly and nods at Gabe and leaves without saying goodbye. His efficiency and composure are truly impressive; as with Gabe, he gives off the air of a man who, regardless of what problem you bring to him, will have seen far worse. We hear the front door close and his exit leaves an awkward silence; I have a strange sensation, with Gabe leaning against the kitchen counter watching me, as if I am a child and now at last is the dreaded time when I have to explain myself.

'Got any more Scotch?' I say. Gabe brings the bottle over to me and I pour another shot. 'Thanks. Was he in Afghanistan?'

'Not with me,' says Gabe. 'I know him from Iraq. That corporal? He was in my company. Lucky little fucker.' Gabe sits down next to me at the kitchen table. 'Want to tell me what happened?'

'Baldwin. His men jumped me, knocked me out. Next thing I know, I'm chained to a workbench under some arches.'

'The policeman?'

'Yeah. Fucking policeman. He cut my finger off.'

'Only your little one. And only a bit of it.'

I give Gabe a look that would make most men bow their heads and try to pretend they weren't really there but he doesn't care, just smiles. But his pale eyes are not amused. 'Why? Why the fuck is a policeman torturing you?'

'He wanted those discs. The footage, you know? When he beat up Terry.'

Gabe frowns, looks sceptical. He shakes his head. 'Nah. Sorry, no, I'm not having that.'

I nod. 'I know. Doesn't make sense, does it?'

'Kidnap a civilian, torture him, cut off his finger, all because he beat up one of his colleagues? What's the worst's going to happen to him? The police are a closed shop, they look after their own, right? He'll get a warning, might even lose his job, but you can bet your bollocks he'll keep his pension and it'll be hushed up.' Gabe picks up my glass, swirls the Scotch around, thinking. 'No. Doesn't make sense.'

'You want to ask him what it's all about? Be my guest.'

Gabe ignores me, still thinking. 'And why, right, Danny...' He looks at me closely. 'Why the fuck didn't you just tell him where they were? What's it to you?'

'Didn't like the way he asked,' I say.

Gabe laughs, stops himself, looks back at me and laughs hard, laughs for a long time. He shakes his head. 'Danny, Danny, you're not a normal man, you know that?'

Later we are watching *Scarface* on the television and I am drunk and soon fall asleep. I dream of a wolf snapping at my fingers and keep jerking them away, imagining I am up a tree and it is leaping at me. When I wake up, it is light and I am on the sofa and Gabe has put a blanket over me. I must stop sleeping on sofas, I think to myself, then remember my finger and look at the bandage, the events of last night slowly separating from the fears of my dreams until I recognise that it really happened, men really cut off my finger. Last night I was concussed and in pain and part of me had felt fortunate to be alive. Today is a different story. Today I feel cold and murderous and the loss of my finger prompts me to form curious rationalisations; I tell myself that, since I have lost it, I have generally less to lose and hence should go gunning for Baldwin with even less caution.

But after talking to Gabe last night, there is a mystery lying at the heart of last night's events that gives me pause. Gabe was right; Baldwin's actions make no sense. He is risking everything, his career, prison, to get back footage of what is, essentially, a minor crime. The violence he has visited on me, on my father, on Terry's sister; he has left a trail of brutality that seems way out of proportion to the situation he is faced with. And my impression of Baldwin is not that of a man lacking in control or judgement; he is a professional bent copper, probably has been for years, and he must have his reasons. But what are they? Confronting Baldwin makes little sense; he is not a man it will be easy to threaten. If I want to get to the truth, I will have to find another way.

Gabe is still asleep so I scribble a note of thanks and leave quietly. He has his own problems; I will take care of mine alone.

19

AS FAR AS I am aware, the safest place in Essex to stash those discs is in Gabe's house. Breaking into his home would be as suicidal as burning the Koran at Mecca. He has an arsenal of weapons that would shame an African despot and he knows how to use them; worse, he is prepared to use them, which is far more important. I remember reading that in World War One eighty per cent of shots were aimed high because soldiers did not want to take another man's life. Gabe would never aim high. In many ways, my life has been a journey from savagery to civilisation; the course of Gabe's life has been the perfect opposite. As a child, he was a bright, kind and thoughtful middle-class boy. The Gabe I know today is a haunted killer, all traces of liberal angst drilled out of him, replaced by a cold steel I do not think I have ever possessed. It is as if his years in the Army gradually distilled his personality, his softness evaporating away until only a hard centre remained. Though I do not love him any less for it.

I am back in my office and I have the discs on the desk in front of me; I took them with me when I left Gabe's. I do not know what I expect to find but I feel a little like a physicist who has a theory and now has to put it to the test. Intellectually I feel sure there must be something more on these discs than footage of one policeman fighting another. My missing finger tells me that. But I will not know until I have watched them. I have three discs to watch; Terry kept his reasons for wanting the footage to himself, asked his contact at the police station to copy everything from that night, not just the car park. So I have one disc of the station's secure car park, which I have already watched with Terry, seen him getting beaten up. The second contains footage from a camera outside the front of the station looking into the street; the third is from a camera aimed down at the main desk.

I start with the footage of the street, insert it into my DVD player. There is a date and time code at the bottom of the screen and the footage begins at four p.m., in bright daylight. The police station faces a park, with a street between the station and the park's iron railings, cars parked along the kerb on the park side of the street. The camera covers the road outside, perhaps ten metres of pavement as well as the door to the station itself. There are ten steps leading up to the entrance of the station, which is a three-storey Victorian red-brick building. Because of the camera's height it is hard to make out faces, only the tops of heads. The footage is in colour but the colours do not seem true, the reds too red, the blues too garish, standing out from the pavement, which, because of the bright sunlight, looks white. It reminds me of a twenty-year-old holiday video, over-saturated and hard to watch.

The station is not busy, with perhaps fifteen people arriving and leaving each hour, a mix of civilians and uniformed police. I try to count them in and count them out but I soon give up; some of the civilians could be plain-clothes policemen walking into the station for the evening shift. Do they have their own entrance, around the back? I don't know. I watch for half an hour before the pointless-ness of the task hits me, watching a procession of faceless people arrive and leave. What can this tell me? I fast forward up until the time of Terry's arrival in the car park at 10.28, the time I remember from the time code of the footage I watched with him when he was here in my office, battered and bruised and angry. But the exterior of the police station is quiet for the ten minutes before and after this time and there is nothing to see. He must have been dragged into the station by a back entrance; makes sense, given the state he must have been in. I sigh, eject the disc. Two hours and I have found nothing.

I am about to put in the disc I watched with Terry, when my phone rings. I pick it up and my bandaged finger brushes the desk, making me wince. Before I can say anything, Eddie's voice cuts in.

'Missed you yesterday.'

'I was out,' I say. 'Business.'

'Mr Halliday wants a progress report.'

There is no progress, has been no forward movement. I have not even looked through the paperwork Eddie left with me. After what Xynthia told me, the only thing I want to do for Halliday is break him. But I do not think that is what Eddie wants to hear.

'Just going through the papers now,' I say. 'I'm waiting on some land searches. I'll chase them up today, get back to you.'

'So, what shall I tell him?' Eddie sounds anxious; he isn't enjoying his role of overseeing my work. He can see trouble ahead, and he's not sure he wants it. Good.

'Tell him what you want,' I say. 'Tell him these things take time. Tell him to get off my case and it'll get done. That do you?'

'Just…' Eddie does not know what to say; he is out of his depth. He has just realised that I hold all of the power in this exchange; he doesn't know how conveyancing works, how much paperwork, chasing, waiting on other people is involved. I almost feel sorry for him, stuck as he is between the unreason of Halliday and my indifference. 'Just pull your fucking finger out,' Eddie says. 'Mr Halliday ain't what you'd call a patient man.' Is he trying for my sympathy? Eddie, please.

'I'll call when I've got more to tell you,' I say. 'Now, want to leave me to it, or keep wasting my time?'

'Call me tomorrow,' says Eddie, and hangs up. He can't get off the phone fast enough. I smile to myself. That round definitely went my way.

I leave my office to pick up a coffee from the Italian café three doors down, come back and put in the disc covering the car park, which contains the footage of Terry being beaten up. I cue it forward to just before Terry arrives in the van, then sit back to watch.

The footage doesn't get any better second time around; Baldwin's casual elbow in Terry's throat, the other policeman beating him to the ground, Terry's defiant lashing out and their collective, frenzied onslaught. They drag him off into the station and I continue watching for ten minutes, but they do not reappear. I take it out and insert the last disc, from the main desk of the police station. Again, I start at the beginning, at four o'clock, though this time I put it on fast forward and watch people walking at high speed in and out of the station, the sergeant behind the desk disappearing into the back office and coming back out like a cuckoo in a clock. Terry was taken, or rather dragged, away at 10.37 p.m. Baldwin and his colleagues re-emerge into the main area of the police station at 10.51, meaning that they had been alone with Terry for almost a quarter of an hour. I remember Terry's battered face, the bruises and stitching; these people are sadists, of that I have no doubt, men who have developed a taste for causing others pain, for demonstrating their power in savage and bestial ways. I slow the footage down to normal speed. Baldwin is now in shirtsleeves and he is gesticulating, his colleagues following him like dogs around a shepherd. I cannot tell whether he is angry or amused, whether his gestures are of triumph or annoyance. But then, I don't believe that it is possible to ever work out what Baldwin is thinking. His thought processes have nothing in common with normal people's.

Baldwin reaches over the desk and takes a tissue, wipes his hands. He gestures to his colleagues and they go to leave but before Baldwin can get to the front door of the station he stops and backs up, as if confronted by a man even bigger than himself. He walks back into the middle of the shot and I sit forward, examine the screen. Baldwin has opened his mouth; he is speaking to somebody out of shot. He presses his hands to his chest in a 'Who, me?' gesture, and shakes his head. The other policemen with him do not react; they look like a bunch of schoolkids caught smoking, heads down, hands in pockets. Baldwin takes a look behind him at the main desk but there is nobody there. Suddenly a figure enters the shot, the unseen person he has been talking to. It is not a big man, it looks like a teenager wearing a hood and he is holding something in his hand, holding it up and in front of him as if it is a crucifix and he is warding off some dark satanic force. Baldwin tries to snatch it but the teenager is too quick and puts it into the pocket of his hooded top. The angle of the camera doesn't let me see the teenager's face but he seems agitated, a dark blur of gesticulating arms, a hand pointing, both hands held out in a questioning gesture. He tries to push past Baldwin but Baldwin stops him, both hands on the figure's shoulders as if he is trying to prevent him from seeing some terrible sight. The figure struggles and Baldwin turns him and this is the first time I can see his face and I realise that the teenager isn't a boy at all, and then I realise that it is Rosie O'Shaughnessy.

Baldwin manhandles Rosie out of the police station and I eject the disc and put back in the disc covering the outside of the police station. I am in a hurry and my hands are clumsy; as if, should I not get the disc into the machine quickly enough, something dire will happen. I fast forward up to 10.45 then slow it down. The street is very dark, vague shapes in the blackness and three streetlights that are white areas of brilliance. I see a figure walking along the street, up the steps and into the station, purposeful strides as if the figure is on some kind of mission. Rosie disappears from view and I watch the screen; she can only have been inside for a minute at most. One minute and thirteen seconds pass by and she comes back out, Baldwin's arm draped around her shoulders, and in the darkness it almost looks like she is supporting his weight, as if he is a drunk she is helping home. You cannot tell it is Rosie; you cannot even see that it is Baldwin next to her. They walk clumsily down the stairs outside the station, turn right and disappear. She has not been on the screen more than a few seconds and already she has gone and I sit there watching the view of the deserted street outside the police station, and I wonder what mystery awaited her off-screen.

I pick up my telephone and call the local paper; I know one of the reporters on it, a man named Jack who was a gifted student and debater at my school and who was on course for an illustrious career in journalism until Fleet Street's wine bars became more important to him than the news floor. After drying out, he took a job closer to home, perhaps comforted by the familiarity of the stories he now covered. I have noticed his by-line on the paper's coverage of Rosie's disappearance; he has more experience than anybody else on the staff, even if his career has taken a drink-fuelled nose-dive, and he still gets the juicy stories. The receptionist transfers me and Jack picks up immediately; he sounds happy to hear from me.

'Danny! The only person I know who can throw a career better than me.'

'Hi, Jack. How are you?'

'Yeah, good. Working on a story about a twenty-one-year-old dog. Know how old that makes him in human years?' He does not wait for me to answer. 'Hundred and forty-seven. Hang on.' I hear silence for a few moments. Jack comes back on. 'You hear that?'

'No.'

'Sound of the bottom of the barrel being scraped, Daniel. Long and hard.'

'Listen, Jack, I need a favour.'

'I'm skint, if that's what you're wondering.'

'No, no it's about Rosie O'Shaughnessy.'

'Oh yes?'

'What date did she go missing?'

'Twenty-seventh July. Poor fucking kid.'

'And, if you know, what was the last time she was seen? Exactly?'

Jack's been a newsman for enough years to catch the scent of a story pretty quickly. 'You got something?' he asks, his version of humour put to one side for now.

'Don't know. Just, do you know the time?'

'Tick.' I hear papers rustling and Jack comes back on the line. 'Yep. Ten-sixteen. Got the time from CCTV when she walked into the park. Never to be seen again,' he adds in a cartoon-scary voice. 'What have you got?'

'Yeah, I've got to go,' I say.

'Come on. Top line?'

'Call you back.'

'You better.'

I hang up on Jack and look at my screen. I rewind the footage to the point where Rosie is hustled down the steps. The date stamped at the bottom reads 27.07, and the time is 10.55. Thirty-nine minutes after Rosie O'Shaughnessy was officially last seen alive.

20

'WHERE'S YOUR GUV'NOR?' I ask the young policeman, Dawson, the constable with attitude who had shoved Gabe into the interview room after his arrest, and eyeballed me on my doorstep when Hicklin had come to question me over my father's assault. He was in uniform both times then but today he is wearing shorts, trainers, a Hollister T-shirt, and an irritating air of disdain. He ignores my question, taking in the view through his shades. A lot is said about the attitude of young people nowadays and I do not take any notice of most of it. But this young man exudes a sullen entitlement I cannot help but take against. I had called his boss, Hicklin, the day before but he had not been there; Dawson had sighed, grudgingly promised to pass on a message and I had explained that I had some information on the disappearance of Rosie O'Shaughnessy, but that I would only deal with Hicklin in person. He might have interrogated me on my doorstep that day but the way he had dealt with Gabe had impressed me; he exuded the air of a proper, old-school straight-down-the-line copper and it was him I trusted.

I told Dawson that I would meet Hicklin at the band-stand in Gaynes Park; although I trusted him, that trust was not unconditional and I did not want to meet him or any other policeman in anywhere but a public place. What I possessed, what I had discovered on those discs, had me feeling as exposed as a tethered goat in a jungle clearing. Baldwin had been the last person to see Rosie alive; did that mean he had been responsible for her death? What had she said to him in the police station that had caused him to walk her out before anybody else could hear? Was it worth killing for? All I wanted was to get rid of the discs and let the machinery of the state take over, grind Baldwin away to nothing, into a bad memory of our capacity for wickedness. This was bigger than me and I wanted nothing to do with it.

It was only when I arrived at Gaynes Park that I realised I was in the same place as Rosie had officially last been seen, though on reflection perhaps it was as appropriate a meeting place as any. Where better to deliver justice for her than in the park where she first disappeared?

Dawson is watching a trio of knights walk past, men dressed in leather tunics, chainmail, metal breastplates. We are surrounded by a medieval village of tents, suits of armour arrayed on the grass and pots of food cooking on open fires. There is a re-enactment of the Battle of Bosworth Field going on and the Houses of Lancaster and York are scheduled to meet in under an hour's time. The gathered knights are in character and there is a cheery air of good-humoured antagonism, rustic and anachronistic epithets thrown carelessly through the bright sunshine. It

166

is cruelly hot and the men must be suffering under their costumes and several are incongruously carrying bottles of Evian as they clump around, their swords and armour ringing with each footstep. Amongst these knights ordinary members of the public are strolling; the scene is bizarre and yet strangely reassuring, as if my community has been, for one day only, united by a shared eccentricity.

'What the fuck do they think they look like?' says Dawson.

'Hicklin,' I say. 'Wasn't he supposed to be here?'

'Thing is,' says Dawson, 'he's busy and he thinks you might be full of shit. So he's sent me. When I could be watching the football. So thanks for that.'

As Dawson says this, he looks about him and there is something furtive in the way he glances around, as if he is expecting somebody and they are late, that I do not trust. 'Anyway, what've you got?' He nods at the canvas bag I am holding.

'It's...' Why tell him? 'Doesn't matter.'

'Nah go on. We're here now.'

'It'll keep. Tell Hicklin I only deal with him.' I turn to go. 'Looks like we've all had our time wasted.'

'Hang on, whoah,' Dawson says, taking out his phone. 'So fucking important, I'll give him a bell.' He takes his phone out of his pocket with one hand, calls a number, holds the other hand up to keep me where I am. A man in a red tunic and thigh-length boots walks up and good-naturedly puts a leather-gloved hand on Dawson's shoulder.

'No mobile telephony in the fifteenth century, young squire,' he says in what he imagines to be a medieval accent, part Oliver Reed, part rural yokel. Dawson, phone still to his ear, digs out his warrant card and flips it open with one hand in the man's smiling face.

'Police. Fuck off,' he says. I have an urge to cram his warrant card into his mouth. 'Yeah, Dawson,' he says into the phone. 'Yeah, he's got… Dunno what it is, won't say. Nah, in a bag.'

I am backing away; I no longer want any part of this. He sees me leaving and holds his hand up, more urgently now, commanding. I ignore him and knock up against the back of a man in chainmail who is practising his sword strokes, carving figures of eight in the air, watched by some young kids. Dawson is walking towards me and we are in that moment when he is not yet chasing me and I am not yet running away; I keep backing away and he keeps advancing. There are people everywhere and tents and I catch my heel, almost trip on a guy rope. Dawson is shaking his head at me, eyes unreadable behind his sunglasses. I turn and pick up my pace, past tables selling leatherware, pewter jewellery, crystals. There is a smell of frying burgers in the air. There are so many people I cannot walk in a straight line, have to pick a path between them. I look back and see that Dawson is still following me. As I turn, I glimpse something and do not believe what I see. I look again and there, emerging from between a hot dog van and a stall selling Thai food, is the policeman with the moustache from the workshop under the arches. He is walking towards me on a different trajectory to Dawson and now I have to change my direction, pick another escape route. There is a roped-off arena for a jousting contest in my way and I skirt the edge, mingling with the people waiting for the show to start. I cannot see Dawson or the other policeman but I know that they cannot be far behind. I am looking for them and not looking where I am going and almost walk into a small child with its face painted like a tiger's. I apologise and am about to turn when a genial voice from behind me says, 'Now look who's here,' and even before I can turn I know it is Baldwin and that Hicklin never got my message and that I have been set up from the start.

'Got something for me, have you?' Baldwin says. Dawson and the thin-faced policeman break through the crowd and now I am surrounded, Baldwin behind me, the other two in front of me and either side. Baldwin is so close to me that I can feel his breath in my ear. It makes me shiver. I turn and I can see the pores in his skin, so defined in the bright sunlight that it is almost as if I am examining them under a microscope. His head seems even bigger this close up, on a different scale from other people's. His doughy skin is loose and his eyes as incurious and free of emotion as a lizard's. I have not seen him since he had me cuffed to the bench underneath the arches; I will my eyes to meet his, to not show the emotions I am experiencing, revulsion and fear and rage. Behind Baldwin is the policeman with the moustache and drinker's face who is trying to control his own fury.

'Where's Gary?' I ask.

Baldwin's face twitches slightly and I know I have scored a point, sucker-punched him just like he had caught me off my guard in my office. But he recovers quickly.

'How's the finger? Giving you any trouble?' He smiles guilelessly. I do not respond, do not know how to. He took my finger; he knows that he is so far ahead on points that there is no real contest.

'You, son, are as much use as tits on a nun, know that?' he says to Dawson. Dawson swallows, looks down at the grass at his feet. The other policeman chuckles. People have drawn back from the drama that is unfolding, sensing the aggression and confrontation in the air. Baldwin looks to be in his element.

'Give me the bag,' he says.

It is hopeless. Outnumbered by three policemen. I am a lawyer. We should be on the same side. I have no options. Yet I cannot simply hand the discs over.

Baldwin rolls his eyes. 'Dawson. Make yourself useful.'

Dawson sees this as his opportunity to atone for his earlier failings. He saunters up, grins at me. 'Bag.'

I ignore him, turn to Baldwin. 'What did you do to her?' I say. 'You kill her?'

For an instant, I have Baldwin wobbling, back on the ropes, but he is not a man who can be rocked for long. He steps towards me, too close so that he is invading my space and it is all I can do to stand my ground, to not edge away. He leans in closer still and puts his mouth to my ear. I can feel the warmth of his breath now and I wait for whatever he wants to whisper to me but instead he just stands there, breathing softly into my ear and, just as I did underneath the arches as he caressed my face, I have the feeling that I am being violated in some subtle yet obscene way. The man has an animal force that disgusts me and that I do not know how to deal with. He exhales into my ear with a sigh that sounds almost post-orgasmic and sticks his tongue gently into my ear. I step quickly away, shaking my head and involuntarily shuddering. When I look at him, he is smiling, his eyes unfocused; his abuse of power seems to work on him like an aphrodisiac. Men or women, girls or boys, I believe it is all the same to him. The abuse of power is what turns him on, regardless of the victim.

I am still recoiling from his violation when Dawson snatches the bag from my hand. Baldwin smiles.

'Now what are we going to do with you?' he says.

'Nothing,' I say. I keep my voice steady, despite what Baldwin has just done to me.

'Oh,' Baldwin says. 'Now I wouldn't say that.'

'Here? Now?' I look around at the people surrounding us, every one a witness. Look back at Baldwin. Shake my head. As I shake it, I can feel his saliva, cold, inside my ear. I suppress a shiver. 'I don't think so.'

Baldwin clicks his tongue. 'You, my boy, have got a target painted on your back. Big one. You know that?'

I do not answer, watch him.

'And the thing with me is, I see a target? I never miss.' He laughs, a short snort. 'Never.'

Dawson hands the bag containing the discs to Baldwin deferentially. Baldwin takes it, smiles at me again, but there is no warmth in his eyes. I experience a moment of absolute stillness as I hold his gaze and an understanding passes between us that nothing is going to happen right now, but that we are not finished with each other. I back away then turn and walk towards the watching crowd and as I reach it the people part and I walk past knights, women in smocks, step over ropes holding their tents in place and keep walking until the crowd thins and I reach the gates of the park and walk back into the real world, free. At least for now.

21

CHANGING THE DRESSING on my finger is painful. I unwind the gauze and it comes off in stages, tacked to my skin by a yellow sticky fluid that is leaking through the black stitches of Major Butler. My finger is red and swollen and the end of it looks like a badly darned sock. I hold it under a warm tap and regard myself in the mirror. I look bleak and ugly and gazing at my reflection I get the impression I am trying to outstare a hard man and the thought makes me smile despite myself. The running water eventually cleans the stump of my finger; I do not have the will to touch it myself. I smear on some antiseptic cream and wrap it back up, gently.

I am in Gabe's bathroom. I cannot go home. Baldwin is not going to go away; he might be sitting outside my house now, waiting for me to show. Or one of his men. I do not know what resources he commands, how many people he has working for him. Have no idea who I can trust. I realise that I have been standing still in front of the mirror for minutes, going over my options, trying to think of a way out. But I cannot find one.

*

Last night I had told Gabe about the footage, about seeing Rosie. He had no better idea than I did about what to do, but his lack of connection with the real world meant that he saw it as less of a problem than I did. Either let Baldwin get away with it, or deal with him, now, definitively. Like gunning for a policeman was no more problematic than attacking an insurgent camp, a question of logistics, tactics, nothing more. The question of justice for Rosie did not concern him; she was dead, so it did not matter any more. I am amazed by Gabe's lack of sentiment, but I suspect that it is something the Army teaches you. Deal with problems, don't waste time worrying about moral aspects. I wish I could do the same but I know that, just as I am haunted by my mother's disappearance, so too will I be haunted by Rosie's death.

'This Baldwin,' says Gabe.

'Yeah?'

'Listen, it's like I said. The solution is simple. Do nothing, or get rid of him.'

'Bit extreme?'

'You see a middle ground?'

'Nail him. Find evidence. That thing called justice our society is predicated on.'

Gabe laughs. 'Christ. I never had you pinned for a crusader.'

'I'm not. I'm a lawyer.' I so want to believe in Gabe, believe he can help me. But this is not the way. 'What I'm definitely not is a fucking assassin.'

'Anyway, you had evidence. Then you lost it.'

'Yeah. Thanks for the reminder.'

But Gabe is right. I have lost the discs incriminating Baldwin, and with it any kind of hold over him. He will get away with whatever it was he did to Rosie; he will do whatever he likes with me. The thought makes my hands clench; I want him brought to justice, crushed, destroyed. And I want justice for Rosie; I did not know her well, only by sight, but I am the sole person who knows what might have happened to her, and I have failed her. But these feelings of guilt and remorse have no practical value. The reality is that, without those discs, Baldwin can do whatever he likes. He is untouchable.

Gabe shrugs. 'Just trying to help.' He regards me levelly over the top of his coffee cup then looks away, nothing more to be done. Tough love indeed.

In my car on the way to my office I think about what Gabe said, and about my options. I am no angel but I am not in the business of knocking off policemen, regardless of what they might have done. I was telling the truth when I told Gabe that I wanted to bring Baldwin to justice; I just do not know how. Without the footage I have no evidence, and without any evidence I have nothing.

I am paranoid enough that I drive past my office twice to make sure that nobody is waiting for me, and park a street away. I have not done any work towards Halliday's property purchase, and so spend the morning in the dull paper chasing of conveyancing, organising searches from the Land Registry and ordering surveyor's reports. My heart is not in it but it is only work and I can see no point in antagonising Halliday, with all the other problems I have got at the moment. A day too late, I call Eddie to tell him about my progress, feed him some legal jargon, which he doesn't understand but which seems to pacify him. I give him a timeframe of a fortnight to get everything in order which he tells me is much longer than Halliday expected but I can tell that he is pleased to be able to tell Halliday something, anything.

I leave my office at a quarter to two and head for the hospital. My father has been moved from Intensive Care and he is now on a ward, his tubes removed and just a drip feeding into the back of his hand. He is awake when I arrive and I am amazed to see his face brighten momentarily as he sees that it is me, his son, who has come to see him. I have heard that near-death experiences can have profound effects on people's personalities, but I have never before seen my father pleased to see me. I sit down next to his bed and look at him. On his back, his skin seems to be slipping off his face as if it is not sufficiently well anchored and he looks old. His hair is greasy and I can smell it from where I am sitting. He turns his head to look at me, doesn't sit up.

'All right?' I say.

'Better,' he says. 'Nearly died.'

'Yeah, well...' I know that I am expected to deliver comforting words but I cannot. 'Who were you fighting?'

'Someone got the drop on me. Didn't see them.'

'No faces?'

'Can't remember.'

'Didn't say anything?'

'Said I can't fucking remember, didn't I?'

He turns his head away; it did not take long for the old antagonism to resurface. We sit in silence for a while. Fuck it, I think.

'Went to see Xynthia Halliday. She told me about my mother, about what happened.'

My father does not respond and I watch the back of his head resting on his pillow, wonder what's going on in there. I am about to say something else when he slowly turns his head back towards me.

'She told you, did she.'

'You let Halliday sell her?'

'Think I could have stopped him? Least he didn't kill her. Or me.'

'You could have tried.'

My father closes his eyes, perhaps replaying the situation back to himself, asking himself if he could have done anything differently. But he is not one for self-examination and he opens them again, this time looking defiant.

'What do you want?'

'I want to find her.'

'How you going to do that?'

'Don't know.' I don't, and suddenly the futility of it hits me. What can I do? She could have gone anywhere, done anything. Anything could have happened to her. She could be at the bottom of a canal.

'Why'd you want to find her, son?' my father asks softly and I look at him in astonishment, this gentle tone one I do not believe I have ever heard from him before.

'Wouldn't you? She's my mother and I never got to know her.'

'So long ago.'

'You never told me anything. You think I didn't always wonder?'

'Couldn't say anything. Fucking pointless.'

'I want to know.' The word 'closure' springs to my mind but of course I do not say it; my father knows nothing about such things. He sighs deeply and closes his eyes again, for such a long time that I wonder if he has gone to sleep.

'Dad?'

He opens his eyes. 'Some Irishman,' he says. 'In Manchester.'

'Irishman?'

'Took your mother.'

'Took her. You mean, was sold her.'

My father ignores me. 'Fucking ex-Provisional or something. Only met him once. Horrible cunt.'

'Got a name?'

'Connolly. No, Conneely. Sean Conneely. He was forty then, probably dead now.'

This is more than I had ever expected. A clue, a step towards my mother, a name from thirty-seven years ago, shining up at me like metal from under the sea. 'You sure?'

'Sure.' My father lets out a long ragged breath. 'Never found out what happened to her. Couldn't...' He blinks and a tear rolls out of the corner of his eye, past his crow's feet, on to the pillow. 'Tried to forget.'

'How could you forget? I was there.'

My father looks at me and in his eyes I can see that the anger that was always there has gone and that instead there is a pain which seems fathomless. 'You were,' he says. 'Always.'

Manchester. Sean Conneely. I have a name, a destination, somewhere to go. He may be dead. He may not have anything to say to me. But this is all I have and I will follow it through until I know for sure. What I will not do, what I cannot do, is wait like a cornered animal for whatever Baldwin is planning for me. I can still feel his tongue in my ear; my finger will not let me forget his existence, out there, a lurking horror. As a child, I would listen for my father's return home; the feet on the stairs, the twist of the door handle, the widening shard of light. But, as afraid as I was back then, I never thought I would be killed. Hurt, yes, but in my small bed, underneath my blankets, the possibility of death never crossed my mind. But Baldwin has killed, and I am sure more than once; behind his easy smile and genial manner is a murderer entirely without pity. Nowhere is safe for me any more. I believe he means to kill me; he has got under my skin, into my head. And perhaps it is merely because I am tired, and it is late. But I can think of nothing that will stop him.

Still, I will not call what I am about to do running away, merely a strategic withdrawal. I drive to my office and leave a message on my answerphone explaining about a family emergency, then home and pack a bag, lock the windows, close the curtains. All the time I tell myself that I will be back, that this is just temporary, that I am not being run out of town. But if I stop to think about it, I cannot see any way back.

22

I ARRIVED IN Manchester yesterday, having driven up the M1 doing a hundred and more, looking in my rear-view mirror with a sick feeling of paranoia right up until I hit the M1 and left London far behind. Every car that came up behind could have been Baldwin. Once a Porsche driver tailgated me flashing his headlights and I felt a dread, as I pulled over and willed him to go past, which caused me to clench my teeth so hard my jaw ached. As I drove north and passed exit signs bearing the names of towns I had never visited and never would, I wondered whether I would ever be able to go back to Essex. But fear, like any emotion, cannot last for ever, and with every passing mile my feeling of dread lessened. It felt reassuring to be caught up in this tide of people with places to go, their own business to take care of; the number of cars on the motorway was so great that I could not help but feel diminished by them. I became comfortable in my insignificance.

For some parochial reason I had expected colder weather, perhaps drizzle as I headed north but the sun continued to blaze and I wondered how long it could be until it rained.

The countryside that I drove past looked as parched as the South of France, yellow grass and trees that seemed exhausted by the effort of standing up in the heat. I stopped off at the services for a coffee and drank it in the bright sunlight surrounded by families in cars loaded up with bags and bicycles and towing motorboats or caravans. Although I was headed for Manchester and not the Cote d'Azur or Miami, I still shared, in some small way, that feeling of escape that only a holiday can give. I was going to find somebody; but nobody would be able to find me while I was away.

There were only four people named Conneely in the phone book for Manchester, and only one of them had the initial S. I thought about calling the number, but there are some things it is best to do in person and, anyway, I did not want to scare him off. If I turned up out of the blue in person, there would be little a man of his age could do to get rid of me.

The only person who knew where I was going, and why, was Gabe; I'd passed by his place after I left my house and thanked him for putting me up, told him what was going on. I must have caught him on one of his more empathetic days as he took the time to engage with what I was saying.

'Sold her? Jesus. I guess it explains why your dad wasn't keen on discussing her. Christ, Daniel, every time I think your background can't get any more fucked up.'

'Yeah. Well.'

'Think you're going to be able to find her?'

'Have to try.'

We were standing up in Gabe's kitchen and he sat down at the table, indicated that I should too. I pulled out a chair and sat down opposite him. His pale eyes looked concerned.

'Listen, Danny, you sure about this?'

'Why wouldn't I be?'

'It's been an age. A lifetime. Think you're going to find anything you like?'

'I could find *her*.'

'Whoever that is. She didn't ever try to track you down, right? I mean, shit, Danny, it's not as if you ever moved. You live about a mile away from where you grew up.'

I shrug. 'Could have had her reasons.'

'Sold her.' Gabe shakes his head. 'You ever read the story of "The Monkey's Paw"?'

'Nope.'

'This couple's son dies at work, gets chewed up in some machinery. They use this monkey's paw to wish him back to life, right? So immediately there's a knock at the door but the father, he suddenly realises how messed up his son was by the accident, how horrific he will look. Uses their last wish to wish the kid back in his grave.'

I give Gabe a stern look. 'Please. Be careful what you wish for?'

'Just saying. It's been a long time. You've got no idea what you'll find. Her life, Danny, it must have been fucking horrific. You can't imagine.'

'You think I can stop? Now?'

'Probably not,' says Gabe, getting up and stretching, sermon over. 'No point trying to tell you anything anyway. You'll do what you want.' He yawns, arms extended over his head, something feline in his dismissiveness. 'Try not to get killed.'

'I'll try.'

Conneely lived in Salford, on the west of the city. I could have gone and visited him then; it was only four o'clock and it would not have taken me long to get there. But the hotel I was staying in had a bar and a roof terrace, and I had been driving all day. And the truth was, I was not mentally prepared to confront a man I had never met before, who might well have caused my mother immeasurable pain and humiliation. I put my bag in my room, took the lift up to the bar, ordered a vodka and tonic. The terrace filled up and soon I was surrounded by people drinking, talking, laughing. I felt camouflaged by their presence, lost within this new city where nobody could find me. I drank too much and of course my size attracted glances, curious from the women and appraising from the men. But I was left alone and I felt safe and eventually when a group asked if they could share my table I went back down to my room and slept more soundly than I had done in weeks, lulled to sleep by a show in which men and women entered and left an apartment and talked with each other and the audience laughed.

Now I am standing in front of Sean Conneely's address in Salford. He lives in a red-brick terrace house with a small front garden, on a street in which half the houses are vacant and have perforated metal sheets fixed over the windows. There are no cars parked in the street unless you count the burned-out shell of a Mercedes half on, half off the kerb three houses down, resting on its disc brakes, its tyres melted away. There are small squares of broken glass everywhere so that it crunches wherever you walk. A group of kids on BMXs are swearing at the end of the road, throwing stones at a streetlight that is already smashed. Sean Conneely's front garden is overgrown with weeds and his front door is wide open. There is an armchair in the front garden amongst the weeds and an old man who I assume is Sean Conneely is sitting in it and my immediate suspicion is that he is quite mad.

'Mr Conneely?'

'And who the fuck would want to know that?'

I push open the green peeling metal gate and walk into his front garden. He is wearing a brown suit that is heavily stained and he does not have any shoes on. He is smoking a cigarette and on his head is a trilby. As he talks, I can see that he is missing several teeth and he is thin, haggard even, the skin on his throat hanging down like pale curtains of flesh and he has big saggy bags under his watery eyes. His legs are crossed and the cloth of his trousers looks like it is draped over tent poles, so thin is he. He does not look like a trafficker of women who was once connected to the Provisional IRA; but then, he must be knocking eighty.

'My name is Daniel Connell,' I say. 'I was hoping we could have a chat.'

'A chat he says.' He looks around at some imaginary person over his right shoulder and leers at them. His accent is pure Ulster, as thick as stout. 'Well why the fuck not? Sit yourself down.' There is nowhere to sit, so I remain standing. He does not seem to notice. 'Now, why would a brute like you want to visit a man like me?'

'I'm looking for my mother,' I say. 'I wondered if you might know what happened to her.'

'And how,' Conneely says as he takes his cigarette out of his mouth and bends forward and carefully stubs it out on the ground, 'would I happen to know anything about your fucking mother?'

He says this without a trace of the madness with which he'd greeted my earlier questions and I am suddenly sure that it was an act and that Sean Conneely is very much in control of his faculties, despite the fact that he is quite clearly dying. Cancer of some sort, I imagine. I wonder how long he has got.

'She worked for you,' I say evenly. I swallow after I speak; it is hard for me to say, to normalise in words, the hell he must have put her through, to call it something as anodyne as 'work'. But I want answers and until I get them I am prepared to mind my temper.

'She worked for me?' he says in surprise and touches both his shoulders with his fingertips. 'And tell me, Mr I've-never-fucking-met-you-before-in-my-fucking-life, what is it this mother of yours did for me?'

'I don't know,' I say. 'A man called Vincent Halliday sold her to you. You tell me.'

'Halliday.' Conneely fishes around in his inside pocket and comes up with a pack of cigarettes. He offers the pack to me, eyebrows raised. I shake my head. He takes one out and lights it. I believe that Sean Conneely was a wicked man, but he does not seem wicked now, merely rascally. Can evil, I wonder, become attenuated with age, lose its cutting edge? 'I knew a man called Halliday,' Conneely says. 'A boxing fella. From down south there.'

'Vincent Halliday. Essex.'

'Essex.' Conneely tuts to himself. 'Halliday. That's your man.'

'My mother's name was Marcela. Marcela Cosma. Here.' I take out a photo of my mother and walk towards Conneely. He looks up at me, eyes wide in mock fear, and snatches it out of my hand, examines it carefully.

'Marcela. Christ and I haven't seen her face for a while. Marcela? Now what did we call her?' He closes his eyes and looks upwards as if he has smelled something, trying to think back over the years for the whore's name he had given my mother as if he is trying to catch a scent. He is so atrophied I imagine I could literally tear him apart. He opens his eyes again and says, 'No fucking idea!'

'You recognise her?'

'I believe I do.'

'She's my mother.'

'She do much mothering?'

'No. Because Halliday sold her to you, and you fucking destroyed her life by pimping her out, you skinny little Irish prick.'

'Ah,' says Conneely, wagging a finger at me. He does not appear to have much to lose. 'Now. And I was supposed to know she was your mother, was I?'

'Just tell me what happened to her. Is she alive?'

'And how the fucking hell would I know the answer to that?' Conneely says in an indignant squeal. 'She's not my fucking wife. Or mother.'

I look at Conneely in exasperation. He is a man in the latter stages of some nasty terminal illness and I doubt that snapping one of his fingers will have much effect. If I am to be honest, he does not excite much violent feeling in me at all; he is simply too pitiful. Yet this is the man who took away my mother. This visit is not working out as I had hoped.

'When did you last see her?'

'Ah. Ah, now. Let me think.' He closes his eyes and takes five or six rapid puffs on his cigarette, eyebrows jumping up and down in time, and I know that he is mocking me. But when he opens his eyes he does not look quite so manic. 'She was your mother, you say?'

'She left when I was born. I never knew her.'

'So what in fucking hell are you doing looking for her now?'

'She's my mother.'

''Course she is. If you say.' He closes his eyes again, takes more crazy pulls on his cigarette, looks at me. 'I would say, it would have been nineteen eighty-one. Around that time. Your mother, she wasn't like the other girls. No drugs, no drinking. A fucking lady, she was. Had to get rid of her. She...' Conneely's eyes lose their focus as he looks back into his past. 'She was too good for all that,' he says quietly.

'What did she do after? After you got rid of her?'

'Haven't a fucking clue,' says Conneely. 'Went back to wherever she came from?'

'Romania.'

'Was it? Well fuck me.'

'Who the fuck are you?'

I turn around and see a young man in a white wife-beater vest and low-slung jeans and Reebok trainers. He has gold hoops in his ears and tattoos on his arms and he has that kind of trapped energy that manifests itself in uncontrolled twitches and a too-fast walk and suggests that pointless violence can be unleashed at any time, for any provocation. He looks like the kind of person who will be in prison, not within years but within months or very possibly weeks.

'Ah, now then, Daniel, this here is my grandson Brendon. Brendon, this gentleman is after asking me questions about things that happened, oh, fucking years ago.'

You old cunt, I think. Drop me right in it, will you? The young man snorts and spits on to the path, an act I can only imagine he conceives as threatening. Anyone can spit, I want to tell him. Wow-wee. But instead I keep my mouth shut. I still want more information from Conneely, if he has it.

'Want me to get rid of him?' Brendon asks. He has a nasal Mancunian accent and for some reason I find it extremely irritating, so much so that I forget my good intentions and without reflection imitate him like a child would in a playground: *'Want me to get rid of him?'* So much for keeping my mouth shut.

Conneely cackles and slaps the arm of his chair but Brendon does not see the funny side. He walks towards me and pushes me. It has little effect; I weigh at least half as much again as him and, anyway, what is the point of pushing somebody? Hit them or don't has always been my view. I smile and punch him in the face. I don't hit him hard but he still staggers backwards. He puts his hand to his nose and when he takes it away it has blood on it. I turn back to Conneely and do not notice Brendon take a knife out of his pocket. I sense rather than see movement and turn back to him but it is too late. He stabs me in the outside of the thigh, but because I was turning it does not penetrate deeply. He takes the knife out. It is a lock knife, black handle, four-inch blade. Blood begins to seep through my jeans. This person, this boy, has stabbed me? I am almost too surprised to be angry.

Brendon is coming back to stab me again. He has a manic hatred in his eyes. As his hand arcs over to cut me, I catch it. My hand engulfs his. I hold his knife hand up high and with my other hand punch him in the armpit. I punch upwards, so hard that his feet leave the ground and the blood leaves his face. Already the fight has left him but he stabbed me, so I punch him again, this time in the face. I hit him hard and feel the crunch of the cartilage in his nose. He sits down heavily on the path just inside the gate and looks stupidly around him, as if he has dropped money in the dark. It is all I can do to not move in, hit him again, humiliate him, really hurt him. How dare he? The leg of my jeans is soaked with blood. They will have to go in the bin.

Conneely looks at me with a newfound respect. 'Well now, that was nicely done,' he says, but he is interrupted by a woman who runs out of the open front door. She is perhaps sixty-five and wearing a dressing gown. Conneely cackles again. This is turning out to be some morning for him. The lady runs down the path and bends down and puts her arms around Brendon whose chin is resting on his chest, blood staining his wife-beater, his legs straight out in front of him. She looks up at me in fury.

'What have you done?'

I can do nothing but shrug. Brendon attacked me; not only that, he stabbed me. And this is my fault? But sometimes there is nothing to say.

'He's after looking for his mother,' Conneely says, wheezing. 'Marcela. Show her the photo.'

'I don't want to see any photo,' the lady says, dabbing at Brendon's nose with a handkerchief. 'Just take yourself away.'

'Take a look,' Conneely says, and there is a snap to his voice that I have not heard before. The lady clearly has though; she reacts as if struck, turns, looks at me.

I take out the photo and show it to her. 'She's my mother.'

She reaches up for the photo from where she is crouching next to Brendon, takes it, looks at it carefully. 'Your mother?' she says incredulously.

'You know her?'

'I did. I recognise her. Of course I recognise her.'

'Do you know where she is?'

'No. No, I don't. I don't.' Who is this woman, I wonder. If she is married to Conneely, I have only sympathy for her. I take out a business card with my name and number on it.

'If you know anything, anything at all. I do really want to find her. Very much.'

She takes the card from me, then looks back at Brendon who is showing signs of life. 'Go on,' she says, handing back the photograph. 'Go. Go.'

I look at Conneely but he just raises a hand in friendly farewell. I am too confused by the events of the last few

191

minutes to feel disappointed that I have not come away with more than I have. I walk out of Conneely's front garden and down the street, looking back when I reach the end and I see that Brendon is now standing up and being fussed over by the woman. Conneely is lighting another cigarette and when it is lit he shakes his fists at the sky, for what reason I cannot guess.

I have to walk a long way until I find a minicab firm that can take me back to my hotel; this area of town appears to be about as affluent as Mogadishu. The driver looks doubtfully at the blood on my jeans; he looks more approvingly at the fistful of money I wave at him. On the way back, I reflect on the little I have learned from Conneely. My mother worked for him for only a handful of years before she got out; that in itself is better news than I had expected. That he did not know what happened to her afterwards, though, is devastating. Apart from a measure of peace of mind, I have discovered nothing from my strange experience with Conneely. Right now, my mother seems as far away as she has ever been.

Back at the hotel and faced with the silent reproach of my empty suite, I realise that I have no reason to stay in Manchester, no leads left to follow. I do not wish to return to Essex; I have told what clients I have that I will be away for a week and figure that I might as well stay away for that long at least. But for a man with some financial resources and five days to kill, the choice of where to go is bewilderingly wide, nowhere on the planet out of his reach.

I do not have any family except for the father I do not want to see and, possibly, the mother I can't find. I do not have any close friends living overseas who are due a visit. However, my conscience is nagging away at me and I realise that I can kill two birds with one stone.

Terry Campion is still, as far as I know, hiding away in Marbella but he does not yet know what I do, that Baldwin wanted the footage back for darker reasons than a mere case of police brutality. Terry needs to know that, rather than blow over, this problem will never go away and that perhaps he might want to consider staying in Spain until Baldwin ceases to pose a threat. I have tried his mobile again and it is disconnected; I have called his sister who claims not to know where he is. The only lead I have is that he told me when I called him that he was in his mate's bar; Marbella is not a small place but, still, I should be able to find it.

I head down for reception, to check out and call a cab for the airport. I have never been to Spain before and what self-respecting Essex man makes it to the age of forty without having visited the Costa Del Crime?

23

I BELIEVED THAT in England we were suffering from a heat wave of unparalleled intensity but in Spain the air is so hot that breathing in feels like a hairdryer is blowing down my throat. As I leave the plane, it is as if the air has been replaced by something denser so that walking through it feels like a struggle. It seems impossible that life can survive in such a hostile atmosphere, that plants can grow, that people can function. The sun is so bright that I cannot look at the tarmac of the airport runway without my eyes squinting and pricking with tears. The baggage reclaim area is half-heartedly air-conditioned and already I can hear the English muttering to themselves that it's hot, too hot, how can people stand it? The security staff and customs officers look at us with unconcealed contempt, as if we are a fresh batch of prisoners being shipped into a third-world prison. I find my bag and head outside to get a taxi.

On the flight out, I had sat next to a drunk young man with innocent blue eyes who told me that he had been to Marbella fourteen times and that if you wanted pussy then there was nowhere better to get it, although saying that his brother had gone on a stag weekend to Bratislava and reckoned he'd had a threesome with two six-footers. The young man was called Jim and Jim was with a group of seven other young men who were all equally drunk and sitting in seats behind me and across from me and in front of me. The harassed trolley dollies were clearly counting the minutes until we landed, wearing fixed smiles that did nothing to conceal the fact that they were, basically, terrified by these people they were meant to be responsible for. Even I did not fancy asking them to please shut the fuck up, not in a confined cabin thirty thousand feet up, so instead I smiled and told Jim that I had never been to Marbella but that I had a mate who had moved there, only the problem was I didn't have his address. I asked him about bars where I was likely to find him and unwittingly provoked a loud and tedious discussion amongst Jim's friends about what the best bars in Marbella actually were. None of the places they suggested had Spanish names; I suspected that neither would any of them serve Spanish food or even Spanish beer. I have enough middle-class pretensions to try to sample a country's culture when I visit it, but Jim and his friends had no such designs. Nor, if I knew him at all, would Terry. I left the plane with a list of bars and an invitation to join Jim and his friends on the pull that night.

My taxi driver is listening to some music that I do not recognise on a tape deck, a toothpick in the corner of his mouth jigging up and down as he sings fragments of the song in a language that is not Spanish. We are driving past an industrial zone of aluminium-sided warehouses and supermarkets and chain restaurants; I see an enormous McDonald's and a Carrefour the size of an aircraft hangar. I do not wish to emulate my countrymen in complaining about everything that is foreign but I do not believe that I have ever experienced worse driving in my life, my driver stamping on the accelerator as if it is an especially resilient cockroach that refuses to die. The seats of his taxi are made of plastic and I can feel myself sweating against them. The sky is so bright it is no longer blue but white and the sun has bleached everything so that the landscape looks like it would in an overexposed photograph. I have never been to Marbella before but I am an exception in my corner of Essex; for many it is an ideal of heaven on earth, a corner of Spain that will be for ever England. Looking out of the window, I have to wonder why.

Growing up with my father, it was inevitable that I should hear about the wonders of Spain; I know of four of his friends for sure who left England in a hurry before the police caught up with them, heading for Spain and its lack of an extradition treaty. Although Spain is now only too happy to extradite criminals, it is no longer a simple matter to find them; there are going on for half a million British expats living in the south of Spain and their population is disproportionately represented by the criminal class. I am aware that an English version of Omertà is the norm amongst the community and that aiding any authorities brings with it severe repercussions. Punishment beatings and fish and chips; the Spanish must love us.

We are approaching the city now and passing half-finished apartment buildings, cranes standing idle next to windowless façades that lack a roof as if it is the day after the apocalypse. The motorway gives way to boulevards, black tarmac and white kerbs with palm trees standing in the middle of roundabouts and soon the unfinished blocks are replaced by concrete houses, then huge white mansions with lush grass and bright flowers in their front gardens, spilling over white walls. My driver blows through a red light and nearly kills two boys on a scooter; they have to swerve to avoid him and turn so tightly their knees almost touch the ground.

We turn a corner and suddenly we are on the seafront and the Mediterranean is the bright blue of a stained-glass window, luminous and beautiful; the enormity and serenity of it affects me immediately, soothing me somehow. Even with the driver's strange music in my ears and the ragged hot air blowing through the window, the sight of that expanse of water acts like some kind of balm. I take a deep breath and feel the oppression that had been sitting in my pores lift and dissipate. Regardless of whether I find Terry Campion or not, that simple view means that this trip will not have been wasted.

My hotel is on the seafront, an orange concrete behemoth that steps further away from the sea at each floor making it look like the superstructure of a ship emerging from the hills behind it. I can watch the sea from my balcony, which has a table and chairs and a parasol. The tiled floor under my bare feet has been cooled by the air-conditioning. I walk out on to the balcony, again shocked by how hot it is; my skin immediately pricks with moisture. On the horizon is a tanker, a hundred thousand tons of steel rendered hazy and ephemeral in the distance. Directly below me four lanes carry cars and scooters up and down the seafront, two lanes either side of a green border in which flowers grow. Beyond that is the beach, which is covered with people, the top halves of young men and women sprouting out of the shallow water. The seafront curves away from me and the buildings facing the sea are mostly hotels or restaurants or bars. I look at the list of bars that Jim and his friends gave me on the plane and already I can see one, The Banana Tree. I am in Marbella and evening is on its way and I need a drink. The Banana Tree seems as good a place to start as any.

I draw a blank at The Banana Tree, same at Jake's, Reflections, Room 8, Den's Den, O'Malley's, Oxygen and The Tiger Club, which has the distinction of a real stuffed tiger behind the bar. I spend the afternoon threading my way in between outside tables occupied by drunk English people with sunburns and dozy chaotic expressions as if they have just been woken up to be told that their house is on fire. Lager and forty-five-degree temperatures do not seem to be an ideal mix, particularly for young men and women accustomed to a sixty-watt sunshine. Next on my list is JoJos, no apostrophe, a waterfront bar with blacked-out windows and red ropes threaded through brass stands leading the way to the main door. Inside, I could be back in Essex; there is a long black bar with backlit spirit bottles on glass shelves behind it, leather-covered booths and three pool tables in the back. It is not busy and I stand at the bar. A blonde woman in a bikini top comes over; she is nearly fifty and the tanned skin on her chest looks like the hide cover of an old book. Her pink lipstick is fighting a losing battle at standing out against her orange skin.

'Pint of...' I scan the pumps. 'Carling.' She pours and I look around but there aren't many people in the bar and none of them is Terry.

'I'm looking for a friend of mine,' I say. 'He had to leave England in a bit of a hurry.'

'Oh yeah?' She is chewing gum and she blows a small bubble which pops untidily against her pink lips.

'Name's Terry Campion. Wouldn't know him, would you?'

'No, love.'

'Couldn't miss him, he looked like he'd had a fight with a bear. Black eyes, stitches. Skinny, about this high.' I put the edge of my hand against my chin.

'You haven't got a picture?'

'No.'

'Might not have noticed, but this is summer.' She puts my pint down in front of me, licks the last of the bubble gum from her lips. 'Lots of people. They come here on holiday.'

I nod, acknowledge her sarcasm. She has a point. Finding Terry might not be as simple as I had thought it would be. He cannot be the only Englishman in Marbella with a bruised face and if I am to be honest Terry is not the world's most memorable man. I drink and decide that for the rest of the evening I will try to enjoy myself and push my search to the back of my mind. But it seems that try as I might I cannot put Essex behind me because I feel a hand clap me on the shoulder and a loud voice says, 'Put your hands up or you will get it, son.'

I turn around and see Jamie DeLaney, a twenty-five-year-old wastrel from my neighbourhood who could have played tennis at national level if it was not for the fact that he was born without sense, like some people come into this world without sight. He is grinning happily but then I have never seen him do anything else; I have in the past found myself resentfully jealous of his incapacity for gloom. He has blond hair and a well-fed face that would be handsome if not for the puppy fat, and he is as stupid and friendly as a Labrador.

'Jamie.'

'What you doing here, Danny?'

'Holiday. Lots of people come here on holiday.'

Jamie grins. 'I'm on holiday too.'

'Amazing.' Jamie's father owns a company that makes the uPVC surrounds for double-glazed windows and I don't believe that Jamie has done a day's work in his life. He is a professional gambler who once dropped £200,000 on his team, Chelsea, to win the league. When they didn't, he laughed and paid for everybody he knew to go on a three-day bender. But I am not being entirely fair; apart from that error of judgement, the word is that he makes good money, mostly from playing poker in big tournaments. Probably nothing significantly bad will happen to him in his entire life.

'Drink?' he says and I hold up my full pint.

'No thanks.'

'Oi, darling? Pint of Carling.' He turns to me. 'So, who you here with?'

'Nobody. On my own.'

Jamie looks at me like I've confessed to molesting children. 'Yeah?'

'Couple of days. Change of scenery.' I take a drink and Jamie notices my finger.

'Jesus, Danny, you in some kind of bother?'

'Nah. This? Shaving accident.'

Jamie nods. He's streetwise enough to know when not to push something. There's a brief pause but Jamie's never been one to put up with a silence for long.

'Tell the truth, it ain't just a holiday. I've got a poker game too.'

'Yeah?'

'At the Four Seasons. You should see it, Danny, it ain't like round here. Two sides to Marbella innit, and over there it's proper classy. Lamborghinis, Ferraris, fuck me you can't move for it.'

'When does it start?'

'Yeah, started actually. Been playing the last four days, got a day off today so, you know.' He hands money to the woman, picks up his pint, takes a healthy swig. 'Getting on it.'

'You winning?'

'Yeah, not doing bad. Cost me ten grand to buy in but we're down to the last four. Two Yanks and some woman from the Philippines, looks like she should be cleaning my room but she plays like fucking Yoda.' Jamie's guileless face chucks out this racial slur as if it is meant as a compliment. He leans in close to me. 'I've got two hundred and sixty grand in chips,' he says. 'Definitely got a sniff at winning the lot.'

'How much would that be?'

'Million and a half, but it's in Euros, so, fuck knows. Probably buy a villa here if I win anyway, so... Don't matter, does it?'

'I guess not.' I look Jamie over but I cannot discern in any part of him the steel he must possess to consistently win at high-stakes games.

'So, anyway, tonight I am having it,' he says. 'You coming to the party?'

'Party?'

'Oh, do one, Danny, what, you come all this way and you ain't even heard about it? You know Bernard Leavy?'

I know Bernard Leavy. He's been living in Spain since the robbery of a post office depot in Dagenham over a decade ago, a post office depot where his brother-in-law worked for a year and left shortly before it got knocked over. As far as I know, there's no warrant out for his arrest but, if you wanted to find somebody steeped in criminality, Bernard would be your man. He is such an accomplished thief, if you cut him open I would not be surprised to see that he had helped himself to somebody else's blood. 'How do you know Bernard?' I ask Jamie. 'Bit before your time, isn't he?'

'Loves poker,' says Jamie. 'Treats me like I'm fucking Bono or something. Here, why don't you come with me? Might want to change first, but it'll be a good *craic*.'

Although my notion of a perfect evening doesn't involve hanging around with Essex faces, I can think of worse companions than Jamie. If you want to forget, for a time, that life is a shabby, cruel and dangerous place, Jamie could have been designed specifically to help make it happen. His disposition is sunnier than the weather outside. And besides, if anybody might have heard about Terry Campion, might know where he is, chances are it'll be Bernard Leavy. From what I have heard about him, he's connected to anybody worth knowing and many, many people you would never want to know.

'Yeah, go on then.' I tell him where I'm staying and he tells me he'll be round in a couple of hours, meet me out the front, pick me up. We finish our drinks and talk about people we know back home and I walk back to my hotel as the sun goes down and the streets empty out, the city resting before the evening's onslaught of binge-drinking and pointless sex and violence.

24

JAMIE PICKS ME up in a purple Ferrari that he has hired for the week. It is convertible and the roof is down and it has white leather seats. I get in next to him and he turns and smiles behind mirrored Ray-Bans.

'Fucking sweet or what?'

'Yeah, it's nice, Jamie. Didn't have one in gold?'

'Cheeky cunt. Here, check it out.' He floors the accelerator and the Ferrari feels as if it is a toy being tugged on a string by a godlike child. I am pressed back into my seat and Jamie screams into the night sky with a primeval abandon that is infectious. I smile and find that I am looking forward to hanging out with Jamie at Bernard Leavy's villa. We turn away from the seafront and head through town, past neon signs and shrieking women in tiny skirts and gangs of young men striding around as if looking for revenge. We hit a neighbourhood full of bigger mansions and the street heads up into the hills, zig-zagging behind haciendas hidden behind gates and tall walls. We turn a corner and see a pair of gates wide open, the street jammed with cars. Jamie sounds his horn and shouts to people he knows then drives further up the hill to park.

Bernard Leavy lives in a white villa that sits behind a wall that is half again as tall as I am, topped with terracotta tiles. I wonder what he has stolen recently to pay for such opulence. The house is set back from the road and there is a lush lawn both sides of the drive leading to it, spotlights showing the way. Yellow light spills out of the open front door of the house and I can hear music, Spandau Ballet's 'Gold', which I have not heard for years. We walk through the door and into an open-plan living room, which has a square sunken area in the middle of it, big enough to hold two large leather sofas and a rug. Throughout the room, men in linen shirts and high-heeled women in tiny dresses, mostly metallic, gold and silver, are talking and drinking.

'Jamie! Over here, son.'

I look over and see Bernard Leavy walking towards us. It has been at least a decade since I last saw him and he seems to have done well in that time; he has thick white hair brushed straight back in waves from his brown face, and his gut pushes out his silk shirt. He is a short man but solid and is wearing black-framed glasses; I don't know why but he makes me think of an aging film director with a Napoleon complex. He holds out his hand and takes Jamie's, puts his other hand on top. 'Still winning?'

'Yeah, so far,' says Jamie. 'Ask me tomorrow night.'

Bernard laughs and shakes Jamie's hand, two downward jerks like he's pumping water. He lets go, turns to me, holds out his hand. 'Bernard Leavy.'

I take his hand. 'Hi, Bernard. I'm Daniel, Frankie Connell's boy.'

'Frankie's boy? Fuck me.' He steps back theatrically and looks at me, up and down as if I am so big that it is straining his neck to take me all in. His eyes are warm and crinkled and he has a natural way of making me feel at my ease. 'What happened? You fucking eat him?'

'I said it'd be okay, him coming,' says Jamie.

''Course it is, fuck me, 'course it is. Here –' he looks at me seriously. 'I heard your old man weren't well.'

The Essex grapevine clearly has a long reach. 'He's out of danger,' I say. 'His heart.'

'You send him my best,' says Bernard. 'Tell him to come out here. Convalesce.'

A woman with thick black hair that is clearly dyed and too much make-up walks up and takes Bernard's arm. On her hand is an enormous diamond ring and her nails are bright pink, like her lipstick. 'Bernard? Out of Champagne. Again.'

Bernard pats her hand and gives us a smile. 'Grab yourselves a drink, boys,' he says. 'Steal the silver. Do what the fuck you like.'

I had not realised but amongst this crowd Jamie is nearly a celebrity, both men and women in thrall to the glamour of his gambling lifestyle. I soon lose him to a group who hang off his every word and walk out on to the patio. Bernard has one of those swimming pools that looks like it is spilling off the edge of a cliff, no back wall to it. It is lit from within and is a beautiful cool limpid blue. I am on my own but I am quite content, drinking a vodka and tonic and looking out over the lights of downtown Marbella, glistening through the heat below me like ten thousand flickering candles. I do not recognise anybody at the party and have not drunk enough to be garrulous; I will have a couple more drinks then walk back to the hotel. I turn to refill my glass and meet Bernard at the patio doors, where he is talking to two men. I move to walk around them but Bernard calls to me.

'Danny! Danny, come here, over here.' He beckons exaggeratedly with his arm and I stop and turn back. The other men he was talking to turn away to talk amongst themselves, and Bernard reaches up an arm and tries to hang it over my shoulders. 'Here, son, it must be, what? Last time I saw you...' He stops, thinks. He is quite drunk. He snaps his fingers. 'That's it, you was a lawyer. You still...?'

'Still. I've got a practice.'

'Amazing. Brilliant, really brilliant. See much of your old man?'

'Now and then. Keep in touch.'

'Good, that's good. Family. That's good.'

Bernard comes from an enormous family of Irish Catholics who are still well represented in my neighbourhood; he probably couldn't avoid them if he tried.

'You're doing all right,' I say.

He smiles knowingly. 'Not bad, not too bad.'

'Beautiful place.'

'Paradise, I call it. I'll die here. And happy.'

He really is drunk. I think about strategies for leaving, but he keeps talking, swaying slightly. 'Marbella,' he says without the slightest trace of irony, 'is the most beautiful place on earth.'

'Seems nice,' I say, at a loss for how to respond to such a proclamation. A young woman walks by us and pinches Bernard on the cheek; he tries to respond by slapping her on the bottom but misses. She laughs at him over her shoulder and sticks out her tongue. He watches her go wistfully, then turns back to me.

"Course it's full of Spaniards. They're arseholes, but what're you going to do? Their country I suppose.'

He admits this grudgingly, as if he's doing them a favour, allowing them their sovereignty on sufferance. 'And the blacks don't cause no trouble, too shit scared of getting deported. Where we went wrong back in England, giving that lot passports.'

I do not answer. I am willing to bet that, out of any of the recently arrived ethnic groups on Spanish soil, it is the British who create the most headaches for the Spanish authorities. Bernard finishes drinking in his Mediterranean paradise and turns to me.

'I had a lot of time for your old man,' he says. 'He keeping busy?'

'Semi-retired, I'd say. Working on his drinking.'

Bernard laughs, head back. 'In't we all, son? He was a good man in his day, handy man to have around. You can tell him that, tell him I remember him. Frankie Connell. Fuck me.' He sighs and looks out over Marbella, shakes his head as if overwhelmed by the sight. 'So what you doing here? Over on holiday?'

'Yeah... No. Actually I'm looking for someone.'

'Anyone I know?'

'Heard of a guy called Terry Campion?'

'Can't say I have.'

'Son of TJ, had a car dealership?'

Suddenly the lights go out in Bernard's eyes and he loses interest, starts looking around the room, our conversation over. The problem with company like this is you never know when you're starting to stray on to unsafe territory, turn over stones that should be left as they are. What involvement Bernard had in Terry's father's life I don't know, and do not want to know. But it is clear that it's not something Bernard is keen to revisit. Still, I have started so I might as well finish. I didn't fly a thousand miles to worry about treading on anybody's toes.

'He's a policeman. Terry. Last thing I heard he was over here.'

'Like I said, can't say I've heard of him. Him or his old man.'

'If you do hear anything...'

'Oh yeah, 'cos I've got a lot of time for coppers,' says Bernard. He looks at me and he does not seem friendly any more. 'Listen, be lucky, Danny son, yeah? Say hello to the old man.' He looks me up and down carefully, shakes his head, turns and walks back into the house, weaving slightly. I get the feeling I should be thinking about leaving. I look for somewhere to put my glass down and as I turn a man approaches me, another man just behind him. They are the two men Bernard was talking to before I spoke to him. They are both perhaps forty-five, trim, in good shape. The first one has dark hair, the other fair, look like they play a lot of golf, work out in the gym. Watch what they eat. The way they are standing, tense, as if expecting trouble, puts me on guard.

'Nice evening,' I say coolly.

'Don't live here?' says the dark-haired man.

'Visiting. Holiday.'

'Yeah? How're you finding it?'

'Heard you asking about Terry Campion,' the fair-haired man cuts in. He speaks fast, aggressively. He's still standing behind his friend, which makes me suspect he isn't as brave as his tone suggests.

'That's right,' I say. 'I'm looking for him.'

'Why?' the dark-haired man asks me. He has an easier tone, but there is still an edge to his question.

'I need to tell him something. Warn him.'

'You a policeman?' the dark-haired man asks.

'Me? No. I'm a lawyer. I'm Terry's lawyer.'

This is clearly not what they were expecting. They look at each other. 'His lawyer?'

'And I need to tell him something. It's important.'

This time they look at each other then turn their backs to me, discuss something between themselves. I do not know who these men are and am beginning to lose patience. Terry is still notionally my client and it is me who should be asking the questions.

'You know where he is?' I ask. 'Because if so—'

'Got any ID?' the dark-haired man interrupts.

'What?' I frown at them. 'Why would you want that?'

'Terry is...' The dark-haired man pauses. 'Might be in a bit of bother.'

'I know. That's why I'm here.'

'But are you here to help him? That's the question, isn't it?' The dark-haired man raises his eyebrows, inviting me to explain myself. But I have had enough of being interrogated by men I do not know. I take out a business card, hand it to the dark-haired man who reads it, hands it to his companion.

'And you two,' I say. 'Who might you be?'

'Friends of his,' says the dark-haired man. 'Looking out for him.'

'You know what kind of bother he's in?'

'Yes.'

'No you don't,' I say. 'You haven't got a clue.'

'Listen,' says the fair-haired man, taking a step towards me. It's a bad idea and the dark-haired man knows it; he holds out his arm, blocking the fair-haired man off.

'Okay,' he says. 'How about we have a sit down and talk about this?'

Andy, with the dark hair, actually knows a bar that has a Spanish name and serves Spanish beer. Not only that but he orders a selection of tapas in what sounds to me like fluent Spanish, which for some irrational reason makes me like him. We sit down at a booth, Andy and his friend, who I have heard Andy call Rob, on one side, me facing them. A pretty waitress places a bowl of whitebait, another of chorizo, on our table.

'*Gracias*,' says Andy. She smiles at him.

'So,' says Rob. 'What don't we know?'

'That's between Terry and me,' I say. 'But he's in danger.'

'We know that,' says Andy. 'From Baldwin.'

'He could be one of Baldwin's,' says Rob, looking at me. 'How'd we know?'

I hold up my finger. 'He did that to me. Last week.'

'Looks painful,' says Andy. 'You must have got on his bad side.'

'You know him?'

'We know him,' says Rob. 'We used to be coppers. Reason we know Terry, too.'

'I thought Bernard didn't like coppers,' I say. 'How come you were at his party?'

'Ex-coppers,' says Andy. 'Over here we do a bit of security work, investigations for people who don't want to use the locals. Bernard puts a bit our way.'

I suspect that Marbella has its own peculiar morality, like other regions have their own micro-climates. Ex-coppers working for active criminals; I do not even try to understand, simply take the information at face value. This is not my town. 'Listen, if Terry thinks he's in danger now, he has no idea. Things have got more... serious. I need to talk to him.'

'No can do,' says Rob. I like Rob a great deal less than I like Andy. 'Incommunicado.'

'He's not in Marbella,' says Andy. 'Hasn't been for a week. He's... He got paranoid. Thought someone was going to get him. You know.'

'Do him,' says Rob. I almost expect him to mime racking the slide on a gun.

'He might be right,' I say. 'Why I need to speak to him.'

'That won't be easy,' says Andy. He looks at Rob. Rob shrugs at him. Andy turns back to me. 'But we might be able to help you.'

25

WHERE I AM sitting, the sun is as bright as if not brighter than in Marbella, but it is windy and the wind is coming straight off the Atlantic, fresh and salty. I am sitting on a low stone wall overlooking the beach and particles of sand are blowing into my hair, sticking to my skin, insinuating their way through the seams in my shirt. Seagulls are circling in the sky, diving down to meet the fishing boats that are coming into the small harbour with their loads of sardines. It is now late in the afternoon and the sea, which had been a bright turquoise, is now a dark indigo except at the horizon where it is starting to redden. There are very few people on the beach; a couple of kids are flying a kite and their shadows are long and dark on the white sand. On the sea is a small boat and in the boat are two figures; they are pulling line in hand-over-hand. They have been out there for two hours at least now; when I got to the beach they were already at sea. But I have been happy to wait until they come back to shore. There is no hurry.

Now they are rowing back and I get up from the wall and take my shoes off and walk down the sand towards them.

The sand is still warm from the sun and it feels glorious, my feet sinking into its cool heat with every step. The men get out of the boat into the water and pull it awkwardly on to the beach. As I get closer, I can see that one of the men is perhaps sixty years old; he has black hair and dark skin and his face is deeply lined. The other man is pulling the boat with his head down, putting his back into it. When he reaches the shore, he looks up and he can't make out my face and his eyes open wide in panic.

'Terry,' I call. 'It's okay, it's Danny.'

I had taken a bus from Marbella to a port town called Algeciras and bought a ticket for the ferry that crosses the Strait of Gibraltar to Tangier; I had found myself in Africa before I had time to prepare for the different sights and sounds, the unnerving absence of anything familiar, the din and the pace. The local Hertz didn't have anything left to rent, but a local had pointed me down an unpaved side street of peeling plaster two-storey buildings where I had handed over fifty Euros to hire a battered white Fiat Panda for a week. It had bald tyres and lacked a wing mirror on the passenger's side, and I hadn't liked the sound of the exhaust, but I figured if it broke down I could simply walk away from it; the man doing the hiring out had not asked for any identification when he asked for my name and address. He was a skinny young man wearing a Metallica T-shirt and he had only one eye; I suspected that the car was stolen and that he did not want it back. I didn't care either way.

Andy had told me that the last they had heard from him, four days ago, Terry had been in Oualidia, a small town in

Morocco on the Atlantic coast. They hadn't heard from him since, didn't expect to; recently Terry had become convinced that Baldwin would come to Spain to find him, and just wanted to disappear. I could not blame him. I recognised the feeling.

Oualidia is five hundred kilometres south of Tangier and I followed the coastal road all the way, the sea a constant presence on my right. The scenery was monotonous, barren scrubby fields sectioned off by low stone walls, the occasional goat, the even less frequent person. At one point, the road disappeared and I drove on bare earth until, around a corner, I came across a road crew with a digger and truck full of hardcore who waved to me as I passed. I stopped off at a town along the way, spent the night in a concrete hotel, which served me a plate of couscous with vegetables, courgettes and carrots in a watery sauce under fluorescent lights. I left at nine the next morning and arrived in Oualidia just after lunch. I walked into the main square, which looked over the harbour; it was empty except for two boats which were being repaired, skinny men squatting down on their decks mending sails and rigging. One of the buildings on the square was a restaurant so I walked into it and asked a shy woman if she had seen a man with skin like me, pinching my skin up and showing it to her to make myself understood. But she didn't, or wouldn't, and scampered off to fetch a man with an important black moustache who spoke English and told me that the man I was looking for was out fishing with Walid. He took me by the elbow and walked me to the seafront and pointed, there. I could make out in the distance a small shape, so I'd walked down to the beach and sat down on the low wall and waited for his boat to come in.

Terry walks with me back to the restaurant, where we sit at a table with a plastic cloth on it near the window and the shy woman I had first spoken to brings us mint tea, smiling uncertainly. I go to pour it but she waves a hand and pours it herself, lifting the metal teapot high in the air so the tea falls a foot and a half into the ornate glass cups she has set down on a silver tray. We are the only people in the restaurant, which has only four tables and a cash register near the door; it has the shabby, scuffed look of a down-at-heel corner store that has had all the units removed, leaving only the lino on the floor and the fluorescent tubes hanging on thin chains from the ceiling. A faded calendar showing the harbour is pinned on the wall behind Terry's head. I have an end-of-the-season feeling, melancholic and lonely, as if we have been left behind by the rest of the holidaymakers, who have jobs and families and lives to return to.

'New career as a fisherman, is it?' I say.

'How'd you find me?' says Terry.

'Your mate Andy. Bumped into him in Marbella, told him I needed to see you.'

'Why? What's going on?'

'Drink your tea.' Terry looks at me apprehensively and drinks. The bruises on his face are nearly gone but I am shocked to see how much weight he has lost. He is tanned and gaunt and he could almost pass for a local.

'You really thought Baldwin would come looking for you?' I ask.

'I dunno, Danny. It's like I can't think straight any more. One morning I wake up and it's fine, by dinner I'm shitting myself and looking round corners. Like I've gone mad or something.'

'Obsessing.'

'Yeah. Totally obsessed, dream about him, wake up in the night and can't go back to sleep. I have these fantasies where I kill him. You know? So I won't have to worry any more. He's fucking crept inside my head and I can't get rid of him.'

I do not know what to do or say. I came to share what I had found with Terry, but I am worried that any more pressure and he will lose what little sanity he has managed to keep. Already he is seeing demons that aren't there; what will happen when I tell him that, actually, they are real and that Baldwin is more dangerous than he ever imagined?

'Listen,' I say. 'That footage... How much of it did you watch?'

Terry frowns. 'What do you mean?'

'Did you watch all the discs, all of it?'

'No, just... Just the bits with me in.'

'So you didn't see anything else on the discs.'

'What, it wasn't enough, Baldwin kicking ten bells of shit out of me?'

He's got a point; why would he watch more? I only went through it all after what Baldwin did to me, after his reaction became so excessive that it aroused my suspicions. 'Just asking,' I say.

But Terry, half-crazy or not, is still a policeman and he knows when somebody is lying; he has dealt with evasion on more occasions than he can remember. 'No. There's something you're not telling me. What? Danny? Fucking what?'

'I watched it all,' I say. 'And what happened to you, that's just the undercard for the main event.'

'What? There was something else?'

'Oh yes. There was something else.'

I had feared that finding out about Rosie would throw Terry into a panic; he was a man who was already on the ragged edge. But strangely, after hearing the news, he seems to calm down. He is no longer the central character in this story; it is about Rosie, not him, and this perhaps gives him a sense of perspective, helps him make sense of what has happened so far. I remind myself that he chose a career in the police and that he is, ultimately, motivated by the notion of justice, of bringing evil people to book. Hearing about Rosie gives him a cause; something to work towards, rather than something to run away from.

'You think he killed her?'

I shrug. 'Don't know. Don't know what happened. But if he didn't, why hasn't he said anything? Why does he want to keep the fact she came to the station a secret?'

'Yeah.' Terry's quiet, thinking. 'But why? Why would he? He's a bent copper all right, but why would he kill that kid?'

'Don't know.' I rub my face; I have not shaved in days.

'Jesus, Danny, what happened to your finger?' Terry says, pushing his chair back from the table in horror. He looks at me. 'No.'

'Doesn't matter what happened to my finger,' I say.

'He do that? Baldwin do that?'

I look at the end of my finger. I need to take the stitches out, have been putting it off. It is bruised but no longer swollen, though it does not look pretty. 'Yeah, he did it.'

'Oh, Danny. Fuck, Danny, I'm so sorry, man. I brought this on you. I did.' He chokes up and brushes the back of his hand over his eyes and when it comes away his eyelashes are glistening. 'I'm sorry.'

'Forget it. It's done. Over.'

'Except it's not, is it? We're, ah...' He snaps his fingers, trying to think of the phrase. 'Loose ends.'

'Probably not you,' I say. 'I'm the silly fucker who asked Baldwin if he killed her.'

'You did?'

'Yeah. To his face. Rattled the horrible bastard.'

Terry looks out of the window of the restaurant. It is almost dark now; Oualidia has no streetlights and outside it is pitch black, the windows of the restaurant acting as mirrors. We could be the last people left in the world. But when Terry turns back to me he seems to have made a decision; his expression is determined and there is a bright excitement in his eyes.

'So okay. It's simple, right? We fucking do him. I'll give the discs to my guv'nor; he'll take it up the chain. 'Bye-bye Baldwin.' He smiles at me. 'No? We've got to do it, right? For that girl?'

Terry is not going to like what I am about to tell him; not one little bit. I put my fist to my mouth, knock it against my cheek. 'I gave them back to him.'

'What?'

'Didn't mean to. Some little bastard called Dawson pulled a fast one. I thought I was giving them to his boss, turns out he's Baldwin's little pet.'

'You don't have the discs.'

'Not any more.'

'Oh.' Terry frowns, looks at me in disappointment. 'That was careless.'

'Well the thing was…' I begin, but Terry interrupts me.

'I leave the discs with you and you lose them? What kind of a lawyer are you?'

'Yeah, Terry…'

He holds up a hand, shakes his head in wonder that he could have made such a bad choice. He leans forward, across the table towards me. Beckons me in until our heads are almost touching.

'You seriously think I wouldn't make extra copies?'

The next morning, after spending a near-sleepless night in what I suspect was the shy woman's daughter's bed and for which she would not accept payment, I say goodbye to Terry and head for my car. Terry has told me who he gave the other copied discs to, an old friend who has long since moved out of Essex. I am still buzzing from the news that Terry made more copies of the discs, and cannot wait to get back to England and pick them up, to make Baldwin suffer. I feel as if I have had a last-minute reprieve, a new chance at life. But Terry is still not his old, defiant self; last night he told me that he did not want to come back to England with me, did not want to help me take Baldwin down. He said that he was sorry and I could see the fear and more, shame, in his eyes; I told him that it did not matter, and I meant it. I selfishly wanted the pleasure of breaking Baldwin all to myself.

I am only a half hour out of Oualidia when my mobile rings. I do not recognise the number and pull off on to the dusty shoulder to answer.

'Daniel Connell.'

'You left me your card.' It is a woman's voice but, although it sounds familiar, I cannot place it. 'You came to see my husband, Sean Conneely.'

'Yes. Yes, I did. Hello.'

'Mr Connell. I am sorry about your mother, about what happened to her. God knows I am.' The words spill out as if they are too hot in her mouth, then she pauses.

'Okay,' I say. 'Was there anything...?'

'You must think me... I am not a bad person, Mr Connell.'

Standing by while your husband destroyed countless innocent lives, I think. Of course you're not. But I do not reply. Perhaps she has been living with the guilt of what her husband did to all those women for too long, needs to unburden herself. I look into the distance, over miles of baked earth, and wait for her to get to the point.

'Mr Connell,' she begins again, her voice calmer. 'Mr Connell, I remember your mother. I remember her to this day.'

'Okay,' I say. 'Was there anything...?'

'And I know where she went. After she left us.'

26

'DANIEL CONNELL.'

'The fuck are you?'

'Who's speaking?'

'Eddie, that's who's speaking. You was supposed to call three days ago. Now, again. Where the fuck are you?'

'Out.'

'Out. Your office is closed, nobody home. You done a runner?'

'I'm away on business. I have other clients.'

'Halliday, that's your client. 'Til you're finished, he's your only fucking client.'

'This conversation is over.'

'No. Don't you fucking dare hang up. I've got a message.'

I debate pressing the button, shutting Eddie up. But I let him continue.

'Mr Halliday is not happy. Not at all. You're making an enemy there, son, and you don't want to do that.'

'You have a message?'

'Mr Halliday says, come back today, get it sorted, and he'll forget that you took off for three days. You don't come back? He'll burn your fucking house down.'

My hand is gripping my mobile so tightly I wonder if I have the strength to crush it. I am in Manchester looking for the mother Halliday sold, yet he is threatening to burn my home. All fear of him has vanished; once again, as in Halliday's bar, I feel that I am about to say something very unwise. But the depth of my anger is such that I do not care.

'You tell Mr Halliday,' I begin. I pause.

'Yes?' says Eddie.

'You tell Halliday that if he threatens me one more time I'll...' But as I say the words I realise how childish this all is, how Halliday is reducing me to the language of the playground. If you do X, I'll do Y, the most primitive of equations. 'Tell Mr Halliday I'll see him when I get back. We'll sort it out then.' I do hang up now, with some relief. I am in Halliday's bad books, I know; but at least I have not threatened him with violence. There may still be a way out, which there would not have been had I said anything rash.

I hear somebody clear their throat and look up and see the receptionist at the hospital's front desk regarding me with disapproval. She points to a sign that shows a picture of a mobile phone within a red circle, a diagonal red line across it. I put my phone away and walk up to her. She is young and quite pretty with strawberry-blonde ringleted hair and freckles, but she has the distracted, frustrated air of somebody who knows that everybody she deals with will come away dissatisfied in some way.

'Help you?' she asks.

'Yeah. I'm looking for my mother.'

Conneely's wife had told me that she knew where my mother had gone. At the side of that two-lane Moroccan road, I had struggled to hear what she was telling me as a bus blew past, pulling a cloud of dust in its wake.

'I don't know where she is now, you understand me? I cannot tell you that.'

'Yes,' I said, pressing the phone so tightly against my ear that my wrist ached.

'But I can tell you this. She was working as a cleaner at the hospital there.'

'The hospital?'

'Saint Mary's. She had a job there, I know that much.'

'When was this?'

'Oh, Mr Connell, this was years ago. Twenty-five years ago it must have been.'

'Right,' I said and I could not help the disappointment sounding in my voice. 'Thank you.'

'You said anything, if I know anything,' she said defensively. 'You asked.'

'Tell me,' I said to her. 'When your husband was forcing women to have sex with men they didn't know and then taking their money, when he was buying confused and scared young girls from criminals. While all that was going on, Mrs Conneely, what were you doing?' I waited for her reply but there was none, and some seconds later I heard a click as she hung up. I had not heard from her since.

The hospital receptionist turns to her keyboard. 'What ward is your mother in?'

'No, she… She isn't a patient,' I say. 'She used to work here.'

She stops, looks back at me. 'Used to?'

'A long time ago. I'm trying to find her.'

'How long ago?'

'Twenty-five years.'

She frowns, confused. 'You haven't seen her since?'

'I've never seen her.'

She tilts her head, ringlets cascading gently, and something softens in her look. I'm willing to bet that she is a sucker for those magazines full of true stories of hope and tragedy, of children lost and mothers found. Now it is happening to her, for real. I could have walked in holding my own severed arm and she would not be more concerned, more willing to help. She folds her arms and leans towards me.

'Were you adopted?'

'Not exactly,' I say. 'She was taken away.'

Her eyes, which are a startling blue, widen. 'By her family?'

'Criminals,' I say, loading the word with as much significance as I can. 'Criminals took her.'

She mouths a silent 'Wow' with her lips. Now that I have her undivided attention I can see that she really is pretty. She shakes her head slowly. 'That's terrible?'

I do not know why she posed that as a question, but I nod anyway. 'I know.'

She sits back up, back to business. 'Twenty-five years is a long time,' she says. 'You'll need to talk to Personnel.'

'Where will I find them?'

She pulls over a plan of the hospital and shows me where Personnel is housed, in a separate building on the other side of the complex. I thank her and head away, and she calls after me. I turn around.

'If you find her,' she says, 'tell me, yeah?'

I arrived back in Manchester last night and went back to the hotel I had originally stayed in, where they recognised me and gave me the same room I had left only a few days ago. I had not driven back to Tangier, instead headed for Casablanca where I had taken a flight home, which stopped at Barcelona on the way. I had left the Panda in the airport's parking; I felt a slight pang of guilt for the one-eyed man who had rented it out to me in Tangier but figured that, even in Morocco, a car in that state couldn't be worth much more than I had paid to hire it.

The weather in Manchester has now changed, sunshine swapped for a persistent drizzle under grey skies. It is no longer hot and the people no longer radiant; it is as if I have returned to a moribund city that has, since I left, experienced a collective minor tragedy. I have to walk for five minutes before I find the building that houses Personnel, a grey, tired prefab that looks as if it was put up temporarily, yet thirty years later nobody has found the money to replace. Here, too, there is a reception desk but behind it is an older woman wearing glasses on a chain and with the flat eyes of somebody who long ago lost the habit of empathy. She looks me up and down, nostrils flaring as if she has smelled a turd.

'Help you?'

'I hope so. I'm trying to trace my mother, who used to work here.'

'She's missing?'

'Kind of,' I say. 'I don't know where she is.'

'I see,' the woman says, but she doesn't; nor does she want to. Already she has me marked down as a nuisance. 'Why do you think we can help?'

'You might not be able to. Only, all I know about her is that she used to work here.'

'Recently?'

'I don't know. She was certainly here twenty-five years ago.'

The woman exhales through her nose with annoyance. 'Twenty-five years?'

'Could have been more recently.'

'We're a hospital,' the woman says. 'Not a missing persons' bureau.'

'But maybe somebody would remember her,' I say. 'Even know her. I would like to find her.'

'Have you asked the police?'

'Why?' I say. 'What would they do?'

'So instead you come here,' she sighs. 'What did she do here? At least tell me that. Was she on the staff?'

'She was a cleaner,' I say.

The woman cocks her head in surprise. 'A cleaner? Twenty-five years ago?' She shakes her head and removes her glasses, lets them hang over her grey cardigan. 'We wouldn't have any record of that. Not now. And anyway, most of our cleaners come through an agency.' She leans closer. 'Most of them are foreigners. Somalis, Poles, God knows where they come from. But they don't use their real names, they don't pay taxes. I don't get involved.'

'You're telling me that my mother is not worth finding?'

The woman does not like my tone. 'I am telling you that there is nothing I can do.' She laughs unkindly. 'Twenty-five years ago.' Like I've asked her to perform alchemy.

'You won't look? Check? I have her name.'

'It won't do any good. Our records won't go back that far. Everything was computerised.'

'I have a photo. If I could show people…'

'Mr…'

'Connell.'

'Mr Connell, I am sorry but we are talking about ancient history. This is a hospital, not a museum. If you have lost your mother, then I am of course very sorry and wish you all the best. But there are proper channels and you cannot just appear at my desk and snap your fingers.'

I look at the woman's hand and notice that she is not wearing a wedding ring and wonder whether she has been unloved for so long that her capacity for emotional engagement has atrophied, withered like an unused arm. I know that she will not help me, know that there is no better nature to appeal to. In any case, she is probably right; to find a casual worker from a quarter of a century ago is an impossible task. I nod and walk away but as I go she says, with a sharpness which I believe entirely unwarranted, 'And I would thank you for not wasting the time of the hospital staff with your enquiries.' She will be reflecting indignantly on my intrusion for hours, stewing until her microwave pings to announce dinner for one. I am tempted to wrench the door of the prefab off its hinges but instead I let it swing closed. Some people are lost causes.

I walk the corridors of the hospital and pass several cleaners polishing the linoleum with big machines like benign lawnmowers or towing trolleys loaded with sprays and cloths, but none of them is old enough to have been working twenty-five years ago; looking at them, the futility of my search hits me. I am chasing a ghost, somebody who may well have cleaned the corridors I am now walking but who did it a lifetime ago. I see a sign directing me to the exit and decide that there is nothing that I can do, that I might as well give up. As I pass through reception, the pretty girl from behind the desk sees me and calls out.

'Did you find her?'

I shake my head and keep walking but she runs out from behind the desk and catches me up, ringlets bouncing.

'You didn't find her?'

'No.'

'You went to Personnel?'

'The woman there wasn't much help.'

'She's a bitch.'

I smile. 'That's the word I was looking for.'

'What did she do here, your mum?'

'She was a cleaner.'

The receptionist is quiet for a time. 'It's such a long time ago,' she says.

'I know.'

'Thing is with this place, cleaners are here, like, for a month? Nobody remembers them.'

'Yeah.'

'Even other people, doctors, twenty-five years... Did you talk to Nurse Abbotts?'

'Who?'

'She's been here for ever. Nobody knows how long, it's like a joke. Only she's nice, yeah, she's lovely.'

'You think she's worth talking to?'

'You're not just going to give up?'

'I don't know.'

She looks at me in amazement. 'When you're this close?'

'This close? I'm looking for a cleaner who probably worked here for a week, before you were born.'

She flaps a hand. 'Someone'll remember her. You just need to keep trying.'

'You think?'

'You'll find her,' she says. She puts a fist to her heart. 'I just know it.'

I am not a superstitious man and of course I did not take the receptionist's words seriously; yet on another level, her enthusiasm for my lost cause gave me at least the strength of purpose to find this Nurse Abbotts and ask if she knew anything. The receptionist, who told me that her name was Maggie, showed me where I could find Nurse Abbotts: on the delivery ward which she ruled, and had ruled, for as long as anybody could remember. Maggie even put a call through to the ward for me, telling whoever was there that I was on my way and could they help. When I get there, I explain to the nurse guarding the door of the ward against desperate fathers unwilling to wait for visiting hours why

I am here. She tells me to hold on, she'll go and find Nurse Abbotts for me.

I expect a bosomy woman with pinned-back hair and a severe expression, a *Carry On* harridan with all the humanity of a stone. But instead Nurse Abbotts is a small, slender black lady with short hair and gentle eyes and an air of calm efficiency. She holds her hand out and I shake it; it is small but her grip is strong and she gives my hand two brisk pulls.

'What is your name?' she asks. She has a slight accent but I cannot place it, though I think it is from the Caribbean somewhere.

'Daniel. Daniel Connell.'

'Well, Mr Connell, come with me.' I follow her down a main corridor, her quick steps making me feel as if I am lumbering behind her. On either side of the corridor are four-bed wards with women sitting up, many holding babies to their chests. She opens the door to a small room with a coffee machine and a sink and a table, around which are four plastic chairs. She sits down at one, invites me to take another. She puts both elbows on the table, hands clasped as if praying.

'Now, the nurse tells me that you have lost your mother.'

I nod. 'She was a cleaner here, a long time ago.'

'Child,' Nurse Abbotts says, 'cleaners come and go. One week they're here, the next they're gone. You know that, don't you?' She looks at me and I can see a kind concern in her eyes; she has no more expectation of success than I do. I suspect that she is practised in delivering bad news to people in this room.

'I understand. But this is all I know about her.'

'How long ago we talking about?'

'Twenty-five years ago.'

'Goodness me,' she says. 'Goodness. Did she have a name, this mother of yours?'

'Marcela,' I say. 'Marcela Cosma.'

'Not much call for second names, not round here,' she says. 'Marcela. You have a picture of Marcela?'

I take out the shot of my mother holding her sunhat to her head, in the yellow mini dress. Nurse Abbotts takes it almost reverentially, for which I like her enormously. She looks at it for some time, then back at me.

'I believe I remember a Marcela,' she says. 'But she didn't look like this lady, no-uh. Nothing at all like this beautiful woman here.' She passes the photograph back to me. 'But I believe it is the same person.'

'You do?'

'A sad lady, this Marcela. She told me she had once had a child herself. The look in her eyes as she saw all these mothers, with children themselves...' Instinctively, Nurse Abbotts reaches across the table and puts her small hand over mine. 'I did so feel pity for her.'

Something in the way she says this makes me think that she is speaking of my mother in the past tense; Nurse Abbotts must notice the alarm in my eyes because she squeezes my hand and hurries to go on. 'Oh, child, no, the last time I saw your mother she was well. As well as I ever saw her.'

Nurse Abbotts asks me if I would like a coffee; I say no, but she tells me that she would, that she has battled with caffeine for over thirty years and that she is ashamed to confess that caffeine has always been the victor. She tells me that she will not drink the coffee from the machine in the nurses' station, that there is a Starbucks not five minutes away. I have to walk fast to keep up with her as she strides briskly down corridors, greeting people along the way, down a flight of steps and we are outside, and then out of the hospital grounds completely. She does not talk and I do not ask her any questions; I believe that she has something to tell me but wants to do it in the right environment.

She is known in Starbucks and they ask her if she wants her usual; I order a cappuccino but when I try to pay nurse Abbotts will not allow me.

'As bad as drinking alcohol,' she says. 'Lord knows I try, but without my coffee I'm useless as a hen.' She sighs to herself in disappointment at her weakness and we wait in silence while our coffees are prepared. We take them to a table and now I cannot wait any longer and I say, 'Please. What do you know about my mother?'

Nurse Abbotts smells her coffee, then looks at me. She has a small silver crucifix around her neck and I can see the shape of her collarbones underneath her skin.

'She was a good cleaner, your mother,' says Nurse Abbotts. 'Ordinarily I wouldn't remember a cleaner, but Marcela, she was with us a long time. Years, maybe, goodness, maybe five years it would have been.'

'Was she okay?'

'She was a sad woman. I believe that she had led a difficult life. We all knew that she had lost a child, but she never

236

told us how it happened.' She looks at me. 'But she didn't lose you, because here you are as large as life. Even larger, goodness knows.'

'She was taken away from me. Against her will.'

'Oh, Lord,' she says. 'The poor girl.'

'But she wasn't... hurt?'

'Hurt? No, least, not physically. She was a beautiful girl but I so rarely saw her smile.' Nurse Abbotts tries her coffee and exhales with pleasure, then remembers where she is and puts it down. 'I would ask for her, on our ward,' she says. 'The only time, in thirty years here. But your mother, she had a way about her.' She pauses, losing herself for a moment in thoughts of the past. 'She would always work nights. Never days. Never saw her during the day, in all those years.'

Nurse Abbotts drinks more coffee and I am silent; I do not want to interrupt her reminiscences, as if she is in a trance, which, if broken, will cause me to lose my mother for good. 'There are two kinds of nurses,' she says eventually. 'There are the kind who see it as a job, and those who... You know what I mean by a calling?'

'A career you are naturally adept at,' I say.

Nurse Abbotts chuckles. 'One way of putting it, child,' she says. 'I have never heard it described that way before.' She chuckles some more. 'Your mother was a cleaner, but her way with people, she was naturally adept. Yes she was. I would have her on the ward and my nurses, they would give out pills, do their job. But your mother, she had the touch. The number of times I saw her with her arm around some poor new mother, reassuring her, just talking.' Nurse

Abbotts shakes her head sadly and her right hand instinctively caresses her crucifix. 'Just talking to them, and her with no child of her own.'

'So what happened to her?'

'We had a pregnant girl on the ward, her baby was not well. The heartbeat, we kept losing it. We gave her an emergency caesarean but it was too late, the poor baby died before we could get her out. There is no sound more distressing than the cries of a young mother who has lost her baby, the grief. Of course we hear it all the time but there is so much pain, so much... And we have so little time, we are always so busy...' Nurse Abbotts looks out of the window, into the street, lost again for a moment. She turns back to me with a smile. 'Your mother stayed up with this poor girl, stayed with her until her parents came the next morning. The next night the same thing. I believe the third night she was not supposed to work but she came in anyway, and of course I did not say anything. I was glad to have her.'

A man in a suit holding a coffee nudges past our table, jostling Nurse Abbotts as he passes. He does not apologise and I am half out of my seat before I feel Nurse Abbotts's hand on mine again. I look down and she is chuckling. I am no great admirer of religion, but clearly Nurse Abbotts's faith makes her impervious to fear; or perhaps it is simply her innate nature. Either way, she reacts to my latent aggression with an amused indulgence.

'What are you doing, child? Sit yourself back down.' She tuts to herself. 'I can see you're an angry one.' The amused light dies from her eyes. 'But what am I saying? Poor child like you, and growing up without a mother.' She wags a finger at me. 'Get you in trouble much, that temper of yours?'

'Now and then.'

'Now and then he says.' She tuts some more. 'I should think so. She wouldn't be impressed, let me tell you.'

'She', Marcela, my mother, had formed some kind of bond with the bereaved girl over the course of those three nights, Nurse Abbotts explains to me. Perhaps it was a shared sense of bereavement; perhaps my mother really had found her calling, offering comfort to a girl she could identify with, whose pain approached the levels of her own. Whatever connection they forged, it carried over to the girl's parents. They were well off, Nurse Abbotts did not know what it was the father did but he spoke well and drove a big car, and they too found comfort in my mother's presence. Just a fortnight later the girl's father showed up at the hospital and offered my mother a job as their housekeeper; a job, he made clear, and a place to live. A home.

'Penelope, the poor girl's name was,' says Nurse Abbotts, and I cannot help but admire her capacity for empathy, that memory which retains individual names over years, decades. 'The surname... Of course she had no husband, no boyfriend.' She clucks her tongue, in sympathy rather than disapproval. 'So hard, for them all.' She sets down her cup, takes a moment, lost in contemplation of the pain she has witnessed over the years. She comes back to the here and now with a smile of suppressed triumph. 'Latimer. All three of them, Latimer. I remember, I admit I asked about them. For Marcela's sake. But they were respectable.

Decent people.' She nods, satisfied that she acted properly all those years ago. And satisfied that her memory has still not betrayed her.

'And that was the last I saw of Marcela,' she says. 'I thought of her often, prayed for her for years. But I never saw or heard from that dear girl again.'

27

'SO TELL ME, Mr Connell.' Mr Latimer dabs at his mouth fastidiously with a white linen napkin, then folds it shakily back on his lap. He raises his eyebrows, inquisitive rather than interrogative, and picks his knife and fork back up. 'Why now? After all this passage of time?' He talks slowly with the ponderous, portentous air of a man who is used to people hanging off his words; a cardigan-wearing academic of some obscure and irrelevant subject. My regard for him is plummeting by the second.

Next to him, his wife gives me a quick encouraging smile but her innate middle-class good manners cannot hide her abiding suspicion. Her daughter, Penny short for Penelope, does not bother hiding her hostility; she is drinking from a wine glass but I can see one eye glaring at me from behind it, the other obscured by her tipping hand. Mr Latimer has not waited for an answer before going back to sawing at his steak, as if to reassure me that this is not the third degree and that he does not expect an answer immediately, our dinner is just as important. The atmosphere around the table is as crisp as the white tablecloth, as fragile as the wine glasses.

'There was a lot of secrecy,' I say. 'I was discouraged.'

'By?' Mrs Latimer tries to soften her curt question with a smile but we both know where we stand. I am as welcome in their comfortable lives as a cowboy builder trailing dog shit.

'My father. I believe that he was ashamed. He was complicit in her... In what happened to her.'

Mr Latimer nods, a slow nod of absolute understanding as if my account tallies with various other similar stories he has heard or experienced. But he has the serene air of a man who has lived an entire life sheltered from such brutal realities. He has soft white hair like a cat's fur and lines at the corners of his blue eyes as if he is accustomed to smiling and having much to smile about and he has told me that he is a retired auctioneer. I imagine he lives in a large house that sits up a gravel drive behind high hedges. He is merely being polite; he cannot understand a single thing about me.

'And so what happened to make you seek her out?' he asks. He puts down his knife and fork, plants his elbows and steeples his fingers, folds them together. His daughter Penny slurps wine loudly, finishes her glass and sets it down clumsily. All three are looking at me and I get the strange feeling that I am an interviewee and that I had better satisfy their questions or this is as far as I will get.

A waiter comes into our small room and hovers; Mr Latimer flicks his fingers at him discreetly, dismissing him with the practised gesture of a man who is used to dealing with underlings. The waiter disappears as noiselessly as he arrived, leaving us alone again in this small panelled room, a private dining room off the main restaurant. It is in a converted bank and you have to climb wide stone steps to get through its heavy wooden doors, to step echoingly on its black-and-white tiled floors. A woman met me and when I gave the name Latimer showed me to our place of honour, crossing rows and rows of white linen-covered tables under a high domed ceiling, some kind of battery-chic dining, which Manchester somehow seems to believe is exclusive. But the food is not bad, modern British and price-wise falling narrowly the right side of taking the piss; the company, so far, is vinegary and strange to my coarser palate.

'My father had a heart attack,' I say, answering Mr Latimer's question. I will spare these people the details, of my crossing the path of Vincent Halliday, of my meeting with his ex-wife. Already the story of my mother and me is dirty enough. 'And with it, a change of heart.'

'Is he on the mend?' Mrs Latimer asks, her good manners too deeply ingrained to be forgotten, even now.

'He's out of danger, yes,' I say. 'I thought she had left me. Voluntarily. I never knew that it was not her choice.'

'And so here you are ready to make everything all right.' Penny speaks with the lurching imprecision of somebody who is not used to drinking. She sits back in her chair and shakes her head in frustration. She is in her late-fifties with the immaculate, starched blonde nest of hair I associate with country-living, Range Rovers, children at good schools and church on a Sunday morning. Her fingernails are immaculate; I notice them as she sits forward again and reaches for the wine bottle. She could be a politician's wife, about to disgrace him.

'I am here to find her,' I say. 'That's all. It's thirty-seven years too late to make everything all right.'

Mr Latimer apparently likes this answer; he nods his head at his plate as he chews his steak. I am surprised by how spry and alert he is, despite his age. He must be in his eighties, his wife too.

'You understand,' he says, 'that Marcela became very dear to us. Very dear indeed.'

'I understand,' I say. 'But I cannot help that she is my mother.'

Penny blows out her cheeks petulantly as if she is a child who has been told she can't go to a party. But Mr Latimer points a knife at her with a liver-spotted hand, waves it admonishingly. 'Penelope. Mr Connell has a right, whatever you may think. He has come this far. We owe it to him to hear him out.'

I'd left Nurse Abbotts savouring the remains of her coffee, sighing happily to herself, lost contentedly in a past that was, apart from perhaps an over-dependence on caffeine, entirely blameless. I headed back for the hotel under a persistent drizzle; I did not have a coat or umbrella and by the time I had found a taxi I was soaked. It was early afternoon but already cars had headlights on, beams reflecting off slick black roads in the grey light as if autumn was giving us a sneak preview of the misery to come, dousing our summery optimism in its pearly gloom. For the second time I looked through Manchester's phone book, but this time my task was more difficult; while there had been only four Conneelys there were over forty Latimers, and none of them had the initial P. I had asked for the hotel's directory and I smiled at the girl at reception as I tore the page out; she raised an eyebrow but did not say anything. I took it upstairs to my hotel room, stretched out on the bed and called the first number. A man answered.

'Hello?'

'Hello, I'm trying to get in touch with a Penelope Latimer.'

'Don't know anyone called Penelope, pal. Who are you?'

'A friend.'

'Yeah? Good luck.' He hung up and I reflected on the suspicion I had heard in his voice. The malicious, sinister caller infiltrating our homes and insinuating himself into our lives is a media bogeyman feared by all; I was going to need to use some finesse. But fear is a useful emotion to exploit, and I am better used than many to intimidation.

'Hello?'

'Good evening. My name is DCI Travis, and I'm trying to contact a Penelope Latimer as a matter of some urgency. We believe her identity is being used as part of a money-laundering operation.'

I reached thirty-one of the forty numbers, and drew a blank with each; people were concerned that their identities and bank accounts were at risk, but none admitted to being related to a Penelope Latimer and I believed them. Why would they have any reason to lie? I lay back on my hotel bed and looked at the ceiling, projecting the story Nurse Abbotts had told me on to its blank whiteness. She had described the young woman who lost her baby all those years ago as a 'girl', unmarried; a wealthy girl gone off the rails? Anything could have happened since, she might have married and changed her family name, might have married, divorced, remarried, widowed. Which left me with nothing but a first name, Penelope; not the most common first name, but not nearly enough to track her down. I felt as if I had arrived at a train platform only to see my train pulling away without me; no matter how far I travelled, the spectre of my mother remained out of reach.

I called Gabe to tell him what I had found, reassure him that I was alive and that I had not caused anybody any significant harm. But his phone rang and rang and even my closest friend felt impossibly distant; I was in Manchester and I was making a fool of myself. I wondered where he was, how he was doing, if he needed somebody to speak to. But Gabe was Gabe and he would be all right, or not, on his own terms. There was nothing I could do. Next I called the hospital where my father was; he was comfortable, the nurse told me, though I have never known my father to be comfortable in his whole life. I hung up, looked at the phone in my hand; I realised that there was not a single other person in the world I could call at this time, who I could ask for reassurance, who I could share my doubts with. I lay back and tried to sleep and pulled a pillow tight, hoping it would offer some solace against the mocking darkness.

The next day, I went back to the hospital's reception, the red-brick building crouched underneath a bleak grey sky that seemed lower than it should be, making me keep my head down, my shoulders hunched. Maggie was sitting behind the desk reading a garish magazine printed on cheap, thin paper, a headline proclaiming that 'I Married My Own Brother', her hair pinned up and little curls escaping past her ears giving her the innocent air of a benevolent pixie. The reception area was empty, last night's victims of drunken misdemeanours bandaged up and sent home, all evidence washed away by the hospital's imported workforce, blood, vomit, imperceptible tears. Maggie looked up at me and beamed, put her magazine away.

'I was just thinking about you. You find her?'

'Not exactly. Maybe.'

'She remembered your mum? Nurse Abbotts?'

'Yeah. She remembered her.'

Maggie leaned forward, blue eyes wide. 'Told you. So go on. What happened?'

'She was a cleaner here, Nurse Abbotts recognised her from the photo. Said she was a good person.'

'Don't tell me she's dead.' Maggie put a hand to her mouth and looked at me with guileless horror. 'Don't say she's dead.'

'I don't know. Nurse Abbotts couldn't say. She told me, she said my mother helped look after a young girl who lost her baby, here in the hospital, and the girl's family took her in.'

'Oh my God,' said Maggie. 'So amazing.'

'Yeah. Only I need to find that young girl, and I've only got her name from back then.'

'You Google her?'

'Yeah. Unless she's a sixteen-year-old gymnast from Jericho, Texas, I can't find her. But you could.'

*

It took Maggie thirty seconds to call up the medical records of Penelope Frazier, *née* Latimer. She wasted even less time worrying about the morality of what she was doing, or wondering whether I was perhaps a predatory sadist with a sinister agenda, rather than a lost child. She wrote Penelope Frazier's most recent telephone number on a piece of paper, scribbled 'Good luck!' underneath, the dot of the exclamation mark a small circle with a smiley face inside.

Back at my hotel I picked up the telephone as if it was a crab which could pinch. I dialled the number, hesitating at the final digit, knowing that this was as close as I would ever get to finding my mother. I heard a ringing tone, broken by a brisk, strident woman's voice. I imagined her standing in a large tiled hall, fresh from delivering orders to a coterie of servants.

'Penelope Frazier.'

'Mrs Frazier? My name is Daniel Connell.'

'No, I'm sorry but I don't have the time...'

'Please, I'm not selling anything.'

'But of course you are. And I am extremely busy...'

'I am trying to trace my mother. Marcela Cosma.'

This silenced Penelope Frazier, a feat which I suspected was not straightforward. I heard nothing and I wondered whether she had hung up, feared that she was no longer there.

'Mrs Frazier?'

'Marcela?'

'Yes. I believe that she is my mother.'

Another silence, this time longer, but I could hear Penelope breathing. I pictured her holding the receiver tightly, trying to process the information delivered by this disembodied voice.

'She doesn't have a child.'

'I'm sure she must have told you about me.'

'She told me her child was dead.'

'I'm not.'

'This is... You cannot just call me up. Out of the blue, this is not the way to do things.'

'How would you prefer I do things?' I asked, a hint of impatience. I wondered whether I had disturbed her from a game of bridge and could feel the tidal wash of resentment flow through me.

'Why are you calling me?'

'I traced my mother through the hospital. A Nurse Abbotts, she remembered you.'

'My *God*.' She said this petulantly, as if I had told her that not only did she need to change her worn tyres, but that her exhaust needed replacing too and that it wasn't going to be cheap. 'How dare you dig around in my past, Mr...?'

'Connell. It's my past too.'

'So you say,' Mrs Frazier replied snappily; already she was rallying, marshalling her thoughts after my surprise attack. 'If you are indeed who you say you are.'

'Why would I lie?'

Penelope didn't say anything, just emitted a sarcastic snort as if the answer to that question was beneath her answering. I liked her less and less.

'Tell me, Mrs Frazier. Is Marcela Cosma rich?'

'No.'

'Is she famous? Influential?'

'*No.*' Again the petulance.

'So then why, if you'll excuse me, the fuck else would I be calling you, if I wasn't her son?' But I did not reach the end of the sentence before I heard the dialling tone in my ear and I worried that, once again, the legacy of my father's temper had closed one more door on me.

'My father was connected with the local underworld,' I say. Mr Latimer raises his eyebrows in polite interest. Mrs Latimer is busy skewering a skittish new potato, and Penny is exhaling loudly and looking at the ceiling. 'He would do odd jobs for criminals, hang around their circle. He wasn't very successful, but it's what he wanted to be.'

'In Essex,' says Mr Latimer.

'In Essex,' I say. 'One man, Vincent Halliday, used to run girls. A pimp, I suppose he was, though that was only one of his sidelines. Anyway, he was put away for twelve months for attacking another man. While he was inside, my father started a relationship with my mother. With Marcela.'

'Who was one of his girls,' says Mrs Latimer, the statement sounding odd coming from the mouth of an elderly matriarch with cut-glass consonants.

'Yes. And by the time he got out, it was too late. My mother was nearly ready to give birth. Halliday had no choice but to wait until I was born.'

'This is… horrible,' says Penny. 'I won't listen.'

To his credit, Mr Latimer ignores Penny. 'I suppose the question is, why should we believe your story?' he says. He looks apologetic. 'One can't take chances.'

'He has her eyes,' says Mrs Latimer, again surprising me. 'Oh, he's her son.' A quick look across at Penny. 'I'm sorry, dear, but he is.'

'You know how much pain you've caused her?' Penny asks.

'Penny,' says Mr Latimer. 'Mr Connell can hardly be blamed for that.'

'And now here he is, and what? Dad? It's not that bloody simple.'

Mr Latimer nods, acknowledging Penny. He holds up a palm to her and his attention mollifies her for the moment. He looks back to me.

'Mr Connell, this issue… It is not quite as clear-cut as it seems. Not from your perspective, I grant you. If you are Marcela's son, then of course you naturally wish to see her. The question is not, will she want to see you? The question, I suppose, is more, ought she to?'

After Penelope had hung up on me I had tried to call her back immediately, and had listened to the ringing tone ten, twelve, twenty times. I had tried again, and again, taken a shower, tried again. I was angry with myself for losing my temper, for letting her prim outrage get under my skin. I left my hotel room and sat at the bar, asked the boy behind it for a vodka and tonic. He had acne and when he reached up to the optic his hand was shaking and I didn't know whether it was because it was his first day or if it was the expression on my face, the way I had ordered my drink. I tried smiling at him when he put my drink down on the bar but he did not want to meet my eyes. I drank and wondered what my next move should be.

I could track Penelope down without a problem, make her tell me where my mother was or, if she was dead, at least where she was buried. But I had had a vision of a gentle, poignant reunion; I wanted to leave the nasty baggage of my violent past behind me, not taint my mother, or her memory, with what I had become in her absence. I wanted to do it right.

I finished my drink, headed back to my room, decided to give Penelope one last try. The phone was picked up on its second ring by a well-spoken man with a suspicious tone.

'The Frazier residence.'

'Hello. My name is Daniel Connell.'

'Ah yes. Mr Connell. I am Penelope's father.'

I could imagine the drama; Penelope demanding her father come over to deal with all these beastly phone calls, right *now*. I needed to tread gently.

'I'm looking for my mother.'

'Penelope told me. Marcela.'

'Yes.'

The man did not say anything for some moments, as if he was thinking. 'Mr Connell, may I ask you a question?'

''Course.'

'Are you sure you wish to find Marcela?'

It seemed an odd question but it was asked without malice; if anything there was something tender, solicitous in his tone to which I could not take offence.

'I'm sure. I need to know. What happened to her. About her life.'

The man sighed, paused again, two, three, five seconds. 'You have given this a lot of thought.' A statement, not a question.

'A lot.'

'Very well. Do you have a pen?'

I picked up a pencil from the desk in my room. 'Yes.' He gave me details of a restaurant, told me that he would be happy to meet me there the following evening, seven o'clock. He wished me a good day and put the phone down and I sat there looking at the address and tried to tell myself that I was, without a doubt, doing the right thing.

'For a mother to lose her child is a terrible tragedy,' Mr Latimer says. He has stopped eating, laid his knife and fork together on his plate. 'For a mother to lose her child, only to find him again, could be an even greater one.'

'Really?' I ask. 'I think you'll need to explain that statement.'

Mr Latimer takes his napkin from his lap and folds it carefully, keeping me waiting. I imagine giving him a quick slap on the top of his head, wonder whether that might hurry things along. But when he looks at me I can see nothing but compassion in his eyes; perhaps I am being uncharitable, judging him too harshly.

'Mr Connell, please, we only want what is best. And of course we have no right to stop you from seeing Marcela. We would not dream of it.'

Penny lets out a snort and for the first time Mr Latimer loses his composure; he rounds on her, holds up a finger.

'Penelope, for pity's sake, stop acting like a bloody prima donna', he says. 'Mr Connell hasn't come all this way to listen to you sulk.' Penny's mouth stays open, but she does not reply. Clearly even in his eighties Mr Latimer wears the trousers.

'Excuse my daughter,' Mr Latimer says. 'I hope you can understand that in many ways Marcela has been like a second mother to her. She has lived with us for twenty years. Oh.' He puts his fingers to his eyes, rubs them, pauses for a long while before he trusts himself to speak again. 'Goodness, this is difficult, is it not?'

There is something about his unconcealed distress, his lack of affectation, which instinctively makes me revise my opinion of him; more, makes me sure that he has not just mine but everybody's best interests at heart. Mrs Latimer leans over to rub him gently on the back. Penny looks shamefaced.

'I just—' begins Mr Latimer, but I cut him off.

'Mr Latimer,' I say as gently as I can. 'I am no gold digger. I'm not looking for a hand out. All I want is to know, to have some idea...' To my horror I can feel tears coming to my eyes; I am not Mr Latimer and I cannot let them be witnessed in public. I stop, collect myself. 'I do not wish to cause my mother any pain. However you would like to manage this situation, I will willingly go along with it.'

Mr Latimer nods, but now it is Mrs Latimer's turn. She places her napkin on the table. 'Mr Connell, Marcela has always believed that she lost an angel. It is quite apparent to me that you have not led the easiest of lives... I wonder...' She is struggling to find the words, a way to sweeten the medicine, but presses ahead regardless. 'Will, can, your turning up like this, out of the blue, bring her happiness?' She pauses. 'Peace?'

'I'm not dead,' I say. 'I have a house, a business, friends. My life is not an irredeemable failure.' I smile at her –

reassuringly I hope. 'That's got to be better than nothing. Right?'

To her credit, Mrs Latimer smiles back, bows her head. Mr Latimer sits up, places the fingers of both his hands flat on the edge of the white tablecloth.

'Well, it's decided then,' he says. 'Thank goodness for that.'

28

THE LATIMERS HAVE built a fully equipped medical suite in a first-floor room at the back of their house, a large brick-and-timber building constructed in the thirties with leaded windows and two chimneys emerging from a charmingly shingled roof. The house is set back from a quiet road behind tall evergreens, exactly as I imagined, and as I stepped out of the car on to the gravel I could almost smell, underneath the freshly mown grass and jasmine that grew over the porch, the peace and complacency of the place; it was as unfamiliar to me as a foreign country.

My mother's room has a large picture window at the end, stretching from floor to ceiling and almost from wall to wall; the garden, which the room overlooks, feels part of the room itself. There are polished hardwood floorboards and a flat-screen television attached to one of the white walls on an ugly black frame. In the centre of the room is my mother's bed, huge and with the clean plastic-and-tubular-metal lines of an artefact from the set of a science-fiction film. She is plugged into a drip that feeds a clear liquid from a plastic bag down into the back of her hand, and next to her a machine displays numbers and lights on a blank black screen. Another machine the size of a photocopier lurks next to it; I hate to imagine what its purpose might be. I am sitting on a dining chair next to the bed, bent forward, watching her. I have been here for hours.

Mr Latimer told me that my mother had already survived pancreatic cancer once, that she had put up a courageous fight and had beaten it through force of character despite the doctors initially giving her little chance. But five years later it had returned with an aggression that even my mother's tenacity and bravery could not face down and had quickly metastasised, reaching her kidneys and stomach. She needs dialysis daily, morphine rather more often, he explained to me. She is as comfortable as possible but I believe that she exists in a pain-filled purgatory nobody should have to endure. Anybody who disputes the rights of the individual to a dignified end should be forced to witness the degradation of body and spirit that cancer can visit on a person. It is shabby, humiliating and cruel.

My mother is asleep, a thin woman with greying hair fanned out on the pillow, a fine proud nose made all the more prominent for the wasted sockets of her eyes and lined, pinched cheeks. She is breathing but only just, her blanket rising almost imperceptibly as if she is a small animal playing dead. She is emaciated, tiny, and I cannot conceive of how a brute like me could have emerged from something so insubstantial. I look out of the vast window and can see a squirrel darting in spasmodic jerks down the trunk of a large conifer.

'Is it you?' Her voice is a whisper, the wind in the trees.

'Yes, it's me,' I say as gently as I can.

She sighs, lies quiet. Watching her, I have the impression of a desperate skeleton crew rallying somewhere within her core, a marshalling of final reserves inside some fading, corroded, fleshy engine room. She does not have much left to give but whatever still lingers, I sense, she wants to save for me. I regard her, her eyes closed, and can see only a failing mechanism that has experienced too much careless and rough usage over its lifetime. That it has survived this long, unbroken or at least still limping along, is already, I believe, remarkable.

Then her eyes open and, suddenly, everything changes. My mother's eyes are dark and intelligent and human and filled with a tender warmth that makes my nostrils and throat swell and I experience a dizzy feeling as if I am freefalling back through the dismal years of my loveless life, back into a lap I have never sat on, into arms that have never held me, eyes that have never laughed with me. I absently notice that tears are running down my cheeks and that it is a sensation I cannot recall. She regards me with a look of adoration and wonder as a young woman would her mewling new-born child and I realise that here, lying on the bed, is truly my mother, a woman who has loved me and not stopped loving me, devotedly, sorrowfully, for nearly forty years. I can conceive of nothing so glorious and, at the same time, so unutterably sad and desolate. The sudden thought of all those years of grief, which could, which should have been filled with happiness, threatens to derail me completely. I do not know how to act or what to say.

But I believe that my mother knows what I am thinking and she smiles at me and, although the smile has some sadness, it is tempered by an emotion in her eyes that I think may be joy.

'Daniel. Oh, my son, yes. It was worth the wait.'

I try to imagine just how overwhelming it must be for my mother to be confronted with the thirty-seven-year-old reality of somebody she has, for all those years, only imagined as a new-born boy. My ingrained insecurities immediately trouble me; I worry that she will see a rough, unlovable creature, a grotesque substitute for the innocent and vulnerable child of her memory. Under the scrutiny of my mother's eyes, I am all too aware of how I appear to others, the intimidating and unapproachable air that I project; how can she be anything but disappointed?

'I am so sorry,' she says.

'For what?'

'She told me you were dead.'

'Who did?'

But my mother does not answer. She is still looking at me almost reverentially, a miracle she dare not believe. I have never before been looked at like this but it causes me no discomfort or self-consciousness; I have never felt so liberated from myself. I gaze back at my mother and, although she looks tired and weak, I can still see traces in her face of the life, the vivacity that shone through in her photos.

She reaches out a hand, the hand that does not have the drip in the back, and I take it. It feels like a cloth just beginning to harden from lack of water, light and flimsy. It lies in mine and from the discrepancy in size we could be two different species.

'You grew,' she says.

'Everybody does.'

'So much. Are you married?'

'No.'

She sighs audibly now, a regretful *'Haaa'* fading away quickly from lack of breath. But she has the strength to wrap her small fingers around the sides of mine and squeeze them softly. She has an accent, which only makes her stranger to me; she is my mother and is holding my hand but still we have a chasm to cross, of years and of grief.

'Harold had such a hard time to tell me. About you.'

'Harold?'

'Mr Latimer. He worried that the shock would kill me. So long he took, to come to the point.'

'It must have been distressing.'

'Distressing.' She closes her eyes, shakes her head. 'Only the English, only they could think that for a mother to hear her child is alive, that it could be distressing. No, Daniel. It was wonderful, of course.'

'He didn't want to tire you. Make you unwell.'

'So I can die not knowing my beautiful son is alive? Idiotic.' She shakes her head again but I can see that even this conversation is costing her dearly, her chest rising and falling quickly now, her face paler even than it was when I was watching her sleep. Beautiful. She called me beautiful.

'Can I get you anything?' I manage to cough out past the lump in my throat.

'Nothing. Just talk to me. I want to know everything. Everything.'

'There's not so much to tell.'

'Who did you play with at school? Did you break a bone? What was your first girlfriend's name? What is your favourite food?' She smiles. 'All this a mother must know.'

'I played with Ronnie at school, when I was very young,' I say. 'His family moved away to Spain when I was nine. I cried for days, but alone, in my room. Nobody ever knew I even missed him.'

'Crying is not so bad,' she says.

'No,' I say. 'I know.' But in fact nobody has ever told me this in my life and just this, this throwaway comment said without reflection or force, gives me an idea of how enormously I missed her presence when I was young, how different my outlook could have been.

My mother's face stiffens in pain and almost unconsciously she reaches up to a button on the tube of her drip and presses it, giving herself another dose of morphine. Her eyes close as if she is at a classical concert anticipating a particular passage of music and when it arrives her face slackens and when she looks at me again her eyes have lost some of their brilliant focus.

I swallow. 'How long have you got?' It is one of the hardest things I have ever said and I dread the answer. Please let it be months, not weeks.

'How long have I got?' She laughs gently, with not a trace of self-pity. 'Oh, Daniel, I have the rest of my life.'

I sit and hold her hand and watch her fall asleep, her breathing slowing, her face settling back into the drawn lines that seemed to have disappeared when she spoke to me. I wonder at what she has been through, what she has suffered before finding herself here, helpless in this glorious room. Some people's histories are so painful, so wretched, that contemplating them is as difficult as looking at an open wound; the mind flinches away, just as our eyes would confronted by the raw stump of a child's arm. I cannot bear to imagine how terrible my mother's life must have been. I lack the courage.

Mrs Latimer knocks on the door; she is carrying a tray on which is a cup of tea and plate of biscuits – the least, and yet the most, the polite middle classes can muster in a situation like this. I get up from my chair, take the tray from her and set it on the floor.

'She has woken?'

'I spoke to her.'

'She was pleased.'

'I think so.'

Mrs Latimer nods. 'Harold did not mean to dictate to you, Mr Connell.'

'Daniel.'

'He cares, that is all. Marcela is a member of our family and you cannot blame him for perhaps being overprotective.'

'I understand.'

'Penny, when she lost her child... I could do nothing. She was so inconsolable. Marcela, she... She has a gift. With other people. God knows why, after the life that she has had.'

'She seems happy here.'

'Happy? No. No, Daniel, I don't think happy would be the

right word. She found a measure of peace, perhaps. I believe that her history rather precluded happiness.'

'And now?'

Mrs Latimer smiles and I can see that she is as well meaning as anybody can be. 'It's rather complicated, isn't it?'

I cannot help but smile in return. 'Yes. Yes, it's complicated.'

'But, Daniel, no matter what the outcome of your visit, it is right that you are here.'

I nod, grateful for her generosity, for making me feel as welcome as she can do in her home.

'She won't sleep long,' Mrs Latimer says. 'Sit down, drink your tea. She'll want you to be here when she wakes up.'

'Daniel?'

She says it almost with panic, as if our meeting might have been nothing but a cruel dream.

'I'm here.'

She sighs in relief and pleasure, but does not open her eyes. It is evening now and it is just gloomy enough outside that the vast window is caught between a view of the outside and a reflection of our room. I have been watching her for a couple of hours, pacing the floor, looking down into the garden. Being alone has never been easy for me, I am not good at introspection; dwelling on my past never gives me any pleasure. But having my mother here gives me some comfort, softens and takes the edge off my thoughts; it is almost as if her existence casts a benign shadow over my history. I cannot explain it; perhaps it is as simple as the discovery that deep in my DNA exists another personality than my father's and that personality is good. Apparently I am not beyond redemption.

'Was he good to you? A good father?'

My mother asks the question with her eyes still closed and I take my time to consider the question. How should I answer? The truth is so miserable that it can only add a new layer of pain to everything my mother has already had to endure. Yet I have an almost irresistible urge to tell her all, to let out the loneliness and fear of my childhood.

But of course I cannot; already she feels culpable for having left me, despite believing that I was dead. To know that not only did she abandon me but that she also left me at the mercy of an abusive brute would be too much. The least I can do is spare her this.

'He was wonderful,' I say, trying to inject sincerity and levity into my voice. 'Perhaps a little unconventional, but he was a good parent.'

'Really?' My mother is looking at the ceiling, rather than meet my eyes.

'He retrained,' I say. How do these lies come so easily? 'As a plumber. Worked his fingers to the bone to put me through school and university.'

'You went to university?'

'University College. London. It's, a...' I do not wish to patronise her, but a mother deserves some reflected glory. 'It's a good college. I took a degree in Law.'

Now my mother turns to me, tears of pride in her eyes. 'You are a lawyer?'

'Yes. In the City.' I shrug. 'I was a good student. I found it easy.'

At least this is true; at least she can find genuine pleasure in my academic prowess. I suspect that my intelligence all came from this woman; it is her I have to thank for any success I have had.

My mother lets out a long breath and a beatific smile lights her face. 'So, you did not need me. Oh, you cannot know how much of a relief it is. I am so happy, Daniel.'

I did not need her? If she only knew. Again, I fight the urge to lay my past down in front of her, to beg her to reassure me that it was not my fault, that whatever I went through was due to circumstance and not some fundamental defect in my character. God, this is hard.

'My son, a lawyer,' she says in wonderment. 'Oh goodness.'

There is a wardrobe in the corner of the room, on the back wall next to the door. Above a rail of clothes there is a shelf and on that shelf there is a box. I take it down; it is black and once contained shoes.

'This one?'

'Yes. Bring it to me.'

My mother has a remote control attached to a wire and she has pressed a button and the upper half of the bed has raised so that she is now sitting almost upright. I walk back to the bed and place the box on her lap and she takes the lid off. She takes out a folded piece of paper; a newspaper cutting in an old-fashioned font. She passes it to me.

'I am sorry, Daniel. She gave me this.'

'Who did?'

'Xynthia. When I came down to find you.'

'You came?'

My mother looks at me curiously. 'But of course I came. I am your mother.'

'When?'

'As soon as I could. I saved some money, I ran from that Irish man, I came back to get you.' She laughs in quiet consternation. 'You think I would leave you for ever?'

I open the newspaper cutting and read it. It is the story of a child who was drowned in a paddling pool at his home. The child is not named; a toddler from my neighbourhood.

'She told you this was me?'

'And then I gave up, of course. I went back to the Irish man. Where else could I go? It was what I deserved.'

'No.'

'A mother who lets her son die, like that? Oh yes, Daniel, I do think so.'

'But back there? To all that?'

'It wasn't so bad. Really.'

My mother lies back on her pillow and I look at myself in the dark window, which now reflects the entire room; my head and shoulders appear over my mother's bed, which is closer to the glass. I cannot see past it and perhaps it is right that it is hidden from me, that I cannot peer into the darkness and see and understand the full horror of what lies there. I have spared my mother the truth of my childhood; now she is returning the favour. But perhaps nothing matters beyond the window; perhaps all that is important is in this room. Why look further? I reach over to my mother and brush her hair away from her face, her skin dry and cold as if she has just come in from outside. She smiles and reaches up a hand, holds my wrist lightly. I think I can stay like this for ever, even though at the same time I know that it cannot last.

I am in the kitchen of the Latimers' house and Mr Latimer is making me coffee; he is inept but I understand that he is going out of his way, showing me that he, a stranger, cares for me in some measure. He realises that I am meeting my dying mother and that it can be no easy experience, and that it is one I am facing alone. With some difficulty he presses the plunger of the cafetière down; I could help him but sense that he would be mortified. He is wearing a fluffy dark-blue dressing gown and leather slippers and the light is pouring in through the kitchen's leaded windows and on to his white hair, giving him a halo. I stayed most of the night by my mother's side and, though she drifted in and out of consciousness and we did not speak much, I know that I was a comfort to her; she slept with a smile on her face. I caught a couple of hours' sleep in the prim single bed of the room the Latimers have left at my disposal.

'Get much sleep?'

'Some. Not much.'

'How was her night?' Mr Latimer sits down next to me at the table and I can see the sadness in his eyes, too. It occurs to me that perhaps he will grieve for my mother just as much as, if not more than, I will; I realise that I have been remarkably selfish and that not only do I pose a threat to my mother's health and wellbeing, but also that I have stolen some of my mother away from him, after all that he has done for her.

'She seemed well. At peace, maybe.'

Mr Latimer nods at his hands clasped on his lap. He clears his throat and begins, 'Mr Connell, I am sorry if I seemed overly zealous, regarding your mother's wellbeing...'

I stop him. 'Mr Latimer, given the situation, I believe you have behaved entirely correctly. Please, this is easy for nobody. You and your wife are being more than welcoming. I doubt I would be as gracious, in your situation.'

'Yes, well.' He gets up and pours coffee into two cups. The silence is awkward but there is nothing more to be said. He turns to me.

'Sugar?'

The Latimers' garden is enormous and takes hours to mow, but my mother is having dialysis, her blood being cleaned by a machine that Mr Latimer bought himself at a cost I imagine must have been enormous and I would rather be somewhere else, occupied. There seems something brutal and desperate in the idea of her blood being taken away, rudimentarily filtered and then pumped back into her by a humming piece of equipment. Apparently you cannot hire them and he refused to consider a machine that had already been used. With each passing hour, the devotion and love he has for my mother becomes clearer. Perhaps, after the horrors of her youth, my mother found her guardian angel.

I am trying to lay stripes in the lawn, passing first one way and then another, keeping the gaps even, the lines straight. I can look up and see the window of my mother's room but nothing further, but I know that, if she is awake, she will be watching me. It is hot and I am wearing only a T-shirt and shorts; the day is stilled by the heat so that, when I stop the mower, the silence is almost total. I feel marooned in a place with no time, where the outside world has ceased to matter. I wonder how long it can last.

My mother's nurse is a tight-bodied Pole who refuses to smile at me and I am not even sure whether she understands who I am and why I am here. She is checking my mother's drip when I enter the room and she darts a hostile look at me from dark eyes made more alarming by her tightly pulled-back black hair; I am tempted to stick my tongue out at her. Mrs Latimer has given me flowers, fuchsias from her garden, and I walk past the nurse and put the vase on top of one of the machines. The nurse tuts and takes it off, puts it on the bedside cabinet. She bustles about and walks out and I say to my mother, 'Was it something I said?'

'Agata does not like the routine disturbed,' my mother says. She is looking well, better since her dialysis and her face has almost a glow to it. 'She is a good girl, but I think she would also have made a fine Nazi.'

I lean over and kiss her. 'How are you feeling?'

'Feeling? Daniel, I feel like I could dance. Do you dance?'

'Not really.'

'Not really?'

'At all. Imagine if I step on somebody's toe.'

My mother laughs, looks me up and down. 'So big.'

'And ugly.'

'Oh no. Oh, Daniel, you must never think that.'

I flick the flowers with the end of my hand, do not reply.

'I used to dance. In Romania. Of course it was peasant dances, we were not allowed any decadent influence. But here, I went to dance classes. I learned the quickstep.'

'I play tennis.'

'Tennis?' My mother looks at me and laughs softly, runs out of breath and has to take some moments to recover. 'I am sorry, Daniel. You do not look the kind of person who plays tennis.' She stops as if worried that she will cause me offence, but the idea of my playing tennis clearly tickles her and she laughs again. 'In the little white shorts? Oh my God.'

I smile. 'I was pretty good. Still am.'

'I would have gone to see every game,' she says. 'I would have argued with the other mothers. "My Daniel is best. Hush your mouths." Like that, every game.'

'I'm sure.' We are both smiling but of course it does not last, because rushing in behind the words comes the usual tidal wave of lost years and regret. Yet we continue to look at each other frankly; there is no hiding our pain. It is allowed, in the open, acknowledged. This is something we share, our pragmatism.

'You never went back. To Romania.'

'Why? Imagine the shame, Daniel. Leaving my parents for a better life, coming home a whore.'

'No.'

My mother laughs. She laughs easily, though over her lifetime she should have laughed more. 'Oh please, Daniel. It is in the past. And anyway –' and here I see something in my mother which I have not seen before, a mischief which

271

is entirely without inhibition '– I was no good. At being a whore. I was better at the quickstep.' She pauses, shakes her head in private amusement. 'And I was terrible at the quickstep, also.'

'I would have danced the quickstep with you,' I say, but even as I say it I realise how mawkish it sounds.

'No thank you, Daniel,' she says. 'I care too greatly for my toes.'

I stay at my mother's side for three days, and during that time I believe that she shows signs of improvement. Mr and Mrs Latimer are kind to me and I feel welcome, even though their daughter doesn't come to visit. My mother and I talk, and I watch her sleep, and she gazes at me whenever she is awake as if I am a temporary, miraculous visitation that could disappear back into the ether at any moment. And in some ways she is right; though I am happier here in the safety and security of the Latimers' home, at some point I have to leave, to go back and face my demons in Essex. Rosie O'Shaughnessy has parents who have as little idea of what ultimately happened to her as my mother did about me; I cannot leave them to suffer in ignorance any longer. And Baldwin will not keep any longer.

My mother smiles when I tell her that I have to go but her smile is belied by the tears that fall down the sides of her thin head as she looks up at me from her bed. But she regains control and nods quickly and as I bend down she puts an arm behind my head and with more force than I believed she had she pulls me closer, covering my face with quick kisses. I stand up and smile and walk away and there is nothing in the world I would rather do less than close that door behind me.

29

I HAD PHONED ahead and when Xynthia Halliday opens her door she is dressed in a satin shift with a headband to which feathers are attached; she looks as if she is about to go on stage in a play set between the wars. She smiles when she sees me and before I have the chance to say anything she says, 'So? How was she?' I do not answer and after a couple of seconds her face loses its light and she suddenly looks nervous, though she tries to hide it.

'What am I thinking? Come in, come in. We'll sit down and talk. Come in.'

She makes way and I walk past her into her living room, the ranks of photographs still silently charting the success and wonder of her early, pre-Halliday years in theatre. I stand in the middle of the floor and she smiles, though without the brightness of before; she knows that something is up.

'Cup of tea?'

'No thanks.'

'Okay.' She fidgets with her neckline, running a finger inside it. 'Well. You found her.'

'She thought I was dead.'

'Oh?'

'Principally because you told her I was.'

Xynthia doesn't say anything, sits down. She looks at the wall opposite as if it is showing her past. She sighs sadly.

'She came back for you,' she says. 'She wouldn't see sense.'

'It wasn't sense, her wanting to find her son?'

'No.' A flash of anger. 'No, Daniel, it wasn't. What would Vincent've done to her, if he'd found out?'

'Why would he care? Wasn't his son.'

'It wasn't about you. He… So she had a son. Do you think Vincent would have cared about that? She was back, after he'd sent her away.'

'He sold her.'

'And why? Because the alternative was to get rid of her another way. Listen.' She smoothes her shift over her knees. 'As far as Vincent was concerned, she'd made him look stupid. Carrying on with your father, getting knocked up, when she was *his* property. Now she's back, rubbing salt in. You can't see the danger she was in?'

'So you lied to her.'

I see the anger in her eyes again. 'You were a fucking baby, Daniel. You had your life in front of you. Marcela, she was in danger. Right then and there. She wouldn't listen to reason, so I had to make her give up another way. Yeah, I lied. Best thing I could've done for her. I still believe that, even now.'

'You sentenced me to a life without a mother. What gave you the right?'

'Oh please.' She waves a hand. 'Stop being so fucking selfish. At least she's still alive. Look on the bright side.'

I came to Xynthia's door brimming with righteous anger but I can feel it evaporating, leaving only a hollow feeling where it had been. I look at Xynthia's defiant face and I know that, at the very least, she felt like she had done the right thing. She called me selfish and perhaps there is some truth in that; I resent her for consigning me to the uncaring hands of my father, robbing me of the chance of happiness. But perhaps it had been the right thing to do. Certainly, she felt it had been, and I know Xynthia Halliday. She is not a bad person. I sit down opposite her, elbows on my knees, look down at her worn carpet.

'I'm so sorry, Daniel,' she says softly. 'I used to watch you, you know. At school. You looked so sad, so lost. It would break my heart.'

I look up at her. 'She was happy to see me,' I say. But she doesn't hear me, lost in the regrets of her past.

'Poor, poor boy.'

As I drove back to Essex, I had watched lightning stabbing down on to the flat country as a cold front swept in to do battle with the occupying heat that had been sitting sullen and heavy over the land for a month or more. Thunderheads miles high, their edges backlit by the red dying sun, loomed over me as I drove through fat raindrops falling slowly and ominously on to my windscreen. From time to time I would lift my little finger and regard the stump, which my mother's nurse had taken the stitches from; it was shiny and traced with red lines but already it was less angry than it had been. But my anger, my feeling of having been violated by a man as close to evil as I had ever experienced, was as strong as ever. As I thought about Baldwin, my hands gripped the wheel with such force that my shoulders ached, lost in visions of vengeance, which, if I was to be honest, I wasn't sure I had the strength to carry out.

I had picked up the discs that Terry had copied from a man who called himself Frank and whose rustic appearance in a chunkily knitted sweater and rubber boots was belied by his suburban Essex accent. He lived in a stone building in the middle of the countryside on the edge of the Yorkshire Dales and I found him down a rough track, two lines of baked mud with withered yellow grass growing down the middle, which scraped the bottom of my car as I bounced down the ruts. Terry had not told me his story but I had got the impression that Frank was a man with a complicated past, and that he would not be returning to Essex any time soon.

Frank was waiting for me and he came out of his house, if you could call it that, before I had the chance to knock. He had a long grey beard and did not seem pleased to see me.

'You Daniel Connell?'

'I am.'

'Got a call from Terry. Says it's okay to give you this.'

He was holding a carrier bag, which he pushed out at me as if it contained pornography he did not agree with.

'Thanks.'

'Don't thank me,' he said belligerently. 'Just take them and do what you have to do. And don't say where you got them from.'

I wondered about his story and what it was he had run from, but I had had enough of hard-luck tales. Terry, Xynthia, Billy Morrison, Rosie O'Shaughnessy, even my mother; I seemed to have been swamped by a steady stream of undeserving victims and tragic figures, with the result that Vincent Halliday and Baldwin were both out gunning for me. I am a solitary man and thinking back over the chaos of the past weeks I wondered how I had managed to attract so much attention. Certainly, I did not believe that I had gone out actively looking for it; instead, it had been brought to my door by a procession of needy supplicants. Yet I was carrying the entire burden, and it was not a role I had asked for or that I relished. I should have been at my mother's side; instead, I was about to go up against one psychopath in Baldwin, and one borderline case in Vincent Halliday.

I took the bag from Frank and headed back for Essex and whatever awaited me there.

Before I visited Xynthia, I had stopped at Gabe's; I had not spoken to him for weeks and when he opened the door he looked as if he had spent that time drinking with the abandonment of a terminal alcoholic. His face was puffy and I believe it was the first time I had ever seen him unshaven. The drinking seemed to have made his eyes even paler than usual and he stood with one arm against the frame of the door as if it was all that was holding him up.

'So the bottle won.'

'Only the first round.'

'You going to ask me in?'

Inside Gabe's house there was little evidence of his internal disorder; a decade in the Army clearly instilled a discipline that even weeks of hard drinking could not shift. Everything was in its place, washing up neatly stacked on the draining board in his kitchen. I sat down and he made coffee, then he asked me about my mother and I told him everything. As I spoke, his look of hostile indifference changed and his eyes softened; underneath his self-loathing and regret, he still had time for other people. Not a lost cause yet. He asked me about Baldwin and I told him about Terry and the copies of the discs he had made.

'You can stay here, if you like. Keep out of his way.'

'Thanks. But I'm not running anymore. He wants me, he'll find me at home.'

'Daniel, this isn't a fight you need to have. Let the police take care of it.'

'They will. But I'm not hiding.'

Gabe looked at me and eventually nodded, took a drink from his coffee, the cup's rim covering his eyes. 'Your funeral,' he said from behind it, the subject closed. Tough love and short shrift; that's all you can expect from Gabe.

Now that Xynthia's secret is out, that she told my mother that her only son was dead to prevent her running up against Halliday, she opens up to me. She tells me about life with Halliday, about the exciting, glamorous early days of cocktail parties and Ladies' Day at Ascot and sun-soaked weeks on strangers' yachts. But those days were as ephemeral as a four-month West End run, and soon the reality of Halliday emerged; the temper, the psychological abuse, the suspicion and, behind it all, his business. Drugs, blackmail, violence and, worst of all, women.

'Them days,' says Xynthia, 'there was this fucking daft idea that criminals were like Robin Hood or something. Like we were part of the counter-culture somehow. It was the drugs, mostly, like because we were doing them, and so were the bands and the dropouts, like somehow we shared something. But that lot didn't have a clue. Scratch Vincent and you wouldn't find a good-time guy. Scratch Vincent and he'd put you in a hole in the fucking ground.'

She walks to a cocktail cabinet and pours two small glasses of a sweet brown liqueur that I do not recognise but drink out of politeness. The effort of bending down and pouring makes her breathe heavily but she holds up her glass and says, 'To a life of fucking regret.' I smile but feel uncomfortable and, as she drinks and stares unhappily, I look around her cramped living room and her photos and realise that those few years, before the dream went sour, were probably the only good years of her life.

'You want to know, want to really know about Vincent Halliday? I'll tell you about Vincent fucking Halliday.'

I leave Xynthia's flat after two more glasses; I've had enough of the sweet liqueur and dark, grisly revelations she is increasingly drunkenly spilling to me and, besides, I now know enough for what I have to do. I drive home through heavy rain and air that is turning cooler by the minute. Once there, I wait for the end of the thunderstorm. And for whoever is out there, looking for me.

30

I AM AT the place where Rosie O'Shaughnessy was found, a clearing in a stretch of woodland next to a long straight B-road, which sweeps beneath overhanging trees through Epping Forest into the Essex countryside. It is quiet and I have a sense of foreboding that I cannot place; I do not believe in residual energies or spirits or ghosts, but standing in the cool shade I have a sensation of gathering, malevolent forces, which has me turning in a circle, looking into the darkness of the trees for what, I do not know. I hear a noise and a flurry of birds break cover somewhere in the murk and I am so spooked that I almost turn and run.

But I came here for a reason; I hold my ground. I am not a sentimental person but I have felt, over the past weeks, some kind of connection to Rosie, despite barely having spoken to her when she was alive. I have carried the secret of her death with me; I have done my best for her. Now I am standing where she was killed, where her life was taken away by arrogant men who believed they were above the law. If there is a place where I can pay my respects to an innocent, lively, vital young woman who deserved many more years of life, this is it.

There are still some ragged strands of yellow police tape attached to trees and trodden into the undergrowth and, although I am not sure of the exact spot where Rosie's body was found, this feels close enough. I sit down with my back against a tree and think back over the events of the past few weeks, the people I have encountered and the tawdry stories I have heard. Terry Campion, Billy Morrison, Vincent Halliday, Baldwin, my mother; all part of the cycle of criminality and brutality that lies barely hidden underneath the surface of my neighbourhood.

It is cooler today, a wind blowing a chill through my shirt; the temperature has dropped ten degrees in one day and the leaves on the ground are cold to the touch and I shiver against the bark of the tree at my back. Where I am sitting, it is gloomy, the sun beyond the massed branches hidden behind low white clouds, and, although I hear the noise clearly, it is some time before I can make out who, or what, is approaching. My skin prickles in dread and I cannot stand, cannot run. From behind a stand of bushes I can make out the shape of a figure emerging from the dark of the trees, and as it gets nearer I see a face with a strange metallic semi-circle around its bottom half; the face is stained brown and green and only one eye looks at me, the other hidden behind some kind of plastic cover. The figure picks its way robotically over branches and roots and I stand up, the better to see exactly what it is. The skin on my scalp tightens in atavistic horror as I first irrationally think I am witnessing the emergence of some kind of grotesque man-made ogre from the forest's innards; then I realise with a sudden clarity who it is and I think, with a different kind of horror: I created that.

'Hello, Gary,' I say. The last time I had seen him he was barely conscious on the floor of the workshop underneath the arches; the damage I have done to him is dreadful. He looks at me through his one good eye with a desperate hatred.

'You're a fucking dead man,' he says, the semi-circle of metal moving up and down with his lower jaw. This close I can see that it is attached by thin pins, which sprout from the flesh of his chin and jawbone and his entire face is horribly bruised and discoloured. That must have hurt.

'Oh please,' I say. 'You had a look at yourself? You can't want more of the same.'

But before he can answer an arm comes across my throat from behind; there is only one man I know with strength like this and I feel handcuffs cutting into the skin on my wrist and before I can make sense of what is happening my other wrist is cuffed and Gary walks towards me, pulls back a fist and punches me as hard as he can in the face. The arm that is holding me lets go and I fall backwards to the ground, unable to break my fall with my cuffed arms. Gary comes forward and starts kicking me in my ribs and shoulders and he lands one kick in the side of my neck, which closes my throat and makes my vision darken and I hear Baldwin say genially, 'Now then, young Gary, that's enough for the minute.'

I am down for minutes, sucking in great long-winded groans of air through my bruised throat. They are looking down at me, Baldwin, Gary and the man with the drinker's face. I still don't know his name. They wait patiently and there is something I do not like about it. They are in no hurry. What will happen will happen. It has been decided. I am entirely at these men's mercy and it has been too easy, far too easy. I have lost without even putting up a fight. I wonder how long I have to live. Minutes? Seconds?

Baldwin squats down next to me, puts his index finger into my mouth, pulls at my cheek. 'You back with us, cunt?' His finger is salty and large. He rubs the tip over my tongue, pulls it out before I have a chance to bite. I spit his taste out, disgusted. He wipes his finger on his shirt, smiles at me without emotion. I spit again on to the leaf-covered ground with the little saliva I can manage, struggle up into a sitting position.

'What the fuck are you doing?' I say.

'Taking care of loose ends,' says Baldwin. He looks around appreciatively. 'Nice spot you chose.'

'I'm going to make you suffer,' says Gary.

Baldwin snorts, amused. 'He's not quite forgiven you, has Gary,' he says.

'Gary,' I say. Gary looks down at me. 'You're a pussy.'

Gary steps in, foot back to kick. Baldwin, still squatting, puts out an arm, stills him. 'Easy, Gary.' He looks at me. 'Sunshine, you just don't want to help yourself, do you?'

I smile up at Baldwin, try to show some bravado. Baldwin beams a Hollywood smile back down at me. You can never win with this man.

'Been following you,' he says cheerfully. 'Wanted a quiet

word. Right, Gary?' Gary laughs shortly. 'Thought that this might be the time. Away from prying eyes.'

This is where they killed Rosie. And suddenly I need to know how. Exactly what happened. Try to make sense of it.

'How did you kill her?' I say.

'Ah, Rosie,' says Baldwin. He tuts regretfully, picks up a handful of leaves, lets them fall. 'Rose, Rosie, ring-a-ring-a-Rosie. Just one of those things.' Says it like he's describing a failed relationship. Just one of those things.

'Can we hurry up please?' says puffy drinker's face.

'No hurry, Banjo,' says Baldwin. So that's his name. Not one I would have ever guessed. 'Gary's been waiting a long while for this.'

'Why? What had she done to you?'

'Wasn't what she'd done, was it?' says Baldwin. 'It's what little Rosie saw, with those big eyes of hers.'

'Terry?'

'She took a shortcut through the park, did Rosie. Took a peek through the fence and saw us being, being...' He searches for the word.

'Robust,' says Banjo.

'Ah,' says Baldwin, a pleased smile on his face as if he has just tasted something exquisite. 'Just so. Saw us being robust with Terry.'

'Who was a policeman.'

'Hmm,' says Baldwin. 'That was unfortunate.'

'So you killed her.'

Baldwin sighs. 'Silly bitch wouldn't listen. So Gary slaps her. She slaps back. Gary slaps harder. Rosie falls over, cracks her head. The end.'

'She slipped,' says Gary.

'That's what Gary likes to believe,' says Baldwin. He leans closer, whispers. 'It helps him sleep at night.'

'Fuck you,' says Gary.

'Fuck who?' says Baldwin. He stands up, turns to Gary. Gary looks away like a beaten child. 'You fucking prat.'

'She had a broken neck,' I say. 'She did that falling over?'

'That was more of a...' A bird flaps in some branches above us, sound of wings erupting into flight. Baldwin shrugs. 'Seemed the kindest way.'

The statement is so monstrous it barely registers with me. Instead, I ask, 'She was holding something up. On the footage. You tried to take it from her.' I think of Rosie, her arm out, thrusting something towards Baldwin as if warding off evil. 'What was it?'

Baldwin frowns, thinks back, then his expression clears as he remembers. 'Ah yes. Mobile phone. She'd recorded it all, like another fucking Rodney King. Unbelievable.'

So Rosie was killed because she had seen too much; what's more, she had evidence. And, rather than keep it to herself or create some media sensation, she'd decided to take it up with the appropriate authorities, then and there. Perhaps she had believed, in her outrage, that such a flagrant abuse of power would be swiftly and decisively dealt with; that Baldwin's colleagues would be as outraged as she was at what she had witnessed and would give her every support. As she walked into the police station, she must have believed that she was in a place where justice would prevail.

Little did she know that she had wandered into a place of violence and the law of the jungle.

As Baldwin and his colleagues emerged from the cells, laughing and wiping their knuckles with tissues, Rosie confronted them, told them what she'd seen, told them she wasn't going to let them get away with it. At first they tried to reason with her, tell her it was none of her business, that this was the way of the world, that they were the good guys. But Rosie was immovable, furiously sure of her moral duty. Baldwin took hold of her and walked her out of the police station and she must have wondered at his strength; he needed to get her away, reason with her, make her see his side of things away from the eyes and ears of the rest of the station. But Rosie wouldn't listen. Outside in the dark away from the cameras, she tried to get away, to alert a higher authority. Baldwin took her arm, she shook it off, Gary went after her, she said something, he hit her. Instinctively, she hit him back, and by that point it was too late. Things were only going to end one way.

'Okay, let's get this done, can we?' says Banjo. Of the three policemen, he seems the most nervous and I get the feeling that he's not cut out for this, that events have got out of control and he's well outside his comfort zone. He keeps looking around but there is nobody on their way; we are in the middle of a remote forest clearing and he has nothing to fear. I, on the other hand, have never felt so alone.

'It will get done,' says Baldwin easily. 'Why don't you have a sit down? This is Gary's show now.'

Gary walks closer and I can see his face more clearly than ever; it is misshapen and underneath the bruising the skin is broken and I can see bloody cuts where my fists burst his face open. I cannot remember doing it. The semi-circle of metal wraps around his lower face like the beginnings of some foray into cyborg technology, the pins that hold it in place sprouting from his skin as if they grew there. He looks so angry he could cry and I cannot help myself.

'Fucking Robocop. Were the nurses nice to you? Did they give you a lolly for being a brave boy?'

Gary is too furious to respond but behind him Baldwin chuckles softly. 'Eye for an eye, that's what we've decided. That right, Gary?'

'What'll I use?' says Gary.

'Whatever you want.'

'These?' He pulls out his car keys and looks at them doubtfully.

'DNA, Gary,' says Baldwin. 'Use a stick or something.'

'Why create more trouble for yourselves?' I say. 'Just let me go.'

'Trouble?' says Baldwin, puzzled. 'Am I in trouble?'

'You will be if you kill me.'

'I'll probably be investigating,' says Baldwin. 'I'll be honest, I can't see a problem.' Even Banjo snorts in laughter at this. Baldwin's confidence is unshakable; nothing I say will cause him to doubt himself.

Gary has found a stick with a sharp end and he walks back towards me. 'Can you hold him?'

'Can do,' says Baldwin affably. He walks behind me and once more lays an arm around my neck, another across my forehead. Again, I am surprised at his strength. Gary squats down in front of me and puts a finger into my right eye. Regardless of Baldwin's powerful hold, I have enough strength of my own to jerk my head away, hands cuffed and sitting down as I am. Gary is using his thumb and first finger as a pincer; he is trying to pluck out my eye, looking at me intently as if he is having trouble undoing a hard-to-reach bolt. But even though I can only move my head fractionally, he cannot get purchase. His fingers keep stabbing into my eye and it is watering, his one damaged eye peering down at me out of his ruined face like an extreme close-up from a horror film. I do not want this man to take my eye out. He is not a worthy adversary; he is nobody.

'Hold still,' Gary says. 'Stop moving.'

'Use the stick,' says Baldwin. 'Fuck sake.'

Gary picks up the stick and pushes it towards my eye but I jerk out of the way.

'Stop fucking moving,' Gary says tetchily. Baldwin takes an even tighter hold and Gary takes my chin in his hand. My lips twist stupidly in Gary's grip but I cannot move. He holds the stick in the other hand and inserts it so that the point of the stick is in the corner of my eye nearest the bridge of my nose. He rests it there and the pressure of it makes my vision blur. It hurts.

'Smile,' he says, and pushes it forward as hard as he can.

I push back with my heels and take Baldwin by surprise; he is off balance and I lever myself into a half-standing position and rush him backwards, away from Gary and his stick. Baldwin cannot stop my charge and I twist out of his grip and turn, facing him. He looks surprised but not unduly worried. I am still at his mercy, hands cuffed behind me.

'You're too late,' I say.

'You what, son?'

'Terry made copies. And they'll be on tomorrow's front page.'

Copies, copies, copies of copies. Right now there are five versions of Rosie's last actions, five identical documents of her final movements in the possession of five different newspaper editors. Baldwin, supremely confident as he is, is also, right now, utterly fucked.

Baldwin does not take the news well. He blinks slowly, his huge head and body still as the implications course their way through his massive frame. He pinches his nose with his fingers, rubs his mouth and chin. He sniffs loudly, smiles to himself. I feel the nervous anticipation that a child does seeing a balloon inflated too fully. I tense in readiness.

'Oh shit,' says Banjo. 'Oh, Jesus no.'

'Guv?' says Gary. He sounds scared, uncertain.

Baldwin stalks around the clearing like a knocked-out boxer who has just come to in the ring and does not yet comprehend where he is. 'No,' he says, almost conversationally. 'No. No no no.' He passes me and I think he is going to attack me but he just reels past, lost for the moment in his private torment, his world collapsing around him. Suddenly enraged, he pulls at a low-hanging branch, trying to wrench it off a tree but it will not come off so he crouches down next to the tree, puts his head in his arms and starts to moan. Gary walks over to him and this tableau, of Baldwin in dismay being consoled in a forest clearing by a man who looks barely human, is so grotesque I question momentarily whether or not it is really happening. Baldwin, suited and crouched and making strange sounds as he is, makes me think of a bear suddenly and unwelcomely turned human; I have wandered into some hellish fairytale. Gary looks over at me resentfully, as if to say, See, look what you've done to him. The other side of the clearing, Banjo has his hands rammed down into his pockets and his back is arched and throat tight and he is looking up at the sky and crying silently.

Baldwin stops his moaning and shakes Gary's hand off his back and picks himself up; now I am in trouble. He walks towards me and without breaking his stride slams his fist into my face; I fall over immediately, the trees rush past my vision as if it is them falling and not me, until my head is stilled as it lands in the leaves. Baldwin stands over me and breathes heavily. I am on my back with my hands cuffed behind me. I could not be more vulnerable. I twist around but Baldwin puts a foot on my chest, presses down. He takes a knife out of his pocket, a lock knife. He opens it; it has a four-inch blade and reflects the dull light.

'Oh, this knife,' says Baldwin. He sounds manic. 'The places it has been, the things it has seen. Remember when I put it in that Tariq's ear?' He looks around at Gary, who nods. 'I made him look in the mirror and got it in, oh, up to here.' He shows me with his finger, nearly halfway up the blade. 'Man kept screaming. He couldn't believe what was happening.'

I wonder how many people have been victims of Baldwin, how many men and women humiliated and mutilated yet too terrified of his influence to ever say anything. Decades of abuse, hundreds of lives. The man is a monster.

'What are we going to do?' says Banjo.

'That we'll work out later,' says Baldwin. He steps over my chest so that he has a foot each side, then lowers himself on to his knees, sits down on my torso. He puts a hand under my chin and grips it. With the other, he puts the blade of the knife against my lips.

'Say "Aah",' he says. He works the blade in between my teeth; there is nothing I can do to stop him, however hard I bite. The blade is cold and I can feel its edge against my tongue. He twists it, levering my mouth open, the two sides of the blade scraping against my teeth, top and bottom. He is looking down at me intently, like a surgeon assessing a problem.

'This tongue will have to come out,' he says. 'Then we'll see.' He works the blade around and it cuts into the gum at the back of my mouth, below my molars.

'What are you doing?' says Banjo desperately.

'Make sure he doesn't talk again,' says Baldwin. His weight on my body is loathsome. I can feel the heat of his balls on my stomach.

'Do you have to?' says Banjo, plaintively. He turns to Gary. 'I can't look.'

'Cunt deserves it,' says Gary, but he looks sick, disgusted by what is about to happen.

Baldwin has got the blade underneath my tongue and is working away at where it meets my mouth, sawing. Blood floods my mouth. He jabs the point right into the heart of the meat and it hurts, hurts more than I would have believed. Banjo looks away. 'Oh, Christ,' he says. I close my eyes, try to think about something, anything but the fact that a man is trying to cut out my tongue. I try to picture my mother but I can hear Baldwin's heavy breathing; he sounds like a pig at a trough.

Then there is a sharp crack and the pressure from the knife stops and I feel Baldwin's weight lessen. The knife is lying in my mouth now and I shake my head and push it out with my tongue; it drops to the ground next to my head. Looking up, all I can see are the tops of the trees, the white sky through the gaps in the leaves. I lie still for a moment and I cannot hear anything so I raise myself up and Baldwin is lying at my side, one leg still over my stomach, his head a couple of feet from mine. His face is almost intact, but there is a large chunk of his forehead missing above his right eye and one entire side of the top of his head is gone. Something glistens yellow under the bright-red blood. I scrabble with my feet and arms and manage to work myself out from under him and away, his blank eyes watching me. He is as grotesque dead as he was alive.

Gary and Banjo are both looking at him too, shocked, not moving. It is very quiet in this clearing. Gary makes a move forward, stops. Then they both, as if they have reached some silent telepathic agreement, walk quickly away through the trees until it is just the two of us, myself and Baldwin.

I sit there until the birds resume their chatter in the trees, swallowing my blood, then I stand up and walk back to Baldwin's body. Already flies are gathering around the dark pool of blood next to what is left of his head, landing on it, dimpling its viscous surface. I sit down with my back to him and feel through his pockets to find the keys to the handcuffs. It is difficult and takes some time, but eventually I find them. Then, without unlocking them, I head out the same way as Gary and Banjo, not once looking back. I cannot get away fast enough.

31

MY MOTHER'S FUNERAL is in a small country church, which the Latimers have been attending for years; it is made of dingy stone with a large stained-glass window at one end, and they know the vicar personally. He has weather-reddened cheeks and iron-grey hair and he greets me after the service with a sincere warmth, taking my hand in both of his.

'She spoke about you,' he tells me, meeting my bruised eyes unflinchingly, without judgement. 'You were a huge source of comfort to her. I believe you helped her to find peace.'

I nod at him and take my place in the group around the grave. My mother's coffin is lacquered black and resting on a piece of green material like you once found in greengrocers, when high streets still had viable greengrocers. The weather is squally, sheets of rain draping the assembled crowd cowering respectfully under black umbrellas. There aren't many of us; the Latimers, including Penelope who has not spoken to me, and some older people whose lives, they have assured me, my mother touched in some small yet presumably significant fashion.

It had been strange, listening to the vicar's sermon, learning things about my mother that she had yet to tell me. How she had worked with street children, how she had given up every Christmas Day she had to be there for them. How she had been a decent water-colour painter and had even put on an exhibition with other local artists. How she had made people laugh, how she had had a gift for it. All things I should have known myself; how could I not resent a stranger telling me?

My mother died two nights after I left her side, although Mr Latimer has told me that she was happy at the end and that, just an hour before her organs failed her, she had been talking about me; she had called me her miracle. I had been due to visit her again the following day, and Mr Latimer had called me with the news while I was packing a small bag. His voice had broken as he told me that she was dead and I knew that he was crying; he made no attempt to hide it. I had been holding a polo shirt and after I put the phone down I did not know what to do with it. My bag was open on my bed and I stood with the dead phone and shirt in my hand for some minutes before I picked my bag up and threw it into the mirror in my room, cracking it.

Now, my mother's coffin is lowered into the grave and earth thrown upon it. I wonder how I will be able to stop thinking about her; wonder how long before I can forget I ever met her.

*

Back at the Latimers' house, the dining-room table is covered with snack food just out of its packaging and people are balancing plates and glasses in their hands and trying to stand as close to corners as they can. I attract glances and nervous smiles but nobody tries to speak to me, and I cannot blame them. One of my eyes is bloodshot and both are black and the bridge of my nose is split. My tongue hurts where Baldwin hacked at it, and my mutilated finger throbs. They can only begin to imagine how I would respond to a polite greeting.

I stand next to the table, unsure what to do, as uncomfortable as a single man at a nightclub. My hands feel big and clumsy and I don't know where to put them, in my pockets or behind my back, and I pick up a glass of water to give them something to do. I wonder how soon I can get away. I only knew her for three days; we were barely acquaintances. Half an hour should do it.

Penelope is talking to a couple of old ladies, shaking their hands and dabbing at her eyes with a tissue. In the church, she had really let go, huge racking sobs as the vicar gave us some schtick about the immortal soul. She will not look in my direction. Fuck this, I think, and turn to leave but Mr Latimer stops me in the hall.

'Daniel.'

'Harold.' Our conversation is as stilted as that between a young man and the father of the girl whose knickers he's trying to get into. We are still strangers. He is wearing a black suit and he looks feeble, diminished by the events; an old, old man.

'You're leaving?'

'I don't feel like I should be here.'

'If not you, then who?'

I grudgingly thank him inwardly for this unaffected welcome, yet it changes nothing. 'It's difficult for me.'

'For all of us,' he says. 'But before you go, we do need to talk. Follow me?'

He leads me down the hall to his office, a small room with a surprising amount of clutter. I would have imagined a room with polished fitted bookshelves and leather-bound books, leather-upholstered chairs, a desktop covered in leather. But Mr Latimer has an IKEA desk, books and papers everywhere, a tower computer with one side missing. I can see the fan working inside, circuit boards. I imagine he spends a lot of time here, has done for years.

'Your mother left a will,' he says. He opens a drawer of his desk and looks inside, takes out a plain white envelope. He hands it to me.

'A will?'

'Yes. Rather recently, as you can imagine.'

I do not understand. I look down at the envelope in my hand. It is made from thick paper. It looks expensive. 'Well, open it,' says Mr Latimer.

I lever it open with a finger and take out a piece of paper. On it is some writing, and there is a cheque attached. I look at Mr Latimer.

'She saved everything she ever earned, or at least very nearly,' he says. 'Originally it was earmarked for her charity, but then…' He sighs, a light, surprised sound. 'Then you turned up.'

The sum is large. I wonder how my mother ever earned it. 'You paid her?'

'Of course I paid her,' says Mr Latimer, slightly affronted. 'You think I expect people to work for me for nothing?'

'Then this is your money,' I say.

'No,' Mr Latimer says slowly and I can see that he is genuinely upset now. 'No, this is, was, Marcela's money. She earned it and she was free to do with it as she wished. And now it is yours. Please do not insult me.'

I nod and tuck the letter and cheque back into the envelope, tuck the envelope into my inside jacket pocket. I cannot think of one thing to say to him.

'And for God's sake, don't look so angry,' Mr Latimer says sharply. 'You think she'd have wanted that?'

'I don't know.'

'The question was rhetorical. You know very well she would not.'

I do not answer. Anything I could say would only make things worse.

I leave immediately after, without saying goodbye. Why would I ever go back? Why would the Latimers want to see me again? On the way to my car, crunching over gravel, I check my phone and see that I have missed a call. It is Halliday; he has left me a message.

'Connell, Halliday here. You, my son, are trying your luck. Trying my fucking patience an' all. I'll see you tomorrow at the property, ten o'clock. Be late and it'll be your last mistake. Understand?'

I get into my car, adjust the rear-view mirror, look at

myself. I smile and the corners of my eyes crinkle but they hold nothing but malice. Fear is an emotion I can no longer imagine. I start the car and pull on to the road, back to Essex. This, all this, ends tomorrow.

32

ANGER IS OFTEN described as a negative emotion; rage, merely destructive. But as I head into my meeting with Halliday I cannot imagine any emotion that will be more useful, considering what it is I am about to do. I am consumed with fury and part of me cannot wait for our encounter, even though I have no idea how it will pan out and even less whether I will survive it. The death of my mother, the injustice of losing her so soon after finding her, and Halliday's culpability in it all; I would like to tear the skin off his bones. Halliday, untouchable, protected by layers of people and networks of influence and the constant and imminent threat of violence; it means nothing to me. Waiting for him to arrive, I do not feel apprehension, nerves, pre-fight jitters. Instead, I already feel the all-consuming anger that clouds my judgement and renders me impervious to pain; it is as if I am already in the fight, seeing red, charged on adrenalin. My fists are bunched and I cannot stop pacing. Bring it on.

I am standing in the ground floor of the building Halliday intended to buy. It is a large house of red brick just off the centre of town, built at the turn of the century for a now defunct order of nuns. All of the windows are covered with weathered plywood, but inside it is in decent condition; I have been assured that it is a prime rental location and that it represents a potential financial goldmine, although just now, abandoned as it is, it seems merely sad, drab and hopeless, testament to our collective loss of faith in things spiritual. I am standing in the kitchen, which is huge and has three walls of dilapidated cupboards, a sink, a broken cooker. Dust coats everything.

I hear a sound behind me and there is Halliday, wearing only a shirt, although it is raining outside. Behind him Eddie is putting down an umbrella, which I assume he has been holding over Halliday's head. My opinion of him, which was not high before, sinks even lower. Why abase yourself to a man like Halliday? Behind Eddie is another man and I do not recognise him, though I recognise his type. He is about my size with a shaved head and a neck wider than his jaws, perhaps forty; his face looks like it gave up smiling in his teens. He has hands as big as boxing gloves and looks as solid as a freezer. Hired muscle, which probably means two things. One, Eddie has warned Halliday that I am no pushover. And two, Halliday means me harm. But this does not bother me. At least we are both up for the fight.

Halliday walks up to me with his agitated, barely-in-control stride and stands too close, looking up at me with his chin thrust forward and his eyes bright and venomous. He is aggravated.

'Fuck me, you came. Thought you'd dropped off the fucking planet.'

'I'm here.'

'Good fucking job too,' says Halliday. 'Or I'd have sent someone to find you.'

'Saved you the trouble,' I say.

Halliday's eyes flick over my face and, just like in his bar, I have the impression of a snake coiled to strike. Time seems to slow as he weighs up his options, then he steps back, the moment over. He looks over to Eddie. 'Right. What do we need to know?'

Eddie comes over, eye fucking me. Halliday laughs. 'Not your best friend, is Eddie.'

'What's he want, a cuddle?' I say.

'What we want to know, wanker, is whether we're ready to complete.'

'Ah,' I say.

'Ah? The fuck does that mean?' Eddie steps towards me but I stand my ground.

'Interesting place, this,' I say. 'It was built for nuns, you know that?'

'Who fucking cares?' says Eddie. Evidently not a man of learning.

'Then it fell empty, when the order disappeared. Left empty for years, before it was converted into a care home. You know that?' Eddie shakes his head, more in bewilderment than in response to my question. I turn to Halliday. 'You knew that, right?'

'Just get to the point. When's it mine?'

'Well,' I say, 'the thing is, I've been away.'

'So I noticed. Where the fuck were you, anyway?'

'I went to find my mother,' I say.

Halliday doesn't react at first, just watches me, expressionless. I let the silence drag on. Halliday still doesn't react, and Eddie and the muscle soon pick up on something unsaid, something in the air that they're not part of. Things have taken a strange turn and they have been left behind; this is now between Halliday and me. But Halliday is a man to whom bravado is second nature and it does not take him long to regain his composure.

'Yeah?' he says indifferently. 'You find her?'

'I did,' I say. 'She said to say hi.'

'Mr Halliday,' says Eddie. 'Everything all right?'

Halliday ignores him. 'That's got nothing to do with this.'

'How much did you get for her?' I ask.

'Nothing to do with you.'

'She's my mother.'

'You want to leave this.'

'No I don't. How much?'

'Can't remember. Can't have been much.' Halliday smiles. 'She weren't up to much, your mother. Useless bitch.'

I nod to myself. This is the moment. I walk over to the sink and take out a heavy wrench I have put there, cross quickly to Halliday's hired muscle and hit him as hard as I can with it on the side of his shaved head. He tries to put up an arm but he doesn't have time and the wrench makes a meaty sound as it connects and he goes down in a heap.

Eddie looks shocked and I can tell that he has no stomach for this fight, but he has no choice and he walks towards me cautiously and unwillingly like a child approaching a big dog he's been dared to stroke. I step towards him and he puts his hands up to ward off whatever's coming and I throw the wrench at him and, as he ducks away, follow up with a punch in his throat that has him bent over, choking. I drive my knee up into his face and he falls down. I do not know if he is unconscious but if he isn't he's doing a good job of pretending. His face certainly hurt my knee.

Halliday has had enough of this; he is walking towards the door but I catch up and put a hand on his shoulder.

'Uh-uh,' I say. 'Not yet.'

Halliday turns and I don't see any fear in his eyes, just a kind of awed disbelief. These things don't happen to men like him. It doesn't make sense.

'You know you're a fucking dead man,' he says. 'You know that?'

I hit him in the stomach and lower him to the floor where he sits, breathing as best he can. After some time, he takes a long shuddering breath and spits out dribble on to the ground next to him, wipes his mouth with the back of his hand.

'Better?' I say, but Halliday just looks at me with hatred. 'Good. Now then, about this property. A few things have come to light. One of them is that, underneath where we're standing, are the bodies of Michael Connor and Gavin O'Dwyer. But you know that, don't you? Because you put them there.'

Halliday still doesn't answer, watches me warily.

'Must have done it while it was being renovated. What, you knew someone who was pouring the concrete?' I don't wait for a response; Halliday has given up talking for the time being. 'Which is why you wanted to buy this property.

Because if this place is ever demolished, and those bodies are found, you're going down. See, I thought you wanted it to launder money, set up some fake tenants and pay yourself their rent. But you just need it to protect yourself. You've got through one trial. You won't get through another.'

'Who told you?'

'Doesn't matter.' Of course it had been Xynthia, but there is no way I am going to tell Halliday that. She has suffered enough at his hands.

'I'll find your mum,' he says. 'I'll kill her.'

'Too late,' I say. 'She's dead. And say anything more about her and I'll put that wrench down your throat.'

Halliday thinks about saying something, changes his mind. You don't get to where he's got without a sharp instinct for self-preservation.

'But she left me some money,' I say. 'And you know what I did with it?' No answer. 'I bought this place.' I smile. 'Oops.'

'You fucking did what?'

'So I suggest you're nice to me. Because if anything happens to me, like, I get hit by a car, or fall off a balcony, even if I die of natural causes, this place is getting donated to the Essex Police Force. And the first thing they'll do, if they read my will properly, which they will do, is get the jackhammers out.' I am pacing now, and Halliday is following me with his eyes from the floor where he is sitting. 'The second thing they'll do is lock you up and throw away the fucking key.'

Halliday shakes his head slowly, laughs softly to himself. 'Oh, son. Oh dear.'

His attempt to patronise me only makes me more angry and I walk towards him, not thinking clearly, and hold him by his chin, jerk his head up so that he is looking at me. I do not know what to do, and cast about with my eyes. I see the wrench and I pull Halliday across the floor towards it, my hand around his neck. I do not notice his weight; it is as if I am dragging an insignificant piece of luggage. I pick the wrench up and Halliday, for the first time since he arrived, looks genuinely scared.

I think of my mother and her miserable, desolate life, which was all down to this man and his indifference to suffering, his intrinsic lack of humanity, and I desperately want to make him feel something, experience some of the pain he caused my mother and me. I take his wrist and press it to the floor. He is too old to offer much resistance and I pick up the wrench with my other hand and lift it and bring it down on his fingers, once, twice, three times and he is screaming and screaming and it is only then that I realise that I am crying and I don't know how long for. I throw the wrench away and walk out, past a moaning Eddie and the unmoving body of Halliday's ineffective muscle, leaving Halliday bellowing in rage and holding up his wrecked fingers, splay-legged on the floor like a child that's had its toys taken away. Baldwin may be dead. But I have just made an enemy for life.

33

EVEN THOUGH IT is not warm, we are sitting outside the clubhouse because inside Ray has had one too many and started telling his usual lies, before moving on to his favourite subject of immigration. Gabe is drinking Coke and Maria has a glass of wine. Gabe and I have just handed a supposedly up-and-coming doubles pair the battering of their lives and are basking in the realisation that we still have, perhaps, something to offer the game of tennis. Maria is watching us with amusement; boys who can only find self-worth in handing out beatings. She is more right than she knows.

'Nice shot,' I say.

'Which one?' says Maria, who clearly appreciated our performance despite herself.

'Gabe knows which one,' I say.

When I was fourteen, I was challenged to a fight by a boy two years above me, a challenge that involved not only my facing up to the prospect of going toe-to-toe with somebody who outweighed me by over two stone, but also a bus journey across town to the venue of his choice; a clearing in the wooded land of a local park, frequented by drunks and littered with beer cans and the remnants of old fires. I told nobody about the fight and turned up expecting to be battered; in the event, I was not far wrong. But I put in some decent shots myself and it ended with me more or less on my feet. After the older boy and his entourage had left, I was using dry leaves to stem the blood from my nose when, from the higher wooded ground, I saw Gabe sauntering down towards me. 'What?' he said. 'You didn't think I'd look out for you?'

Now Gabe finishes his Coke and gives us a quick goodbye, before disappearing into the gathering darkness. We watch him go because we both know that, once he has gone, it will be just us.

'He looks better,' says Maria. 'Not quite so mental.'

'Yeah.' It's true that the last week has seen a transformation in Gabe. I have heard speculation that he is seeing somebody, but I have no doubt that the truth is darker. Gabe once told me that, when he was in the Army, he spent six months on attachment to a reconnaissance unit where he was taught infiltration techniques, how to lie in one position for days and how to pick off targets at long range, what he described as the zen of sniping. The bullet that killed Baldwin was a 7.62 NATO round, the same used by the British Army. I will never ask Gabe if he shot Baldwin; what would be the point? I know him too well, have known him too long; I know he did it, and he knows that I know. Any mention would only embarrass him and compromise our tacit acknowledgement. He will always look out for me.

But one consequence of his act is that he seems happier than he has for weeks. I know that Gabe loved war, loved the concept of taking lives for the greater good, however abhorrent that idea is to most of us. Perhaps he has got his temporary fix. But his journey did not end with that shot. I have the feeling that it has only just begun, and I cannot help but wonder if it can possibly end happily.

Maria and I sit in an uncomfortable, charged silence, and she shivers as a cold wind blows across the dark courts. It is now a week since Baldwin was shot but the papers are still full of his death, and theories about his involvement in Rosie O'Shaughnessy's murder. It has been speculated that he was killed for what he did to her, and I suppose that, in a way, he was; ultimately, he brought his death upon himself. Even as I think it, I wonder if I am being deliberately glib, simplifying the story to absolve myself of any guilt. But at the same time, I do not care too much. I am no supporter of the death penalty, yet I cannot help but think that the world is a far better place for his killing. It is a hypocrisy that I am comfortable with.

'I was thinking,' I say.

'Steady,' says Maria.

'I'm sorry about before, when we talked. About going out.'

'Oh,' says Maria, and looks down at her glass, swirls it.

'I'm not an easy person to live with,' I say. 'I can be difficult.'

Maria looks at me and her eyes are wide and candid and lovely. 'Everybody can be difficult.'

'I wouldn't want to hurt you.'

'It's just a date, you moron,' she says. 'Tell you what. If you upset me, I'll call a taxi.'

I smile at her easy pragmatism. She is right. Why does everything have to be so complicated? 'Would you like to go to dinner with me?' I say.

'When?'

'Now.'

She downs her drink easily, sets it down exaggeratedly hard on the outside table. 'Where are you parked?'

We get up and she picks up her bag and we walk towards the exit to the tennis club, between dark hedges and into the yellow gleam of a streetlight, and somewhere along the way she puts her arm through mine and for the first time in a long time I think that things might really be looking up.